FELLOWSHIP OF FEAR

The sleek-headed one spoke again. "Now where the hell is it? If we have to cut your gut open to see if you swallowed it, believe me, we'll do it. I *mean* it, you son of a bitch." As if Gideon needed convincing, he removed from his inside jacket pocket a thin, gleaming stiletto, like a prop from an Italian opera, but obviously the genuine thing.

When Gideon did not reply, the man gazed thoughtfully at him, his tongue playing over his upper lip, his head nodding slowly.

"So," he said, his rich voice cordial and caressing, "now we see."

As suddenly as he could, Gideon scraped his right heel savagely down the other man's shin and jammed it into his instep . . .

* * *

"An intriguing combination of mystery and espionage." —*ALA Booklist*

"Sherlock Holmes would be pleased. At last a new detective has come along that looks to small clues, however inanimate, to discover what a man looks like and what his customary behavior may be." —*Houston Post*

"Ingenious and original." —*Library Journal*

"Classic detection." —*Virginian Pilot*

**Also by
Aaron J. Elkins**

The Dark Place

Published by
POPULAR LIBRARY

FELLOWSHIP OF FEAR

AARON J. ELKINS

POPULAR LIBRARY

An Imprint of Warner Books, Inc.

A Warner Communications Company

All the characters and events portrayed in this story
are fictitious.

POPULAR LIBRARY EDITION

Popular Library® is a registered trademark of Warner Books, Inc.

This Popular Library Edition is published by arrangement with
Walker and Company, 720 Fifth Avenue, New York, N.Y. 10019

Cover illustration by Dennis Luzak

Popular Library books are published by
Warner Books, Inc.
666 Fifth Avenue
New York, N.Y. 10103

 A Warner Communications Company

Printed in the United States of America

First Popular Library Printing: March, 1986

10 9 8 7 6 5 4 3 2 1

Book 1: Heidelberg

1

THEY WERE OBVIOUSLY professionals. They worked with a cold precision, item by item, methodical and disinterested. First the obvious places, the places an amateur would have put it: shelves, suitcases, bureau drawers. Everything was put back exactly into its place, every shirt refolded along the original crease marks, the dirty laundry piled carefully into its original disarray.

The taller man spoke. "Nothing. You?"

The other was compact, sleek-headed, with a V-shaped, rodentlike face. "No."

They walked to the door of the room without speaking further and fanned out slowly along the walls, the tall one going to the left, the other to the right. Now they moved to the less obvious places. They uncovered the plates to the two electrical outlets; they fingered the linings of ties, removed light bulbs and looked in the sockets, sought hollow places in the heels of shoes, belt buckles, razor handles, book bindings. They went over the bedding and the bed frame, then carefully remade the bed and put the head-shaped depression back in the pillow. They bent a wire hanger, went into the bathroom, and explored the drain of the sink and the toilet trap. They unscrewed the barrels of ball-point pens and twisted the erasers on pencils to see if they would come off.

It took an hour. Finally the taller man said, "No. If he's got it, he's got it on him. Too bad for him."

"What time?" said the smaller one.

"Nine-fifteen. He's not going to be back for a while yet. Should we turn the lights off?"

"Turn them off."

They sat in the dark for a while. The tall one said, "He's a pretty big guy, you know. Six-one, six-two. Strong—used to box in college."

"So?"

"So he's going to be full of booze. He's liable to get smart."

The sleek-headed man grinned. His neck was long and muscular. The light from a street lamp, coming in through the window, glinted on his teeth.

Gideon Oliver was having a fine time, no doubt about it. With the rest of the new teaching faculty, he had arrived that morning at the sprawling, smoggy Rhein-Main United States Air Base outside of Frankfurt. The long night flight from McGuire Air Force Base in New Jersey, which had made the others grumpy with fatigue, had left him in a state of fuzzy euphoria over setting foot in Europe for the first time.

Dr. Rufus, the college's ebullient chancellor, had been there to welcome the twelve of them with booming voice and hearty handshakes, and had quickly and efficiently bundled them aboard a creaky army bus for the trip to Heidelberg. While the others slept or looked glumly out the window, Gideon watched with pleasure as the air turned clear, the flat land gave way to forested hills, and picture-book villages began to appear.

They had reached Heidelberg a little before 2:00 P.M., and were booked into the Hotel Ballman, on the busy Rohrstrasse. There they were greeted by the cranky proprietress, Frau Gross, who seemed entirely displeased to see them, and by a bored college official who told them about the dinner that evening, gave them directions on how to get to it, and advised them all to get some sleep before then. Gideon was too excited for that, and spend the afternoon strolling along the Philosopher's Walk, *Michelin* in hand, enjoying the clear air and looking down on the Old Town, the busy river, and the eleventh-century bridge. Often he stopped to sit on a bench and drink in the stupendous ruined castle that dominated every part of the town from its hill above the Neckar, its honey-colored stones rich and benign, yet faintly sinister.

In the evening, the entire faculty, new and old, along with the administrative staff, met for dinner in the Schloss Weinstube, modern dining room in one of the castle's ancient chambers Although not basically gregarious, Gideon Oliver was an essen tially civil person, so that when he found himself in an unavoid-able social situation he made the best of it. And when the food and wine were good, the conversation intelligent, and the women reasonably attractive, he had been known to actually enjoy himself. These conditions having been met tonight in varying degrees, he was enjoying himself very much.

During dinner he shared a table with three of the senior staff. Janet Feller alone accounted for most of the evening's intelligent conversation and female attractiveness. She had taught history for three years and was taking the semester off to work at the great library of nearby Heidelberg University, putting the finishing touches on her dissertation. Tall and long-limbed, with a languid grace and a definitely provocative eye, she chatted easily about a variety of esoteric subjects, from the evolution of Paleocene mammals, to polyphonal baroque music, to the chemistry of altered states of consciousness. Gideon, as usual, was fairly quiet, and Janet's attention had been greedily seized by the other two men at the table—not so much, however, that he failed to perceive the asides she made for his benefit, or to note an occasional dark-eyed glance in his direction.

Gideon Oliver was not a conventionally handsome man, and he knew it. He also knew that his big frame, broken nose, and soft brown eyes gave him a gentle ruggedness that many women found attractive.

He was by no means on the prowl. His wife of nine years, whom he had loved with all his soul, had died in an automobile accident two years earlier, and just as he had found no one to compare with her when she was alive, he had found no one since, and he wasn't looking hard. Still, even if not overly susceptible to women, he was by no means immune, and felt, through the wine-induced lassitude, a familiar stirring whenever

7

Janet rearranged her long legs and looked briefly at him with unmistakably friendly intent.

The other two at the table had contributed less to the evening's pleasures. Bruce Danzig, the faculty librarian, was a fussy little man with fussy little hands and feet and a neat little lump of a pot belly—like a cantaloupe—across the exact center of which his belt lay. He delivered his words with irritating precision, pursing and stretching his lips lest a single phoneme emerge incompletely rounded.

On Gideon's other side, between him and Janet, sat Eric Bozzini, assistant professor of psychology. Three times during the meal he described himself as a laid-back Californian, and groomed himself for the part: long hair, neatly trimmed into a sort of page-boy cut below the ears, a Pancho Villa mustache, tinted glasses that never seemed to come off, and an open-throated shirt revealing some sort of canine attached to a thin, gold chain and nestling on a tanned, hairy chest. But at something near Gideon's own age of thirty-eight, the image was wearing a little thin; a widow's peak was discernible under the brushed-forward hairline, the face was a little fleshy, the chest a trifle puffy and soft-looking. Even the bronze skin seemed sun-lamp-induced.

Gideon thoroughly enjoyed the dinner. While Bozzini directed his laid-back charms at Janet with grim determination, and Danzig competed with prissy little attempts at humor, Gideon concentrated on the food, enjoying the ripe German menu terms—*Zwiebelsuppe, Forelle, gemandeltes Truthahnschnitzel*—almost as much as the food itself: clear onion soup, lightly grilled fresh trout, and sautéed turkey breast dusted with almonds. And of course the German wine: live, piquant, and intoxicating. Afterwards came coffee and enormous portions of *Schwarzwäldertorte*—Black Forest cake.

After the tables were cleared, the waiters, gratifyingly obsequious, continued to move about refilling glasses with the luscious wine. This helped considerably during the long speeches by assorted college and military officials. Gideon, like most of the others, sat through them with a pleasant if slightly glassy-eyed

8

expression. Administrators of the United States Overseas College welcomed them to the program, and military officers thanked them for bringing college courses to Our Boys in Europe, joking ponderously about them having all the advantages of army life (PX privileges, base housing, officer club memberships, free movies) and none of the disadvantages (unspecified).

Once, after hearing several speakers use the term, Gideon leaned over to ask Bozzini what a "you-socker" was, thinking it was a military word.

Bozzini laughed. "*You* are, man. A USOC'r." He waited for Gideon's answering laughter, which did not come. "Don't you get it? United States Overseas College; U—"

"I get it," Gideon said.

About an hour into the speeches, Gideon, in a happy, nearly mindless daze, was puzzled to find his tablemates making peculiar faces at him, wiggling eyebrows and jerking heads. At the same time he became aware that the room was quiet.

Finally, Bruce Danzig spoke in a stage whisper, mouthing each syllable extravagantly. "Gide-*on*, stand up!" Frowning, Gideon stood.

"Ah," said the platform speaker with heavy joviality, "we wondered if you were still with us, Professor." Dr. Rufus, the college's chancellor, had an avuncular smile on his pleasant, smooth face.

"Sorry, sir," said Gideon with a sheepish smile. "I was deeply engrossed in mental preparation of my lecture notes."

Laughter and applause came from the other tables, as well as shouts of "Give him some more wine!" Gideon was pleased to see Janet smile.

The chancellor went on. "Dr. Gideon Oliver, whom I am happy to have you all meet, does well to so occupy himself. He has a lot of lectures to give. Professor Oliver, as I mentioned a moment ago—some time ago, actually—is this semester's visiting fellow. He comes to us on a leave of absence from Northern California State University"—scattered applause and a look of surprise from Eric Bozzini—"where he is an associate professor of anthropology. As those of you who are old-timers know, the

9

visiting fellow is expected to cover quite a bit of ground in two months, both academically and geographically, ha, ha."

There was a polite spatter of laughter from the tipsy scholars, and Gideon smiled dutifully.

"Professor Oliver," boomed Dr. Rufus, "will be presenting the Visiting Fellow Seminars in Human Evolution at, um. . . ." He consulted his notes. "Let me see; Sicily first, then back here to Heidelberg, then Madrid, then, ah, Izmir. . . ."

Gideon's mind focused soggily. Izmir? Madrid? Sicily? That wasn't the schedule he'd contracted for. Heidelberg had been on it all right, but the other places had all been German cities too— Munich, Kaiserslautern, some others he couldn't remember. Was Dr. Rufus confusing him with someone else? He hoped not; the revised schedule was tremendously more exciting. But they might at least have checked with him about it.

"As most of you know," continued Dr. Rufus, "we have not had a visiting fellow since the semester before last, ever since . . . well, since the semester before last."

Dr. Rufus frowned and paused, and a small ripple of discomfort seemed to spread over the room. Was Gideon imagining it, or did most of the eyes watching him suddenly avoid contact?

Dr. Rufus had lost his train of thought and did not recover well. "And so," he said, no longer jovial, "and so I . . . with pleasure I welcome Professor Oliver to the USOC faculty for the fall semester. Thank you." Abruptly, he turned from the lectern and went to his seat.

"Hey, man," said Eric before Gideon had quite sat down. "I didn't know you were from California. Northern Cal, where's that at, near San Francisco?"

"About twenty miles south. San Mateo."

"Far out. California. No kidding." He turned to Janet. "Hey, Janet, remember that other guy we had from L.A., Denny Something?"

Janet laughed. "The one who fell asleep after he taught a class on a submarine, and wound up at the South Pole?"

"Nah, that was Gordon Something. I mean the chemistry

10

instructor, remember? Who got stuck in jail in Spain because the border guards thought his demonstration stuff was coke?"

They were both laughing now, well into their cups; old friends excluding Gideon and not paying much attention to Danzig, who sipped his wine and stared into the middle distance.

"Mmm," Janet said, spluttering slightly into the brimming glass at her lips, "what about the time—was it '74?—when they wouldn't let Ralph Kaplan off a base during a big alert, so he swiped a general's uniform and tried to get through the gate?"

"Yeah, with that beard yet!" Eric and Janet both spluttered this time, spraying Gideon with Reisling.

"Ooh," Janet said, "what about Pete Somebody, remember? That funny visiting fellow in Economics, I think it was, the one who didn't show up for class half the time, and then finally disappeared altogether and—"

"Uh, Janet." Eric put his hand on her arm. He made, Gideon thought, a faint motion in his direction. Janet looked confused for a moment, then closed her mouth.

"Look," Gideon said, "what is it with this visiting fellow? What happened to him?"

After an uncomfortable silence, Danzig spoke carefully. "Really, perhaps we shouldn't be frightening off our new fellow with horror stories from the remote past."

"Horror stories?" said Gideon.

"Figuratively speaking," said Danzig, composing a prim smile. "Just your typical war stories. You'll be telling them yourself a few months from now."

Janet and Eric studied their glasses. Bruce added, "Nothing you need concern yourself with, Gideon." He made the statement word by separate word, slowly, as if it were loaded with significance. But then, thought Gideon, that's the way he tells you the time.

He began to ask another question, but changed his mind. If they wanted to play at being coy or whatever they were doing, the hell with them. He was going home. To the hotel, that is. Gideon shoved his chair back from the table and stood up, ready

11

to leave. His high spirits were suddenly gone, the good-old-boy stories did not entertain him, and his half-hatched plans for Janet were somehow no longer of interest. Jet lag had finally hit him; if he didn't get to his bed at the Hotel Ballman very shortly, he'd curl up and go to sleep on the floor of the Weinstube.

He turned from the table without saying good night, catching what he thought was a brief, silent glance between the three of them, and made his way towards the door. Others were milling about, getting ready to leave, and he caught sight of Dr. Rufus self-consciously circulating about, bearlike and jolly, thumping shoulders and shaking hands. When he saw Gideon, he smiled briefly—a twitch of the lips was more like it—and rather suddenly engaged himself in deep conversation with an older man and woman, both senior faculty members.

Gideon waited quietly. There were things that were bothering him, and he was going to buttonhole Dr. Rufus whether the chancellor liked it or not. When the older couple had made their good-byes, Dr. Rufus turned innocently in the direction opposite to Gideon and moved quickly toward another clump of people. Gideon called to him.

The chancellor turned, registering surprise. "Ah, the estimable Professor Oliver! I hope you had a pleasant evening."

"Yes, I did, thanks, but there are a few things I'd like to ask you."

"You bet; certainly. Ask away." He beamed at Gideon, blue eyes twinkling, rosy cheeks shining.

"Well, that schedule of mine. Is that right? I was expecting to go to Munich, Kaiserslautern—"

"Oh my, didn't you get my letter? No? It was a sudden change indeed. Had to change quite a few schedules. When did you leave the U.S.?"

"Tuesday."

"Ah, yes. I believe it was mailed—they were mailed—letters to people whose schedules we changed . . . uh. . . ." He mopped his glistening pink face with a handkerchief. "Mmm, uh, last Friday. Probably passed you going the other way. No inconvenience, I hope?"

"No, not at all. It's rather exciting. It's just a surprise."

"Well, I'm sorry if this has caught you off guard. Happens all the time in this business. Military exercise or an alert, and we just have to change our schedules. Fortunes of war. Here to serve. Well, my boy, good night—"

"Dr. Rufus, what happened to the last visiting fellow?"

The dank handkerchief dabbed once more. "Ah, yes. Dr. Dee. Well. Hmm. That was unfortunate. Yes. Didn't I tell you about it? No?"

Gideon restrained himself. "No," he said.

"Mm. Well, he, uh, died in an automobile accident. Quite sad. Just drove off the side of a mountain. On the Autostrada del Sole in Italy. Near Cosenza, I think. Right off the side of the mountain. Apparently just a case of driving too fast. He'd almost been killed in another car accident a few weeks before. Somewhat odd behavior for a psychologist, really."

There was something wrong with the story, but Gideon was too tired to work it out. Dr. Rufus patted him on the shoulder. "Well, no need for you to worry yourself about it. Get yourself a good night's sleep; you're looking a little worn out, and no wonder. . . ." He began to move off.

"Wait!" called Gideon. "I thought—wasn't he an economist? And I thought he *disappeared*. Isn't that right?"

"Oh my, no." Dr. Rufus wiped his face again. "You're thinking of the fellow *before* last, Dr. Pitkin. Oh yes, that's another story entirely."

"You're telling me that, of the last two visiting fellows, one was killed and one just . . . just disappeared?" Gideon's voice, husky with fatigue, rose to an embarrassing squeak on the last word. "And what happened to the ones before that? Does this sort of thing happen all the time around here? Or just to visiting fellows?"

The chancellor smiled softly and shrugged. Before he could answer, Gideon went on. "Is that why the visiting fellow program was cancelled for a semester?"

"Well, yes, as a matter of fact. To have two such unfortunate occurrences, one after the other . . . well, the program was

13

getting a bad name." He chuckled weakly, frowned, converted the chuckle to a discreet cough, and went over the back of his neck with his handkerchief. "Gideon, you know you haven't slept for almost three nights, and you're obviously exhausted. Get yourself a good night's sleep. Things won't seem so, er, frightening in the morning."

"I'm not frightened, Dr. Rufus, but I am a little . . . troubled. I wish you'd told me about this before."

"Well, I wanted you to take the position, you know. Didn't want to scare you off. Besides, would you have turned down the chance to teach over here if I *had* told you?"

Gideon smiled. "Not a chance. Well, I think I will get off to bed now."

"I think that's a good idea." He patted Gideon's shoulder again. "I'm going too. Can I give you a ride?"

"No thanks. A walk will do me good. Thanks for talking with me, sir." He was trying to make amends for putting the chancellor through an undeservedly uncomfortable time.

"Not at all, Gideon, not at all. Glad to have you on board. Get a good night's sleep now."

The night air of Heidelberg was indeed just what he needed. To step from the noise and stale smoke of the Weinstube into the dark, open courtyard of the castle was like walking into another century—a clear, cool, tranquil century. Gideon knew well enough that the 1300s, when the existing castle had been built, had been no less traumatic than the 1900s. But now, with the courtyard empty and the air, damp with river mist, on his face, Gideon found the scene wonderfully peaceful. His breath came more easily; his nerves almost perceptibly stopped jangling. He stood in the deserted courtyard, thinking of nothing, letting his mind resettle itself into its usual, placid mode.

Slowly, he walked down the curving road that descended to the Old Town, stopping now and then to look out over the rooftops and the glistening river, or to run his hand over the jumbled piles of smooth stone blocks that gleamed like pewter in the moonlight: all that remained of the once-formidable castle outposts.

The jittery, near-paranoid state he had fallen into now seemed absurd and a little embarrassing; he had been unreasonably rude to people trying to be friendly.

When he had been offered the visiting fellowship six months before, he had jumped at the chance and had begun to talk about it as his Great Adventure. And then, at the first hint of danger—if you could call it that—he had developed the raving heebie-jeebies. It had to be the lack of sleep. And all that wine.

The job was perfect; his course material was stimulating, the places he was going were exciting—much more exciting than his original assignment—and his working hours were unbelievable. Each seminar would run for four evenings, Monday through Thursday, leaving the daytime hours free for exploring, and giving him four whole days to travel to the next location and see some more of Europe on the way.

At the bottom of the hill, along the quiet Zwingerstrasse, he looked with pleasure at the scattered buildings of grand old Heidelberg University. Some of the walls were spray-painted with political slogans, a sight that caused him mild pain. It was one thing to scrawl graffiti on the buildings of Northern Cal; but Heidelberg University . . . ! It just didn't seem right. A sign of the times, he thought to himself, then chuckled at the pun. He was more than a little tight, he realized.

Twice during his walk, cars full of mildly boisterous USOC'rs went by on their way from the castle to the hotel. Both times he stepped into the shadows. Not that he was trying to avoid them, exactly, but it was nice to be by himself.

Reaching Rohrbacherstrasse he was plumped abruptly back into the twentieth century. Even at midnight, the traffic whizzed by steadily at the alarming speed that appeared to be customary for city driving. Forty miles an hour? Fifty? With more prudence than he would have shown on a San Francisco street, he waited at the corner for the traffic light to change, looking at the dark, second-floor windows of the Hotel Ballman across the street. He thought he had identified the one belonging to his room, but realized he·was wrong when he saw someone move behind it.

In the darkened room, the tall man dozed in the chair, both hands dangling over the sides, knuckles touching the floor. The other one stood at the window, a little to one side. "Here he is," he said.

The first man stood up at once. "God damn it, it's about time," he said. He moved to the window. "What the hell is he staring up here for, dumb bastard?"

"He's just looking," said the sleek-headed man. "He's plastered; he can't see anything. Don't worry."

"Who's worried?" the tall man said.

They watched him cross the street on unsteady legs. Then, silently, they walked across the room. The tall one stood against the wall to the side of the door, a thin silken cord with a leather ratchet in his hand. The other one stood in the closet alcove a few feet away. They didn't look at each other.

When he stepped into the little lobby of the hotel, Gideon expected to find it full of USOC'rs, but they had evidently gone on to do some bar-hopping, or weinstube-hopping, more likely. Only the landlady was there, dour and indifferent to his nodded greeting. He climbed the stairs wearily, fatigued to his bones. At the door to his room, he searched unsuccessfully through his pockets for the key. He rattled the handle of the heavy door, also without success. For a few moments he remained befuddled, checking his pockets again and again, grumpily lecturing himself on the counterproductivity of fixated behavior. At last he remembered that he didn't have the key. In a scene that had amused some of the old-timers, it had been wrestled from him by the proprietress when he had left that afternoon. Odd, with all the reading he'd done on European customs, he had overlooked the fact that you didn't take your key with you when you left your hotel.

With a grumble and a sigh he went back downstairs and approached the landlady, who watched him with a malevolent eye. He took a breath and drew for the first time on his recent months of self-study.

"*Guten Abend, gnädige Frau,*" he said. "*Ich habe . . . Ich habe nicht mein, mein. . . .*" Here *German Made Simple* failed him. He made key-turning movements. She sat stolidly.

"*Das Ding für . . . für die Tür?*" he said, continuing to turn his imaginary key in the imaginary lock.

"*Schlüssel,*" she said with a disgusted shake of her head.

She turned, plucked the key and its large attached brass plate from the rack behind her, and plunked them on the desk.

"*Ach, ja, Schlüssel, Schlüssel,*" he cried, grinning with his best try at hearty Teutonic joviality, wondering at the same time why in the world he was trying to placate her. She was, as ever, unresponsive.

Then back upstairs, under her suspicious glower, with heavy feet and a stomach beginning to go queasy. The second piece of Black Forest cake had been a mistake. Or maybe it was the twelfth glass of wine. With a hand less steady than it had been even an hour before, he inserted the big key in the lock and opened the door.

When he flicked on the lights, things happened so fast they barely registered. He found himself looking into a taut-skinned face set on a peculiarly long neck. Before he could react, there was a movement behind him and a stunning blow at the base of his skull. A second blow smashed him heavily between the shoulder blades, driving the breath out of him, and something snapped fiercely around his throat. He fell to his knees, clawing at his neck, dazed and breathless, with dimming vision.

As the darkening room began to swirl about him, the band around his throat suddenly loosened, and he dropped, gasping, to his elbows, letting his forehead sink to the floor.

The long-necked man in front of him grasped his hair and pulled his head up. "All right, Oliver," he said, his voice a deep baritone that didn't belong with the ferretlike face, "give us trouble and you're dead, you understand?"

Gideon tried to speak but couldn't. He nodded his head, his mind a jumble.

"All right, you know what we're here for. Let's have it."

Gideon managed to croak a response. "Look, I don't know what this—" The band which had remained loosely about his

17

neck was tugged viciously from behind. The darkness closed in again. Gideon gasped, swayed backwards, and lost consciousness.

He seemed to be out for only a second, but when he came painfully to his senses, he was lying on his stomach. His jacket had been removed. He groaned and began to turn over.

"Lay there," the baritone said. "Try to move and I kill you now."

While they searched his clothing and probed roughly at surprising parts of his body, he lay on his face trying to gather his thoughts and his strength. What could be going on? Who did they think he was? No, they had called him by name; they knew who he was. It wasn't money; that was clear. They were looking for something specific. They knew what they were about, and they had the brutal competence of professional killers, at least from what he'd seen at the movies. It had to be a bizarre mistake.

As a man of studied self-observation, Gideon had never satisfied himself as to whether he was physically brave. Sometimes yes, sometimes no. This was definitely a no. His head hurt ferociously, his neck felt as if it had been seared with a hot iron, his stomach was heaving, and his limbs were completely without strength. And he was just plain scared to death; no arguing with it.

"Look," he said, his mouth against the wooden floor, "this is some kind of crazy mistake. I'm a professor. I just got here—"

"Shut up. Stand up. Keep your hands behind your head."

As Gideon began to rise he became aware of something in his right hand. Something cold and hard. The key. The key and its heavy brass plate. Somehow he'd held on to them all the time. He buried them deeper in his palm. Once on his feet, he moved his hands behind his head, keeping both of them clenched, and stood swaying, his eyes closed, while a billow of pain and nausea flowed over him.

The sleek-headed one spoke again. "Now where the hell is it? If we have to cut your gut open to see if you swallowed it, believe me, we'll do it. I *mean* it, you son of a bitch." As if Gideon needed convincing, he removed from his inside jacket pocket a

18

thin, gleaming stiletto, like a prop from an Italian opera, but obviously the genuine thing.

When Gideon did not reply, the man gazed thoughtfully at him, his tongue playing over his upper lip, his head nodding slowly.

"So," he said, his rich voice cordial and caressing, "now we see."

He nodded more sharply to the other man, who was off to the side, barely within Gideon's range of vision, and who now began to circle around behind him. He was very tall. His eyes down, Gideon waited until he could see the large feet behind his own. Then, as suddenly as he could, he scraped his right heel savagely down the other man's shin and jammed it into his instep. Almost simultaneously he pivoted sharply from his hips with his hands still clasped behind his neck, hoping to find the other man's head with his elbow. It smashed into his throat instead. There was an unpleasant crackling sound and the lanky form collapsed against the wall.

The sleek, ferret-faced man hissed sharply and sprang with athletic speed into a crouch, the knife in his hand, low and pointing upwards. With an unconsciously imitative response, Gideon bent low and thrust the brass plate forward. The other man checked himself for an instant and stared at the plate. He made a gutteral sound low in his throat, then moved in, sinuous and graceful. Gideon hurled the key and plate at him. They flew by his head and into a wall-mounted mirror, which cracked into several large pieces, hung there for an instant, and slid down the wall with a huge crash.

At the sound, Gideon made for the door, but the smaller man, with a crablike hop, was there before him, still hunched over, still pointing the knife up at Gideon's abdomen. They stood looking at each other for a few seconds. Off to the side, the tall man groaned and began to get up, clutching his throat. Gideon's mind was in a strange state. He was certain he was about to die, and almost equally sure it was all a dream. He was calm now, and his mind was focused. He looked about him for anything he might use as a weapon.

His hand had closed on a heavy ashtray when there was a thumping on the door, accompanied by the landlady's agitated shouts.

"*Herr Oliver! Was ist los? Herr Oliver!*"

The three men froze and watched in fascination as the handle turned and the door opened. When Frau Gross saw the extraordinary scene within, she too remained frozen, so that the four of them seemed—to a slightly bemused, not altogether rational Gideon—like a tableau presented by a high school drama group. Here was the hero, doomed and defiant, lithe, ready to leap; there was the villain, cringing and contemptible, glittering dagger in hand; there was his cowardly minion; and there the heroine, hand upon the door handle, mouth open in artful astonishment. . . .

The mouth opened yet wider, emitted a preliminary bleat, and then a full-throated bellow.

"*Hilfe! Hilfe! Polizei!*"

"Quiet!" whispered Ferret-face urgently. "*Ruhig!*" He gestured at her with his knife.

At this, Frau Gross's formidable jowls quivered, seemingly more in indignation than in fear; her hand moved to her breast so that she stood like Brunhilde herself; and she gave forth a shriek that stunned the senses. The two intruders looked at each other, then dashed out the door, shoving Frau Gross out of the way. For a second she stopped howling. Then she took a measured breath and began again with renewed vigor, staring at Gideon with emotionless, piglike eyes.

2

WITH THE MORNING SUNLIGHT streaming through the windows of the Hotel Ballman's breakfast room, and the fragrance of rich European coffee in the air, the horrors of the night had paled to a kind of good guys–bad guys adventure farce, which Gideon was happily describing to a rapt gathering of fellow USOC'rs. He had already gone over the details with the unsympathetic American MPs and the rough, green-uniformed German Polizei who had arrived within minutes after the two men had fled. Now, with a more amiable audience, he was telling things at his own pace, perhaps leaving out a few unnecessary details here and embellishing a little there for the sake of the narrative flow.

He was about to explain how he had carefully palmed the key and brass plate as soon as he had entered his room and found the men, when he saw the husky Oriental come in. The newcomer walked to Frau Gross, who was sullenly laying out baskets of hard rolls and individual little packages of cheese and jam. The landlady gestured ill-naturedly at Gideon with her chin, and the big man—Gideon guessed he was Chinese Hawaiian—walked toward him.

"Dr. Oliver? I wonder, could I talk to you a little?"

Gideon excused himself and got up, and they went to an unoccupied table.

"My name's John Lau, Professor. I'm a police officer." He laid an open card case on the table, revealing a blue, plastic-coated card, and left it there until Gideon had had time to read it.

NATO Security Directorate Identification was printed across the top, and a better-than-average ID photograph was on the left. Then: Name of Employee John Francis Lau; Issuing Department or Agency AFCENT; Ht 6-2; Wt 220; Hr clr Blk; Eye clr Brn; Birth date 7-24-40; Issue date 4-23-70.

Gideon nodded. "All right, what can I do for you, Mr. Lau?"

Lau had made himself comfortable, ordering coffee for both of them, while Gideon had examined his card. Now he flashed a sudden, good-natured smile. "Not Mr. Lau. Just John." He didn't look like Gideon's idea of a policeman. "I'd like to ask you a few questions about last night."

Gideon sighed. "I've already been through it three times with the Polizei and the MPs. . . . But I guess you already know that."

Again the eye-crinkling smile. Gideon liked the man's face, relaxed and powerful. "Sure," he said. "Look, what I want to know is, do you have any idea what they were after?" He had a choppy, pleasant way of talking.

The coffee was dumped down in front of them by Frau Gross. Gideon shook his head slowly while stirring in cream. "No idea, none at all."

"Well, try guessing, then."

"Guessing?"

"Guessing. Pretend you're me. What would be your theory?" It had the sound of a harmless academic exercise. Gideon sometimes used the very same words in Anthropology 101.

"Theory? I don't even have a hypothesis. You're the expert; what do you think?"

"You told the Polizei they were Americans," Lau said. "Is that an inference, or can you support it?" Another Anthro 101 question, Gideon thought.

"I told them *one* of them—the one that spoke—was an American. I could tell from the way he talked."

"What makes you so sure? People speak more than one language."

Gideon sipped his coffee and shook his head emphatically. "Uh uh. I'm not talking about languages; I'm talking about speech patterns. He was born in the U.S., or maybe he came here—I mean there—when he was a kid; five, six, no older."

Lau looked doubtful, and Gideon went on. "I'm telling you, the guy spoke native American; midwestern, maybe Iowa or Nebraska. It's a question of stress, of lilt."

Lau regarded him blankly. Gideon searched his mind for a simple example.

"Do you remember," he said, "when he said to me, uh . . . 'Try to move and I kill you now'? Well, aside from having no trace of foreign pronunciation, he said it the way only an American would. First, there was the rise-and-fall inflection; unmistakable in simple declarative sentences. Medium pitch at the beginning, up on the 'kill you,' and then down on the 'now.' "

"Are you telling me—?"

"That's not the critical part. Some foreigners learn to do that consistently. But the way the words are grouped—the flow, the clotting—that's what tells you for sure. When an American talks,

22

he jams a lot of words into irregular groupings, so the beat's uneven. If you know how to listen for it, you can't miss it."

Lau's expression was anything but convinced. Gideon continued, his teaching instincts warming to the challenge.

"Let's say that he'd used a slightly shorter sentence like 'Move and I kill you now.' In that case he would have given about the same amount of time to 'move' and 'kill you.' Americans and Europeans both do that. But he threw in that 'try to' at the beginning, so that there were a few more words supporting 'move.' Well, a native midwestern speaker of what's sometimes called 'General American' tries to compress all three words into the same amount of time as the one word, and then lags a little in the next word group."

Lau was leaning back in his chair, his arms crossed, apparently trying to decide whether Gideon was a purposeful liar or a simple academic quack. Gideon kept trying:

"Let's say he'd made the sentence even longer—'Just try to move and I kill you now.' Then he'd try to squeeze all of the first four words into the same time as 'move.' It would be "just-try-to-move and I kill-you-now.' Only Americans use that kind of rhythm, and no matter how well you learn the phonemes—the sounds—of a foreign language, you never get the rhythms exactly right. For example, a Frenchman would use a nice, steady beat throughout the whole sentence. He'd say 'Just-try, to-move, and-I-kill, you-now.' A German—"

"What's my accent?" Lau said suddenly. "Do I speak General American?" The challenge was implicit but clear: Do you have the nerve to say I don't?

"No, you don't. There are Chinese overtones. Your individual syllables are a little more separate and even, and naturally there's a little more emphasis on tone, a little less on stress."

Gideon expected him to be angry; instead, he simply looked even more skeptical.

"Look," said Gideon, "I'm an anthropologist. This is the sort of thing I study." The last and least effective argument of the frustrated teacher, he thought.

"I thought anthropologists studied primitive cultures."

23

"We do, but linguistics is part of culture. And we study culture in general, not just primitive ones."

Lau thought it over. Suddenly banging on the table with his hand so that Gideon jumped, he said, "I don't buy it! You're practically telling me language is inherited, not learned. That's ridiculous!" His hands chopped the air.

Gideon was becoming a little irritated. "First, that isn't what I'm telling you," he said. "Second, it certainly seems to me you *do* have a hypothesis. Why are you trying so hard to get me to say he wasn't an American?"

"I'm not trying to get you to say anything. Don't get touchy." Suddenly he was very much a policeman, issuing a steely, unmistakable warning. Gideon's irritation was replaced by a stab of concern. He very nearly asked if he were in some sort of trouble, but held his tongue.

Lau glared at him a moment longer. Then his eyes crinkled, and the mild, affable Hawaiian returned. "I'm sorry. I guess I'm touchy too. We've both been up most of the night on this, haven't we? And my guess is it's been a little tougher on you than on me." Again the friendly smile. Gideon returned it, but now he was wary.

Lau went on. "I've read the report, but there's one thing I'm not very clear about." He held his cup in both hands, seemingly absorbed in its contents. "Would you mind going over how you got away from them after they pulled the knife?"

"All right. I just stamped on the one guy's foot—"

Lau looked puzzled. "I understood you scraped down his shin with your heel and *then* stamped."

"Well, yes, I did, sure, but I didn't think it was important enough—"

"Okay, I just want to make sure I have it straight. Go ahead."

"Then I sort of swung around—my hands were still behind my head—and I lucked out and hit him in the neck. . . ."

Gideon stopped. Lau was smiling cheerfully at him. "Okay," said Gideon, "what now? I'm getting the feeling you know something I don't."

Still grinning, the policeman unbuttoned the flap on the

pocket of his denim shirt and took out a small notebook. "This is from the tape the MPs made of your story. Verbatim. 'Then I pivoted around. I drove my left elbow into his larynx. I caught him on the thyroid cartilage, at the apex of the laryngeal prominence.' Uh, as a simple policeman, can I assume you're referring to the Adam's apple?"

Gideon, on guard, nodded. Lau continued. "That's pretty technical language, isn't it? Or don't tell me you're an anatomist, too?"

"Yes, I'm an anatomist, too," said Gideon, showing more heat than he intended. "My primary field is physical anthropology—that's skulls and bones—" he permitted himself a condescending smile at Lau, who returned it with evident good humor—"and you have to know anatomy for that."

Lau nodded. "I see. Well, what I was wondering . . . that's a pretty fortunate piece of 'lucking out'—I mean accidentally connecting with the Adam's apple—excuse me, the laryngeal prominence—" he consulted his notebook—"of the thyroid cartilage of the larynx. That's a pretty vulnerable spot. You didn't happen to know, I suppose, that an elbow smash there is a standard defensive maneuver against someone who's got you from behind?" Again he had his coffee cup in both hands and was swirling the dregs and carefully examining them.

"No, I damn well didn't know," Gideon said. "What the hell are you trying to imply? I'm telling you I had a lucky—"

"And the business of scraping down the shin with the heel. Very impressive. About the most painful thing you can do to a man without really injuring him. Always effective." He drained the coffee. "Didn't know about that either?"

"Well, to tell the truth—" Lau looked sharply up at him from under his eyebrows, and Gideon continued—"to tell the truth, I read about that in a self-defense book when I was a kid, but I never tried it before."

For a second Lau looked angry. Then his eyes crinkled again, and he laughed with a babylike spontaneity that made it impossible for Gideon not to join him.

"It's the truth, honest," Gideon said through his laughter. Lau kept on laughing. Gideon suddenly remembered something. "Hey, wait a minute. That guy, the one I said was an American. . . ."

Reluctantly, the policeman sobered. "Yes, what about him?"

"Well, he was American all right, but he's spent a lot of time in Europe; in Germany, I think. I just realized it. What was it he said? 'So, now we find out.' No, it was, 'So, now we see.' That's not American syntax. And he said it the *way* a German would: 'So, now . . . we see.' Americans don't do that. The construction isn't American, and certainly the rhythm isn't. Could be he had German parents, but I don't think so. I think he's an American who's been here a long time."

Lau was unimpressed. "I'm not sure I buy that. But please,"— he held up a hand as Gideon began to speak—"I don't think I can handle another linguistics lecture. Doc, are you going to be in Heidelberg a while?"

"No, I leave Sunday morning for Sicily. I have to give some lectures there next week. But I'll be back in Heidelberg the week after. Probably arrive a week from Sunday."

"Fine. I might want to get in touch with you."

"Okay, but I won't be staying here. I'll be at the Bachelor Officers' Quarters. Cheaper. And a lot more convenient to the classes."

"Good idea. The BOQ will be safer, too."

"What do you mean? You don't think they'll come again?"

"No, no," said Lau, "I doubt it." A pause, then the sudden grin again. "I was thinking about your landlady over there by the sideboard. She looks like she'd like to poison you."

Gideon smiled thinly. "Yes. I think she holds me responsible for that broken mirror."

"It's not only that," said Lau. "She doesn't trust you."

"She doesn't *trust* me?"

"Uh uh. She never found the key you broke the mirror with, you know."

"Well, yes, I assume one of those two guys—"

"And she says you tried to steal it from her yesterday afternoon. You know she turned in a police report on that?"

This was news to Gideon. "You're kidding!" he said.

"No, I'm not kidding," said Lau, but he was laughing again, and Gideon laughed along.

3

THE AFTERNOON WAS FREE of business. There was a bus tour to the gardens at Schwetzingen, arranged for the new faculty with the compliments of the administration, but Gideon declined to go. Aside from a constitutional aversion to group tours, he didn't relish the idea of further questions on the attack. He told Dr. Rufus he would use the afternoon to catch up on his sleep. Actually, he was looking forward to spending the time alone, going back to Heidelberg Castle to explore the vast, turreted ruins and terraced gardens at his own leisurely pace.

He lunched at a busy seafood bar on the Haupstrasse, dining happily on little sandwiches of marinated herring—*Bismarck-hering*—at one mark each. When he went back to the hotel to pick up his guidebook to the castle, John Lau was waiting in the lobby, joking with Frau Gross. He actually had her laughing, but Gideon's entrance had its usual sobering effect.

"Hi, Doc," Lau said, sounding glad to see him. "You got some time to go over to NSD headquarters with me? There's somebody else who'd like to talk to you."

"Sure." Questions from the police were a different thing than questions from curious colleagues. He had enjoyed the earlier talk with Lau and looked forward to more of the same, plus an inside glimpse of the NATO Security Directorate.

Expecting them to drive to the USAREUR command complex at the edge of town, he was surprised when John walked him two blocks down Rohrbacherstrasse to a two-story brownstone building, heavy, dingy, and cheerless.

"This is your headquarters?"

"In Germany, yes."

"Boy, as far as I can see, you picked the only genuinely ugly building in Heidelberg. I mean, that is an *ugly* building."

"It figures. It was Gestapo headquarters during the war. I think we got it cheap." He smiled.

Inside there was a small vestibule, vacant except for a few wooden benches and an armed soldier who nodded balefully at Lau's ID from behind a glass partition. Grayish-green corridors ran off in three directions. It looked as if it were still Gestapo headquarters: gloomy, tacky, smelling of disinfectant and old plumbing, and single-mindedly utilitarian. Gideon felt a small shiver at the back of his neck. It was hard to picture John Lau actually working there.

Lau, in fact, seemed subdued once they were in the building. He walked with Gideon down one of the corridors to an office made marginally less bleak by a wall calendar with a color picture of a Bavarian village. A big-boned, middle-aged woman sat erectly at a typewriter near a window.

"Frau Stetten, this is Dr. Oliver to see Mr. Marks," Lau said, his voice, it seemed to Gideon, lacking its usual friendliness. Then, to Gideon's surprise, he left.

"Please sit down, Dr. Oliver. Mr. Marks will in a minute be with you." She spoke without looking up from her typing, with a strong German accent and a distinctly chilly manner. Gideon couldn't help wondering, with uncharacteristic lack of charity, if she had come with the building.

In a few minutes, at some sign that he failed to perceive, she said, "Mr. Marks can see you now. Go in, please." She gestured with her head toward a door behind her.

Gideon opened it and entered a medium-sized office with a single old-fashioned window and plain, fairly presentable gray metal furniture: a desk, three file cabinets, two chairs with cracked green plastic seat cushions. It reminded him of his own office at Northern Cal. A neat small man in suit and tie sat behind the desk. He didn't greet Gideon, but continued to write with a slow, precise hand on a yellow lined tablet. Gideon could see from the format that he was composing a memorandum. He came to the end of a sentence and placed the period carefully.

Gideon waited for him to look up, but the man put the tip of his pencil to his tongue and then began another sentence.

Gideon, who was not slow to take offense when warranted, spoke somewhat sharply. "Mr. Marks? You wanted to see me, I think?"

The man put down his pencil and took a half-finished cigarette from an ashtray before looking at Gideon. He had a natty, carefully trimmed little mustache and short dark hair. Behind horn-rimmed glasses, he made no effort to hide the boredom in his eyes. Gideon didn't like him at all.

"Have a seat. Glad to see you," he said, the words brimming with bureaucratic indifference. "Do you go by doctor or mister?"

"I go by doctor." Ordinarily, it would have been, "Call me Gideon."

"Doctor. Fine. Well, I suppose Charlie Chan told you who I am?"

"Mr. Marks, if you have some questions, please ask them. I have some things to do this afternoon."

"He didn't, I see. Well, I didn't call you in about the incident last night. I'm not in law enforcement."

"You're not in the NATO Security—in NSD?"

"Yes, I'm in NSD, which you're apparently unfamiliar with, so let me give you the two-bit lecture." His weary sigh was so elaborate that Gideon began to wonder if he was being offensive on purpose.

"The NATO Security Directorate is concerned with threats to the international security of the NATO community, with particular emphasis on terrorism and espionage. To oversimplify things—"

"Wait, hold it a minute. What does this have to do with me? Did that attack have something to do with espionage? Were they terrorists?"

Again a sigh, this time an exasperated one. Marks leaned back, put his hands behind his head, and looked at the ceiling. "Dr. Oliver, I've already told you once; I'm not interested in that incident. I've examined it with care, and it is of no interest to me. This interview has no connection with it. Period."

With an effort, Gideon stifled the impulse to say it was pretty interesting to *him*.

"Now," Marks went on, "to oversimplify things, there are four main branches of NSD. Three of those branches deal with espionage, more or less. The other, Safety, functions in effect like an ordinary police department—an international police department, however. It's concerned with protection of life and property. Murder, robbery, that sort of thing. That's your friend Lau's province. Now, the Second Bureau, of which I am a deputy director, is, so to speak, the counterespionage branch. Our job is to counteract enemy agents and terrorists. There is another branch concerned with routine intelligence operations, and then there is Bureau Four, our own little internal secret police."

It was an ill-chosen term to use in this building, Gideon felt, but Marks smiled as if he had said something witty. "The Fourth Bureau keeps us all honest," Marks went on. "It polices our own agents, as well as nationals of member countries who are suspected of spying for the other side."

He stopped abruptly. The two-bit lecture was over. "Any questions?"

"Yes. You've given me an awful lot of so-to-speaks and in-effects. If it's all the same to you, I'd appreciate having my information more precise. And I don't know that over-simplifications are necessary."

"Dr. Oliver, this isn't a college classroom. Everything you need to know, you're being told."

"Damn it, you asked me if I had any questions."

The little mustache twitched, the brow contracted, and apathy suddenly changed to clear-eyed, man-to-man candor. "All right, in all frankness, we need your help, Dr. Oliver. We want you to work with us." He inhaled massively on the stub of his cigarette and let the smoke out through tightened lips: Bogart leveling with Claude Rains in Rick's nightclub.

"Sorry, Mr. Marks, but if you're expecting a yes or no to that, I'm afraid you're going to have to tell me a lot more."

"I know. I'm just trying to decide how much you can be told."

He stood up suddenly and made what Gideon assumed was his momentous-decision face. "I'm going to ask the director just how much we can share with you."

As he walked to the door, he placed his hand on Gideon's shoulder and tightened it in a gesture of trust and conspiracy. Good God, thought Gideon, the man must have been trained in a used-car salesmen's school. Closing Technique Number Four: "Just a minute, I'll have to ask my supervisor if we can go that low." (Smile, shoulder pat.) "I'll do my best."

He sat alone for a few minutes, trying to make something of the conversation so far. Marks might be a buffoon, but this was certainly NSD headquarters, and he had just been asked, as far as he could tell, to spy for them. And all this naturally had no connection with an attack by two professional thugs—spies? agents?—last night. He wondered if they had learned from John Lau of his deductions based on speech patterns or if they shared Lau's apparent suspicion that he was a world champion karate master. No, that was ridiculous; he dismissed the thought. He wished he hadn't gone so long without a decent night's sleep.

In about fifteen minutes, Marks returned with a round, rumply man in his late sixties. Wrinkled gray trousers belted six inches below his armpits and cuffed well above his shoe tops gave him a jolly, elfin quality slightly out of kilter with his watery blue eyes. He moved quickly, reaching out to shake hands with Gideon before Marks had introduced them.

"Monsieur Delvaux, Dr. Oliver."

"How do you do, Professor. Please sit down." With the greeting came an exhalation of cheese and wine. M. Delvaux had been interrupted at his *déjeuner*.

"Do not smoke, please," he said from the side of his mouth to Marks, who raised his eyes heavenward—in Gideon's line of sight, not Delvaux's—and stubbed out his cigarette. Marks seated himself at a side chair, leaving the one behind his desk for Delvaux, but the older man perched on the large windowsill—he had to hop to get up—and began to speak rapidly and softly in a flowing French accent.

"I would like to give you some background on what Mr. Marks

31

has been telling you. For some time now, we have known—this is between us in this room, you understand—about a Soviet action of some sort that is now being planned. We don't know what that action is, but we know that it requires certain secret information from a number of NATO bases. The surreptitious procurement of that information is among the highest priorities of their intelligence machine; its prevention is among ours. We are asking your help in an activity that may be of the greatest service to your country and to the cause of peace. To yourself, there is very little danger, virtually none."

"What exactly are you asking me to do?"

"Simply to tell us if anyone, at any of the bases to which you are assigned—*anyone*—asks you to obtain or transmit sensitive information from that base to himself or to anyone else."

To his faint surprise, Gideon was disappointed. "You're not asking me to *do* anything? Just report back to you?"

"That's correct. *If* the occasion arises." The blue eyes looked steadily at him.

"Well, of course I'll do that. I'd have done it without your asking."

"I'm glad to hear that. Are there any further questions I can answer? If not, I'll leave you in Mr. Marks's capable hands." He hopped down from the sill.

"I do have some questions," Gideon said. "You said there was very little danger to me. Unless I'm missing something, I can't see any risk at all."

"You're quite right. A poor choice of words on my part. My English is far from perfect." He smiled, revealing stumpy, yellow teeth with gaps between them. His eyes didn't smile.

"I imagine the details are secret," said Gideon, "but can you give me some idea of what sort of thing they're after?"

This time the eyes smiled a little. "Ah, we would tell you if we knew, but the sad fact is that we don't know."

"You don't know what they're looking for?"

"We do not."

"Then . . . how will you know if you've kept them from getting it? Or if you haven't? Or how to try?"

32

"Ah, we'll know, Dr. Oliver, but as to how we'll know, I'm afraid we can't share that with you."

"But what about me? I wouldn't know a sensitive request if one bit me on the nose. I mean, unless someone asked me for a hydrogen bomb formula."

Marks snickered. Delvaux ignored him. "We'd like very much to know if someone does. But we think . . . perhaps someone asking you if you happen to have a key to the computer room, or if you can get him the address of one of the officers in your class, or some such thing."

"But you can't expect me to run and tell you every time—"

Delvaux's eyelids flickered. "Dr. Oliver, you are making too much of this. We are not asking you to be some sort of spy or agent. We are merely requesting of you the kindness to notify us if you are approached with a request that strikes you as peculiar and which might in some conceivable way relate to matters of security. Truthfully, we think it extremely unlikely that such an event will occur; we are merely providing for all contingencies. We leave it entirely to your discernment as to whether something is sufficiently extraordinary to notify us."

He rubbed his hands together. "That, I think, is as much as I am permitted to tell you. Will you help us?"

"Monsieur Delvaux, excuse my ignorance. I don't know what sort of authority NSD has. Are you asking my help or ordering it?"

Delvaux laughed. Gideon caught a whiff of cheese again: Emmenthaler.

"Dr. Oliver, the Security Directorate is replete with responsibility, but sadly lacking in authority. We are asking, merely asking. What do you say?"

"Ja," said Marks, "vee are only esking. But uff course ve hef our vays." He screwed an imaginary monocle into his eye.

Delvaux pretended not to notice him. "What do you say?" he asked again.

It was a time to temporize, Gideon knew. There were some elements here that made no sense, and he knew he wasn't thinking as clearly as usual. Moreover, he wasn't the sort of man who went out of his way to find ways of breaking his bones or puncturing his skin. Nevertheless, the proposition stirred his interest. Working with NSD would add a notable dimension of excitement and adventure to the whole European assignment. The probability of real danger—danger that he couldn't cope with—seemed reassuringly low; not, of course, that he took Delvaux at his word.

"Yes, I'll do it," he said.

"Excellent," said Delvaux. "Wonderful. I must get back to my office, I'm afraid. Mr. Marks will explain the details. Good-bye and thank you." Before Gideon could rise, he had shaken hands and darted gnomelike out the door.

"*Le directeur*," said Marks. He lit a cigarette, went back to his own chair, and leaned back in it, looking out the window. He had returned, Gideon gathered, to his bored and abstracted mode.

"Is he French?" Gideon asked. "The accent wasn't quite—"

"Belgian. France isn't a NATO member, as you know."

"Of course," Gideon said, but he hadn't known. Which was ridiculous. He'd have to get his head out of his archaeology texts and see what was going on in the twentieth century; or so he'd been resolving for at least five years now.

"Now," Marks went on, still looking out the window and languidly smoking. "When you have something to pass on to us from the field—from the base you're teaching at—you call back to Heidelberg, to the USOC registrar's office, and say, 'My class roster is incomplete. Could you let me have an updated one?' Got it?"

"Those exact words?"

"That would be dandy, but words to that effect will do."

"All right. Do I speak to anyone in the registrar's office, or must it be to the registrar himself?"

"Herself. Mrs. Swinnerton. No. All you need to do is leave the message with the clerical unit."

"Is Mrs. Swinnerton in on this, then? Is she one of your agents?"

"Classified information. Need-to-know principle. You

wouldn't want me to go around telling other people *you're* in on it, would you?"

Gideon nodded. "Okay, what happens after I call?"

"Then you hang up and wait and see."

"At the telephone?"

Marks had already smoked down his cigarette. He exhaled heavily and, with a large gesture as if he were turning the handle on a meat grinder, he stubbed it out. He stifled a yawn. His eyes moved to the memorandum he'd been working on. "No," he said, "just go about your business. We'll contact you. You'll know it's us because we'll make some reference to your roster." He pulled the tablet into writing position. Gideon was being dismissed, and rather more peremptorily than he liked.

In an undergraduate psychology class, he had once taken a projective test consisting of a series of cartoons. Each cartoon showed a little man saying something irritating to a second person. You were supposed to be the second person, and you took the test by filling in two blank comic strip balloons above his head. In the balloon drawn with solid lines, you wrote your spoken response. In a second balloon with dotted lines you wrote what you were really thinking. Since then, he had often found himself mentally filling in the second balloon when he dealt with annoying people. It kept him from saying things that got him in trouble—sometimes, anyway. Now he wrote in the imaginary box: pompous little fart.

Aloud he said, "All right, I guess I've got it."

"There is one more thing, of paramount importance," said Marks. "This whole thing is strictly between us."

"I understand that."

"You understand, fine. But I mean *strictly*. You, me, Delvaux. That's all."

"I heard you, Mr. Marks."

"That excludes Fu Manchu."

Gideon got to his feet. Cold stares were not his forte, but he managed what he thought was a fairly good one. "I beg your pardon?" Inside the dotted lines he wrote: nerd.

"Fu Man Lau. Nummah One Son."

"Look, Marks—"

Marks pretended to read Gideon's anger as confusion. "I had the impression that you and Lau were getting on fairly well. I just want to make sure you understand. You, me, and Delvaux."

"You don't even tell your own people?"

"John Lau isn't one of our people. He's in the safety side of the house; we're in counterespionage. I told you, we operate on the need-to-know principle. In this line of work, the fewer people who know what you're doing, the better for you and for them. The branches don't tell each other what they're doing."

"Apparently Lau or someone else in safety told you what happened to me last night."

"I needed to know. I thought it might have some bearing. It doesn't."

"You're awfully sure of that. Do you know something about it that I don't?"

"You don't need to know what I know," Marks said with an unappealingly arch smile. "Now, if there isn't anything else, there are some very important people waiting for my recommendations." He gestured at the memorandum.

Gideon made a final entry in his imaginary balloon: self-important twirp. Then he politely said good-bye and left.

4

TYPICALLY, HE WAS A worrier, but the somber, beautiful castle ruins and the grand sweep of the terraces put out of mind the fantastic happenings of the last fifteen or twenty hours. Solitary and relaxed, he roamed over the grounds until dusk.

For dinner he went to a sedate *weinstube* that had been in business, according to a plaque outside, since the 1600s; its dark, polished wooden tables might have been its original furnishings. He made a richly satisfying meal from a bottle of Mosel wine and a plate of *weisskäse*, a creamy cheese served with heavy rye bread and small dishes of paprika and raw onions.

At the hotel, he half-expected Frau Gross to refuse him entrance, but she seemed almost friendly. She wouldn't go so far as to return his smile, of course, but she did give him his key—which had been found under the bureau—and wished him a good night.

He had a moment's nervousness when he opened the door to his room, looking into the alcove and bathroom before closing it. The impulse to peek under the bed, however, he resisted, drawing a firm line between sensible precautions and outright paranoia. He set the alarm for 7:00 A.M. so he could get an early start on the military red tape involved in making travel arrangements for Sicily. By 8:30 he was happily, dreamlessly asleep.

The great stone eagles on either side of the entrance had once gripped laureled swastikas in their talons, but those had long ago been chipped away by young GIs laughing into the newsreel cameras, so that now they did duty as American eagles, guarding the headquarters of USAREUR—United States Army Europe—the heart of America's military presence on the Continent.

The eagles depressed Gideon, as did the rest of the giant complex. Despite the bright USAREUR banner over the gate, the architecture of the huge structures proclaimed them relics of Hitler's Germany, and the vast, cobblestoned interior courtyard conjured up maleficent platoons of gray-jacketed, goose-stepping Wehrmacht soldiers. Fortunately, the paperwork went faster than he had expected. By 11:30 he had his identity card, his military European driver's license, and his travel orders for Sicily. He was also very hungry and knew that at least part of his black mood came from having forgotten to breakfast.

The cafeteria was a relief, dowdy and American, with its noisy young GIs and the friendly smell of grilling hamburgers. Gideon got a cheeseburger, french fries, and a strawberry milkshake, the most American lunch he could think of. Then, as a fitting end to the meal, he had coffee and apple pie.

Much restored, he brought a second cup of coffee to his table and began to go over his interview with Marks and Delvaux the day before. At the time, he had been too tired to think of many questions, but he had plenty today.

If they didn't know what the Russians were looking for or why they were looking for it, what made them think anybody was looking for anything at all? And why did they think that whatever it was would turn up at the particular bases to which he was assigned, as opposed to the hundreds of others in Europe? Or was that what his surprise schedule was all about? Had Dr. Rufus assigned him to "sensitive" bases on instructions from NSD? Could Dr. Rufus be an agent himself? It didn't seem likely.

And, above all, why *him?* Why come to a new, green anthropology professor for this kind of thing? On the other hand, was he the only one? Was it possible that *every* faculty member was being treated to the same routine?

Maybe, but improbable. But then, was any of it probable? He had already put his questions about the schedule to Dr. Rufus and learned nothing except that they made the chancellor nervous (unless that was the way he always was).

When he finally finished at USAREUR, he went across the street to USOC Administration and headed for the faculty library to do some class preparation. He was still mulling over his questions when he passed a door that read, "Office of the Registrar, D. Swinnerton." On the spur of the moment, he went in. Although he didn't expect her to tell him anything voluntarily, she might unwittingly give something away if he were discreet. It was pretty unlikely, but really, where was the fun in being in the spy business if you couldn't play-act at it a little?

At the back of a room in which four or five clerks sat working was a space separated from the rest by glass partitions. Gideon walked over to it.

"Mrs. Swinnerton?"

A plump, round-faced woman of fifty looked up from her desk and smiled sweetly. "Why, hello, Dr. Oliver."

Quick work. He'd never met her, but she knew him by sight. Interesting. "I didn't know you knew me," he said with a smooth smile.

"Certainly. Everyone does, from when Dr. Rufus introduced you at the dinner."

So much for his first coup. "Oh," he said. "Well, I just wanted to meet you, since we'll probably be in contact quite a bit." Clumsy. Not what he'd had in mind as an opening.

"Thank you, it's certainly nice of you to come in and say hello. Not many do." Behind her grandmotherly smile, she looked a little puzzled.

"Uh, you've certainly got a good reputation with the faculty," he said. "I understand your rosters are just about always accurate and on time." Oh, that was even more brilliant, the suave, inconspicuous way he'd slipped that in. The next time he did some sleuthing on his own, he'd take some time beforehand to figure out what to say.

Mrs. Swinnerton was looking more confused. "Thank you," she said again.

"Oh, and I was thinking," Gideon said, "what if I'm teaching at some base and I have a problem with a roster and it's not during working hours? How do I get in touch with you?"

The smile had disappeared now. Her expression was puzzlement and nothing else. "What kind of problem? Why couldn't it wait for the next day?"

"Well, if a roster was incomplete, say. . . ."

"But what's the hurry? You could call us the next day. Besides, the simplest thing would be to tell the education office on the base. Let them tell us. That's their job."

"Ah, I see, yes. Yes, that would be the thing to do." Gideon was perspiring with embarrassment. "Well, thank you so much. It's a pleasure to know you, Mrs. Swinnerton. Got to get to the library now. Good-bye."

He turned and dashed for the door, having arrived at two conclusions: 1) Mrs. Swinnerton was no NSD agent—or she was a very good one, and 2) it was just possible that espionage was not his métier.

At 4:30 he sat alone in the library, coffee cup in hand,

browsing through a pile of anthropology texts. Dr. Rufus and Bruce Danzig came in together, deep in conversation, poured themselves some coffee, and joined him. Danzig blew on his coffee and sipped it, shifting it from cheek to cheek with quick little mouth movements, like a chipmunk eating a nut. Dr. Rufus drank heartily and said "ah."

"Ah," he said, "I'm glad to see you've discovered our library. Very proud of it. Bruce has done quite a job, wouldn't you say?" Even in the quiet library, Dr. Rufus didn't speak; he orated.

"Yes, quite good," Gideon said. "I'm just catching up on this year's papers."

"Did you want to check something out?" Danzig asked without interest.

"Thanks, not this time. These Sicilian lectures are just a basic overview of hominid phylogeny. I think I can get by with my notes."

"As you wish," said Danzig. He chewed up another mouthful of coffee.

"Now, now, now, now," said Dr. Rufus, "some of our students are pretty sharp cookies, after all. Don't you think you ought to have some resources at hand? No charge, you know, and it will make Bruce here very happy."

Danzig didn't appear much concerned, but Gideon didn't want to offend Dr. Rufus, so he said it might be a good idea if he did take along Simon's *Primate Evolution* and Hrdlicka's *Skeletal Remains of Early Man*.

The chancellor beamed abstractedly. "Fine, fine." He finished his coffee and smacked his lips. "Well. Um." All three men rose.

Gideon signed the book cards and gave them to Danzig. "Well, I'm off the Sicily," he said. "I'll see you in a week—that is, if I decide to come back. Some pretty great ruins down there; Syracuse, Agrigento. . . ."

"Yes, fascinating," Danzig said.

"Fine, excellent," said Dr. Rufus. "Have a wonderful time."

Book 2: Sicily

5

GETTING TO THE U.S. Naval Air Facility at Sigonella had taken a full, grueling day: a 3:00 A.M. train to Frankfurt, Lufthansa to Rome, Alitalia to Palermo, an incredibly decrepit bus to Catania, and a two-hour drive in a rented Fiat to Sigonella. Each leg of the trip had seemed tackier than the one before.

The drive from Catania had been the worst. Sicilian road signs were somewhat cursory at best, and the base itself was not on local maps. What should have been a thirty-five-minute trip had taken two hours, made all the more unpleasant by the animated, wild-driving young males who had nearly forced him off the road half-a-dozen times. Three drivers had shouted curses at him and made obscene gestures when he took what seemed to him to be reasonable safety precautions. Although their intent was unmistakable, all the words and most of the gestures were unfamiliar. Once, when he had stopped at a light that was just turning red, the driver following a few inches behind him was forced to lean hard on his brakes and had directed the familiar hand-to-forearm jerk at him. Gideon had noted with an anthropologist's interest the intercultural appeal of this signal, and had tried a middle-finger thrust in return. He had been gratified to learn that it, too, was understood in Sicily.

Once the seminar began, however, Gideon had little time for observations of Sicilian culture. He taught for three hours a day, spent six hours in the library, and caught up on his sleep in his room at the BOQ the rest of the time.

Only once did he leave the base, and then he drove to Aci

Trezza for a solitary dinner at the Vera Napoli, a well-known but plain trattoria at the seashore. At one point during the meal, he happened to look up from his plate of *linguine con vongole* and caught two men at another table off to the side staring intently at him. One, he was sure, had been in the act of making a small gesture in his direction, as if he had been calling his companion's attention to Gideon. Now he pretended that he had been reaching toward a bowl of fruit on the table, removed an apple, and bit into it with a loud snap. Then he let his glance move over Gideon once more, vacantly this time, as if unaware of him, and resumed talking to his companion.

There was something about them Gideon didn't like, even about the way the man had bitten into the apple—with a kind of hardness, a casual brutality. It made him think of the men in the hotel in Heidelberg. He felt a prickle at the back of his neck. Was he in for trouble here, too? This time, if he could help it, he'd be ready. Gideon looked at them from time to time, but they continued to be absorbed in their own conversation, and left before he did.

Aside from this, the days passed uneventfully.

Somebody was in his room.

The quarter-inch segment of paper clip on the worn hallway carpet caught his eye the moment he reached the top of the stairs. He froze with one foot raised and his hand on the bannister, then slowly lowered his foot and placed his lecture notes on the top tread.

Since coming to the BOQ, he'd stuck a piece of paper clip or match stick or cardboard between the door and jamb every time he'd left his room. For three days it had been in its hidden place every time he'd returned. Now it glinted at him like a tiny, malignant exclamation point on the threshold of his room.

He had known that one day he would find them in his room again, but somehow his plans had never solidified beyond planting the paper clip. The most sensible course, obviously, would be to go quietly down to the registration desk and ask the sailor on duty to call the shore patrol. Instead, with his scalp prickling, he got down on his hands and knees and worked his way slowly toward the room. When he reached the wall, he put his ear carefully against it.

There was no sound from within. He could hear the blood pounding in his ears, and a few doors down, two men were laughing quietly. From a television set downstairs, he could hear a parrot squawking, "Ring around the collar!" Nothing else.

Possibly, whoever had been there was gone; Gideon had been in class for three hours. Still, he kept his body low and behind the meager protection of the partition as he slowly turned the handle. The spring latch slid smoothly out with a soft click; the door was unlocked.

Gideon took a deep breath and exhaled. Then he inhaled once more, stopped his breath, and flung the door sharply open, throwing himself full-length onto the hall carpet. The flimsy door banged noisily against the metal bed frame, and Gideon stiffened himself to lunge for the legs of anyone who rushed out.

No one rushed out; the bed frame vibrated, and the door slowly swung a third of the way closed again. One part of Gideon continued to tense itself; another, convinced by now that the intruder had gone, was wondering what to say should anyone emerge from another room to find him sprawled there.

He stood up and looked directly into the room. The light in the hallway threw enough illumination to show him that no one was crouching inside. He walked in and turned on the light. No one was under the bed. No one was in the corner alcove that served as a closet. He checked the door to the bathroom he shared with the occupant of the next room. It was still bolted from his side. He opened it and looked in. It was empty.

He went back to the hall and got his lecture notes, then returned to the room and closed the door. Nothing had been moved, but he could sense that someone had been there. He spent a long time going over the room and trying to determine what had been taken. The intruder, he assumed, must have gotten what he came for, or he would have been waiting for Gideon, as had been the case in Heidelberg.

When Gideon was unable to locate anything missing, he sat

43

down and wrote a list of all the possessions he could remember, down to an underwear count. Then he went through the room again, checking off each item on the list. In the end, he came down to only one thing that wasn't in its place: a plastic bag containing his clean socks.

The idea was so ludicrous that Gideon wouldn't accept it at first. He knew that his memory for everyday things was poor. Nora had often laughed with him about his being an absent-minded professor, though he always protested that his mind wasn't absent but elsewhere, pondering weightier things. Once they had searched for fifteen minutes for a watch that was on his wrist, another time for a wallet that was already in his pocket. But the socks were not to be found, though he went so far as to go down to the car to search for them. When he came back up and stood looking stupidly at the alcove shelf for the fifth time, he suddenly remembered positively how he'd stood right there that morning and taken a green pair of socks from the bag, then changed his mind and taken a brown pair, and finally tossed the bag back on the shelf.

There wasn't any doubt about it. Someone had waited until he went to class that evening, furtively let himself into his room, searched it—and made off with two pairs of blue socks and one of green. Plus the plastic Safeway produce bag that held them.

The man didn't change his position. He remained slouched in the hard plastic chair, his hollow chest depressed and his long, skinny legs crossed at the knees and then entwined again at the ankles, the way women could sit—or men with long, skinny legs. His trousers, rucked up by the convolutions of his legs, revealed unattractive lengths of hairless white calf above beige anklets. His eyebrows were the only things that moved. They went up. His eyes remained on the sports page in front of him.

"They took *what?*" he asked, his voice barely audible above the wooshes and clanks of the washing machines.

"I know," Gideon said, "it's ridiculous. I feel stupid saying it, but that *is* what they took."

It was so absurd that he had almost decided not to bother NSD

44

with it. At eight o'clock that morning, however, he had gone to the Education Office to call USOC—the time was the same in Sicily and Heidelberg—and leave a message about an incomplete roster. Then, feeling both exhilarated and silly, he had had a big breakfast of corned beef hash and eggs at the Officers' Club.

By the time he had returned to the BOQ, there was an old, much-used transmittal envelope waiting for him at the desk. The last entry on it before "Oliver, BOQ" was "Mailroom." He had taken it up to his room in some excitement and had been a little disappointed to find it wasn't sealed, but was simply closed by means of a string wrapped around two dog-eared cardboard discs.

Inside had been a white sheet of letter paper with a navy letterhead, the kind one could buy in the PX for personal correspondence. Typed neatly in the center of the page had been "Laundromat, 9:30 A.M. Re rosters."

He had arrived at exactly 9:30 with a small load of shirts and underwear for "cover," put them into a washing machine, and sat down to wait, choosing a part of the laundromat that was uncrowded. A few minutes later, the gaunt man with the long-nosed, deeply lined cowboy's face had come in, also with a little bundle of wash. When he had set the washing machine going, he sat down near Gideon, lit a cigarette, picked up an old copy of *Stars and Stripes*, and offered a few pages of it to Gideon. Then, after a while, he had spoken without looking up from the paper, the cigarette dangling from the corner of his mouth.

"Roster trouble?"

He had not said any more until Gideon had come to the socks. Now he said slowly, "I don't know whether you're just stupid or you're trying to be funny, but let me tell you something. You're fooling around with the big leagues. Don't play games with us."

"Let me tell *you* something," said Gideon, his ready temper ignited.

"Voice down," the man said. He casually turned a page.

Gideon whispered. "I don't know what's going on—"

"Don't whisper. Just talk quietly."

Gideon opened and then closed his mouth. He didn't really have any reason to be annoyed with this man. "Look, I was asked to tell you people about anything unusual. Getting your socks stolen may be an everyday thing for you, but it's pretty unusual for me. So I told you. Now, is that it?"

"Are you positive they didn't take anything else? Did they maybe plant anything? A bug?"

"Why would they do that?" Actually, the thought had occurred to him earlier in the morning, and he had searched for one. Not knowing what one looked like made it difficult, but he had assumed it would be a button-sized gadget stuck on the bottom of a bureau drawer, or under a window sill, or behind a cabinet. He hadn't found anything.

"You never know," the man said. "Feel around for one under things when you go back."

"I already did. Nothing."

The man uncoiled his knotted legs, got his laundry—two white towels with gray stenciled letters on them—and came back to Gideon. "I like to air-dry these. Makes them smell nicer. I think your laundry's done. Have a nice day." He wished another nice day to a fat, sleepy woman near the door and walked out with a loose-legged gait that Gideon had once heard called a shit-kicker's walk.

6

THE SEMINAR HAD GONE well. On Friday evening Mary Fabriano, one of the students, gave an end-of-class cocktail party at her apartment in Catania. Gideon was forced to accept, inasmuch as he was more or less the guest of honor. As it was, he had a good time. Mary, a young nurse with wildly provocative buttocks, went out of her way to make it clear that she found him attractive and that she was unengaged for the rest of the night. He flirted with her for a while, enjoying himself. As usual, however, when it came down to brass tacks he retreated, as he had been doing since Nora's death.

He left the party at eleven o'clock, depressed and angry with himself and the world. He had wanted to go to bed with Mary, all

46

right. Of course he had. Why shouldn't he? He needed sex like anybody else. He didn't just need it; he liked it—he liked it a lot. At least he thought he did. It had been so damn long, maybe he was forgetting.

When he turned off the highway onto the Dump Road, he was deep in his thoughts. He barely noticed the dark young man watching him so intently from the passenger seat of the car slowly going the other way. Probably he wouldn't have noticed him in any case. His few days of Sicilian driving had inured him to the scrutiny that occupants of passing cars accorded each other. What should have caught his attention, however, was the peculiar fact that anyone at all was emerging from the Dump Road after midnight. The Dump Road—no one seemed to know its real name, but the nickname was apt—was a narrow, backcountry route between Sigonella and the Catania highway, used mainly as a route to work by base employees.

The night was clear, the road deserted and straight. Gideon plunged ahead at Sicilian speed, sunk in gloom. He could have been back at that cocktail party right now, damn it, going through all the delicious rigamarole of the Western pre-mating ritual. Instead, he was zooming down this black, godforsaken road, speeding toward another empty night.

He really had to have a heart-to-heart talk with himself one of these days. It wasn't that he was trying to be faithful to Nora. That would be morbid, and she wouldn't have wanted it anyway. It was just that he needed something—something he couldn't identify—that he hadn't found in anyone since Nora.

There was no shortage of sexy, available women around—that certainly wasn't the problem—but they wanted either one-night quickies or Meaningful Relationships. For him, the one would have been tawdry, the other . . . well, he just wasn't ready. It was funny, really. In his Social Institutions seminar, he separated them neatly into two concepts: the sexual drive was an ancient biological imperative, rooted in the pre-human past, whereas romance was merely a recent artifact, and a dying one at that; a twelfth-century French response to the non-ethics of feudalism. He really believed all that, or thought he did. Yet here he was

47

tied up in knots and going without either sex or romance, horny and love-starved at the same time. Maybe what he needed most—

He saw the dark shape of the car blocking the middle of the road a split second before its headlights went on, blinding him utterly. His foot clamped to the brake pedal, the wheels locked, and he went slipping and sliding toward the stopped car as if he were on ice. Except for the screeching of the tires, it was strangely like floating in a dream.

He was, to his dismay, on a low one-lane bridge with no possibility of turning off the roadway. For the second time in a week, he was sure he was about to die, but with teeth clenched and muscles straining, he stepped on the brake and foolishly pulled back on the wheel. And somehow the weaving vehicle stayed on the bridge and slowed enough so that it finally slid into the stopped car at three or four miles an hour. There was a soft clunk, like a beer can crumpling, and then a gentle, tinkling shower of headlight shards to the ground. Then silence and darkness.

Acting by instinct, Gideon fumbled free from his seat belt, flung open the door, scrambled out, and leaped over the side of the bridge to the gully a few feet below. He landed on his feet somehow, and floundered his way through underbrush and muck, back toward the end of the bridge from which he'd come. Then the flashlights went on and the shouting started, and he ducked back under the bridge and threw himself down into the foul-smelling mud behind a concrete bridge support. He lay on his stomach in the slime, panting and wet. By working his chin a little deeper into it, he was able to look back toward the center of the bridge, where the shouting was coming from.

It sounded like Italian. They were angry, perhaps swearing at each other. His eyes had adapted to the night, and he could see that there were three men. Two of them were gesticulating, appealing to the third: a tall, slender man who stood silent and immobile. The beams from the flashlights darted down from the bridge, playing over the land near where he had jumped. He would be hard to find, Gideon thought. The ground was rough and strewn with rocks, with a lot of bushes big enough to shield him. Unless they happened to search in the right place, he might be able to keep away from them until he made it back to the bank of the gully only twenty feet behind him. Once he scrambled up that, the ground would be flat and easy to run on, with trees to block him from sight until he could get to the little village a mile down the road.

There were, however, two problems, both major. First, the terrain between himself and the bank, lying as it did in the shadow of the bridge, had no protective bushes; moreover, the ground was swampy, full of litter, and difficult to traverse, particularly in the dark. Second, he was crouched in one of the first places they would look once they climbed down from the bridge and saw that the supports at either end provided obvious cover. That is, if they climbed down. For the moment his best bet was to stay where he was until he had a better idea of what they had in mind.

There was a sudden clattering on the pebbles a few feet behind him. Gideon twitched violently, banging his head hard enough against the concrete to see stars. Between the stars he caught a glimpse of a large hare that contemplated him with wide, shining eyes for a fraction of a second and then skittered away. At the same moment the beams swung down to where the hare had been, and there was a flurry of shots—Gideon could hear some of them thunk into the earth—while the lights played frantically over the area. They were shooting from almost directly above him. Gideon could see their pistols, three of them, held out over the side of the bridge, bouncing with the repercussions of the shots.

They were trying to kill him. He had been reacting, not thinking, since the headlights had blinded him, and the thought came as a surprise. They weren't trying to rob him, and they had no questions about "it," no silken cord to force information from him. They weren't shouting at him to stop or to come out with his hands up. They weren't shouting at all; they were just shooting at what they thought was him with guns that made very loud bangs.

Gideon had never been around guns much—not at all, actually—and their loudness stunned him. He jumped at every shot, as he did in a theater when an actor fired a gun. When they stopped at last, after what could have been no more than half a minute, he found that he had his eyes screwed shut.

He opened them to see the light beams sweeping over the gully and along the banks. The hare had apparently gotten away. That's good, he thought. They had been shooting wildly, without ever focusing on or possibly even seeing their target. Now they were back to shouting at each other. He might just possibly have a chance.

Except that he couldn't think of anything to do. As soon as they had started firing, he had changed his mind about waiting them out. He wasn't about to lie there meekly and let them kill him. But without a weapon, or even with one, he was no match for three armed assassins. As for escaping, the moment he moved from behind the support, they'd catch him with their flashlights and mow him down. All he could think of was to toss a rock or a rusty can as far as he could, to engage their attention, and then to run for the bank behind him.

It was hard to get terribly enthusiastic about the idea. A rock or a can bouncing over the ground wasn't likely to fool anyone. It would sound just like what it was, and they would have their beams on him and their bullets into him before he got three steps. But he didn't have any other ideas.

Near his right hand he saw a plastic sack of garbage that was tied at the neck; that, at least, would sound more like a body if he threw it. He reached for it and twisted his head around to assess the run he would have to make. The land was rough and ran slightly uphill, but there were no large bushes or rocks in the way. With all the litter, though, and puddles of ooze, he'd have to watch carefully where he was going. He'd have to get into a runner's starting crouch—there wasn't room under the bridge to stand up—facing the bank a few feet downstream. Then he'd throw the garbage behind him and a little upstream. The moment it hit, he'd run. If they went for the bait, they'd be on the upstream side of the bridge, and the bridge itself would shield him. He'd have to crouch as he ran four, maybe five steps,

50

Groucho-Marx-style. Another two strides would take him over the bank. Then, if they hadn't yet seen him, he'd drop flat on his belly and inch away toward the stand of trees. If they had seen him, however, he'd just run like hell.

Some plan: Option A, crawl like a snake; Option B, run like a rabbit. Still, the rabbit had made it.

There seemed to be some purposeful activity on the bridge now. Gideon could see from the flashlight beams that the men were separating. Chances were, they were splitting up to search for him. Now was the time.

He pushed himself into a kneeling position and grabbed the bag of garbage. It was good to move, to contract his muscles. He could almost feel his autonomic nervous system go smoothly to work, pumping out the adrenalin. More exhilarated than frightened, he was optimistic now about making it, and anxious to give it a try. He longed in fact for a physical encounter, a showdown, but he knew he'd be crazy to try it.

As he shifted his hand to a throwing grasp around the neck of the bag, someone lowered a flashlight an arm's length over the side at the far end of the bridge, where he had jumped off, and swept the beam in a circle. Gideon had to drop flat again, his eye to the space between bridge support and brace. Just before the beam reached him, he realized with a start of horror that he hadn't let go of the bag, that his right arm was out in the open, not behind the support. He had no time to move it, however, before the beam was on him, lighting up his wet and glistening forearm, it seemed to him, like a multi-faceted diamond, throwing reflections and rays in every direction. As the beam hovered for a moment, an icy sweat jumped to the surface of his skin below the warmer layer of muck. He lay, breathless and tight-chested, waiting for the bullets, exerting all his control not to pull his arm out of the light and get up and make his run right then.

And the beam moved on; somehow they had failed to see him. He lay trembling in the slime. His autonomic nervous system seemed to have changed its mind; a physical encounter was the last thing in the world he wanted.

When he raised his head to look toward the far end of the

bridge, he saw a pair of legs dangling from where the flashlight had been shining. The man sat on the edge of the bridge for a second and then dropped to the muddy stream bed with a soft plop. Gideon was surprised to see that the drop was a good six feet. He had been lucky not to break a leg when he had plunged blindly over the side. The first man then helped a second down—the tall, slender one—and they both moved toward the support at the far end, pistols and flashlights in hand. Gideon felt an absurd flash of relief that he had made for this support instead of that one; it gave him perhaps another minute before he was discovered.

He remembered seeing a broom handle nearby when he had reached for the garbage bag. Now, without taking his eyes from the two men, he moved his hands through the filth until he found it. It was only a two-foot length, cracked and splintered at one end; not much protection against two guns.

As he slid it toward him, another pair of legs swung suddenly over the side almost directly above him. Without moving from his place, he could have swatted them with the broomstick, had he wanted to. He quickly gathered himself into a crouch as his nervous system switched on again with a click that was nearly perceptible.

The man above him shone his flashlight down to check the surface. Gideon noted that it was in his left hand. If he had a gun, and Gideon was sure he did, it would be in the right. The dangling legs wriggled a little as the buttocks above them sought a better grip on the edge of the bridge. Gideon could see that the pants were tightly cut and the shoes had high, stylish heels. Finally, the body pushed off with a wriggle of the legs, and the man came down.

Gideon uncoiled and launched himself at the dark figure a fraction of a second before the feet touched earth. He wanted to hit him at the precise moment he landed, when he would, for the barest instant, be concentrating on his equilibrium. Coming at him from behind, Gideon whipped the broom handle down at the back of the man's right hand.

Three things went wrong. First, Gideon's left ankle seemed to

52

give way under him as he came out of his crouch, and he slipped. Second, the bulging, slippery garbage bag somehow got in his way and nearly overturned him. Third, the man landed awkwardly and twisted his body around to try to keep his balance. Thus Gideon's blow was tardy by about a third of a second; the figure was nearly facing him instead of landing with his back to him; and the target—the gun-holding right hand—was flailing around on Gideon's left instead of hanging motionlessly on the right, where it belonged.

The broom handle, as a result, came down on the side of the man's neck, sloppily but hard. The look on his face was so innocently astounded that for a preposterous second, Gideon wanted to apologize. He was only about twenty, lean and powerfully built but smaller than Gideon. Even in the dark, Gideon could see that he was badly shaken.

They stood looking at each other for a ridiculously long time. Then Gideon said suddenly, "Look, this is crazy. I don't want to hurt you—"

The boy leaped back and pointed the gun directly at Gideon's face. Gideon ducked and grabbed for his wrist with his left hand. Instead, he caught the barrel of the pistol. He held it off to the side, pointing away from them and, off balance, tried to twist it free. Somehow, the boy held on to it and managed to fire a shot. Immediately there was a shout from the other end of the bridge.

"Marco!"

Marco, his wrist bent nearly double, but still hanging onto the gun, gave a panicky gasp and hit Gideon weakly on the forehead with the flashlight in his left hand. Gideon sent it spinning to the ground with a backhanded swipe of the stick just as they were both lit up in the glare of the others' powerful flashlights. He knew he had only a few seconds. The other men were no more than a hundred feet away and would not be much deterred by the uneven ground. He had to get the gun away from Marco, and he had to stay close enough to him so they wouldn't dare shoot.

He twisted the pistol barrel with all his strength. Marco's wrist seemed to turn a full, boneless circle, but still he held on and clawed at Gideon's face with his other hand. Gideon hit him in

53

the face with the broom handle. Marco made a dreadful mewing noise but held on and kept clawing. He had gotten his fingers inside Gideon's lower lip and was twisting hard. Gideon felt something give, and hot blood gushed onto his chin. Tears jumped to his eyes with the sudden pain.

"Drop it!" he shouted thickly through the ripping fingers. His cheek flapped hideously. He clubbed Marco again and then again.

The boy's fingers held rigidly onto the gun, although his face was suddenly smeared with blood and weirdly awry. Gideon kept smashing with the broom handle. He was nearly hysterical with pain and horror.

"Drop it, damn you!" he screamed. "Drop it, drop it, please, God, drop it!" Then he heard himself shrieking wordlessly to drown out the rising scream from Marco's mangled, bloody face.

Finally, Marco sagged and Gideon wrenched the gun out of his hand just as the two others got to them. Gideon brushed off a grasping hand and swung the semiconscious Marco around, getting his arms through the boy's armpits so that he supported the limp, moaning form between himself and them. He pressed the end of the gun barrel under Marco's heart and glared crazily at the two men. He tried to speak but couldn't. Marco's damp, greasy hair was against his nose; he could smell sweat and cheap hair oil.

In all his life, Gideon had never been so wildly out of control. He couldn't stop gasping, or maybe it was sobbing, and he was full of an awesome rage. To be hunted down by maniacs with guns; to be standing there in the dark, covered with blood and slime, his lip torn off for all he knew; to be pressing a gun into a boy's abdomen; to be forced to club that juvenile face into a gory. . . .

One of the men addressed him in a lazy, arrogant drawl. "Oliver, if I were you—"

Gideon shouted at him to shut up, only what burst from him was not words but an inarticulate, savage bellow that seemed to come from some beast—some literal, material beast inside him.

So ferocious was it that both men jumped back. Even Gideon

was shocked by its violence; stupidly, he patted Marco reassuringly.

While the two men stared at him with pistols leveled at his chest—at Marco's head, to be more exact—Gideon tried to review his situation. He knew he was hurt and weakened and that his thinking was fuzzy. He wasn't sure how much of the slop on him was blood, nor how much of the blood was his own. He couldn't free a hand to explore his mouth, but he was sure it was terribly lacerated. He thought his face was cut in other places, too. Most important, there had been a sharp pain in his ankle when he had swung Marco around and propped him up. He had done something serious to it, and he knew he couldn't run on it or even drag himself and Marco away on the threat of killing the boy if they followed. Moreover, he wasn't sure that Marco's life would carry any weight with them anyway; they were older than the boy—harder, a different breed. And when it came down to it, he knew he couldn't fire into that helpless, battered body. The other two, he thought, would know he was bluffing.

The older of the two men, the one who had spoken before, appeared to know what he was thinking.

"Oliver," he drawled again, "this really won't do any good, you know. I'd rather not endanger our poor friend there, but if it can't be helped, I assure you I've no qualms about it, none whatever." His speech was English public school, self-assured and superior, with strong Italian overtones.

Gideon didn't answer, but kept the gun pressed to Marco's belly. He had less reluctance about shooting the two others, but he knew he could never get them both. He doubted he could hit even one. He didn't even know whether you had to push back the hammer or simply pull the trigger. From the way they held their weapons, it was clear that the other two were on intimate terms with them.

Marco stirred and tried to plant himself more firmly on his feet. His hands came up to Gideon's forearms and then explored his own face. He groaned; Gideon shuddered, but tightened his hold and braced himself against the boy's body.

"Oliver," the older man said once more, "do let's be reasonable. We'd simply like to talk to you, you see. I'm not really sure how we've arrived at this ridiculous juncture, and I'd be a great deal happier if we weren't pointing these things at one another, wouldn't you?"

He smiled, and it wasn't a bad smile. Gideon said nothing, but kept watching him. He had a lined, high-nosed face, aristocratic in the Italian way, and his smile lent warmth to his eyes. Standing in a Sicilian mud puddle in the middle of the night seemed no more plausible for him than for Gideon.

"I'll tell you what," he went on. "Why don't I put mine away, then?" He did so, slipping it into a shoulder holster underneath a well-cut suit jacket. Then he held up his empty palms.

"Take the light out of my eyes," Gideon said.

The man lowered his flashlight and gestured at the other one to do the same. "There," he said, "is that better? Now suppose that on the count of three, you and my friend here, who is really much more sympathetic than he looks, both lower your weapons until they're pointing at the ground. Then you can both drop them at the same time and we'll have our chat. Now, how does that sound?"

From the way he spoke—slowly and reassuringly, as if he were talking to a child—Gideon knew his own rapidly dimming faculties were apparent. As patently deceptive as his instructions were, Gideon longed to follow them. The pain in his face and his ankle was excruciating, his mind was growing more cloudy each second—he must have lost a lot of blood—and the world was beginning to tilt and slowly spin. He wanted terribly to sit down, but he held on and kept the gun pressed into Marco's ribs, though he swayed on his feet.

"How tiresome," said the cool voice. "Well, old boy, you know perfectly well you're not really going to shoot."

Gideon was having a hard time seeing. He blinked, trying to focus his vision. Suddenly the gun was no longer in his hand. The world turned entirely uside down, and he found himself sitting on the ground at last. He couldn't imagine where Marco had gone.

The slender man was no longer smiling. He said a few quick

words to the other one, who moved toward Gideon, stony-faced. Dimly, Gideon understood he was going to be shot. He sighed and waited, his mind empty.

A light, much more powerful than a flashlight, flicked on from the bridge, capturing them all in its fierce glare.

"Drop the gun! Quick!"

The older man spun and flashed his light at the voice. Gideon saw a familiar face lit up. Now who was it? Let's see . . . it wasn't anyone in his family, not Dad or Saul. Was it one of the kids he played around with? . . . Um, no, because it was a man, and his friends were only kids. Or maybe it was himself? No, that's silly. He giggled. How did his face get so wet?

There was more shouting, and other noises too, but they were a long way off, booming and slow, like a record played at the wrong speed. He giggled again. What was Mom going to say about his dirty clothes? . . . And how did his face get so wet?

7

THE NURSE—LARGE, CLEAN, and handsome—bustled in carrying a tray and exuding a take-charge aura as welcome and natural in Sigonella Naval Hospital as it would have been in Kansas City General.

"Well, how's my favorite patient? Were we taking a little nap? Wake up, sleepyhead. Lunchtime!"

"I can hardly wait," said Gideon, but he was glad to see her. "What color straw do I get today? Can I have yellow again? The kind that bends?"

"No straws today. Doctor says you're on solids now. What do you think of that?" She put the bed tray down in front of him. There was a bowl of dark gray porridge, a cup of light gray pudding, and a glass of milk.

"These are solids?"

"Well, they're not liquids. Would you believe mushies?"

"I'll take 'em. I'm hungry. Which feels very nice." He raised himself to a sitting position.

"We have to be careful with the spoon, now. Try to keep it away from the left side. Your cheek's going to be a teeny bit tender yet. Oh, you have a visitor. He'll be in after you eat."

"Who is it, Sue?"

"Name's John Lau. Nice guy. Says he's an old friend."

"Old friend" was stretching things a little, but only a little, under the circumstances. "Can't you send him in now? I mean, of course, if the rules permit."

"They don't, but I'll make an exception, seeing as how you're going to be such a good boy and eat up all the nice glop."

A few seconds after she left the room, the big policeman walked in with a twinkling smile that was good for Gideon's soul.

"What's up, Doc?"

"I don't believe it," Gideon said. "What are you doing in Sicily? Or am I back in Germany?"

"No such luck; you're in sunny Italy." As always, John's babylike laugh made Gideon laugh too. Then he winced; the stitches had come out just that morning.

"Hey, I'm sorry, Doc. You want the nurse again?"

"No. It only hurts when I laugh." He held up his hand quickly. "Also when you laugh."

John smiled, which was better. "Don't let me stop you from eating. It looks wonderful."

"I'll tell you, it's the closest thing to real food I've had since the shore patrol deposited me here Friday. Five days. Have a seat." He dug into the porridge and gingerly put the spoon in his mouth. Sue was right; it was still pretty raw in there.

John made a face. "What is that stuff?"

"I don't know. Gruel, probably."

"Nah, gruel's thinner." John watched in good-humored silence as Gideon worked his way through the porridge, which tasted wonderful. With hot food in him and a friendly face nearby, he was starting to feel nearly human again.

"Boy," John said happily, "you sure look like hell."

Gideon put down his spoon. He hadn't seen himself since the bandages had come off. "I sure feel like hell. I may as well see the worst. How about handing me the mirror on the bureau there?"

John gave it to him. "You'll be sorry."

"Holy mackerel," said Gideon, "look at that." It had taken twenty stitches to pull together the jagged tear at the junction of his upper and lower lips, and six to close a cut at the side of his left eye, probably from when he'd banged his head on the bridge support. There were another four stitches over his right eye (Marco's flashlight?) and several nasty contusions that had left most of his face brown, black, and purple. Add to this a patchy five-day beard, and Gideon was surprised that he was feeling as well as he was, which wasn't all that good.

John replaced the mirror. "How about the ankle?" he asked.

"Looks worse than it is," Gideon said, indicating the protuberance at the end of the bed formed by a metal framework that kept the covers off his foot. "Sprained a couple of ligaments. I'm supposed to be up tomorrow, but I'll have to use a cane for a while."

"Well, Doc, you sure get involved in some pretty strange situations for a nice, mild-mannered professor-type."

"Amazingly enough, the same thought has been occurring to me. The Curse of the Visiting Fellow, no doubt."

"The curse of the who?"

"You don't know? It's an honorary curse; goes along with my position. The last fellow, two semesters ago, got killed in a car accident, and the one before that disappeared. Or maybe I have them backwards."

John took his notebook from the flap pocket of his shirt and wrote in it. "Go ahead," he said.

"That's all. Dr. Rufus told me about it . . . the chancellor. He was sort of embarrassed to have me even know about it; he didn't exactly gush with information."

John nodded. Gideon saw him print "Rufus" in the notebook. "Okay, Doc. Look, if this keeps up, you're gonna get killed—or kill someone else, more likely. Let's try to find out what the hell is going on. Now, I've seen the police reports and the transcripts of your statements, and I still have some big questions—"

"Wait a minute, John. I've got some pretty big questions myself. I'd like to ask them first, if that's okay."

"Shoot." He flipped the notebook closed and dropped it into his pocket.

"First of all, what are you doing here, really?"

John's injured surprise was clearly genuine. "Hey, look, you've been assaulted with intent to kill. That's a crime, you know, even here, and I'm a cop."

"I know, I know, but why *you*? This is over a thousand miles from Heidelberg. Aren't there any other cops? And why is this a NATO security matter at all? Why not the local MPs?"

John tipped his chair back against the wall. "Let me put it this way: USOC is my beat. The agreement they have with the army calls for protection for the faculty wherever they send you guys. And since the only places they send you are NATO bases, it's natural that NSD has the responsibility. Traveling is no problem for us. We just hop a MAC flight."

"Why do we need protection at all? And why can't the local military police handle it?" Gideon asked again.

"Believe me, it's a lot simpler than negotiating with the local security people every time you go some place, and explaining who and what you are, which isn't always so easy. You're not military, you're not civil service, you're not tech reps—and you go to some pretty weird places."

Gideon hiked himself into a sitting position so that his eyes were level with John's. It took more effort than he expected. "Look, let me level with you, and maybe you'll do the same with me. I'm in way over my head with this spy business I've gotten myself into. What I'm wondering is, are *you* really a cop, or are you a spy or an agent or whatever they call it?" John began to answer, but Gideon cut him off. "And am *I* some kind of a pawn? I don't like being used, especially when it nearly gets me killed."

John frowned, arranging his words. He tipped his chair forward onto all four legs again. "My branch is Safety," he said slowly, with careful emphasis on each word. "Protection of life and property. We're just like the MPs, only we get assignments that cut across their lines. As of this year, I'm assigned to USOC. Before that I was doing the same thing for USAREUR, before that at AFCENT in Holland. And before that I was an ordinary, run-of-the-mill cop in San Diego and Honolulu. I couldn't be more ordinary and run-of-the-mill if I tried. Until you started making my life complicated, that is." It was a long speech for John. He blew out his breath as if he'd been chopping down trees.

Gideon nodded slowly. "I believe you," he said. "Tell me this, John. Do you think there's any connection between what Marks and Delvaux asked me to do and these things that have been happening to me?"

"I don't know what they asked you to do, but I've been wondering the same thing." He gestured at the pudding. "Hey, go ahead and eat your whatever-it-is."

Gideon made a small gesture of impatience. "Is that really true? That you don't know? It's hard to believe an organization could function that way, the right hand not knowing what the left is doing."

"Doc, we have to operate that way. We work on a need-to-know basis. The fewer people who know the dirty stuff, the better. Intelligence doesn't have any trouble finding out what we're doing, because we're not into nasty tricks and sensitive information. But they don't tell us what *they're* doing, and we don't ask." He paused. "We're not supposed to, anyway."

It was the hint Gideon had been waiting for. "Well, I'd like to tell you anyway. All this craziness has to be connected. It's stupid to treat it as a bunch of unrelated incidents." He waited for an invitation to go on, but John just looked at him with a faint smile. "Besides," Gideon continued, "I don't trust Marks. I do trust you."

"Oh, you can trust him," said John, "he's just, well. . . ."

"A nerd. John, would I be compromising you by telling you about it?"

"Yes," said John in a small, stern voice. Then he smiled, and then the smile became the laughter of schoolboys sharing secrets.

Gideon told him about the interview in Heidelberg, the theft of the socks, and the subsequent interview in the base laundry. John listened, walking about the room, neither taking notes nor asking questions. "Huh," he said finally. "How about that?"

"Come on, John, don't be inscrutable with me. It all has to be related, doesn't it?"

The policeman came back to the chair and sat down. "Here's what I would like: I would like it if you would eat your dessert, and if I could please be the cop, and I ask questions, and you answer them. Okay?"

Gideon laughed and winced once more. "Okay."

He spooned up a lump of the gray pudding and pushed it around his mouth with his tongue. "My God, what *is* this stuff? It's insoluble."

"What, the pudding or the case?"

Gideon remembered to catch himself before laughing. "Why, John, that's funny."

Lau accepted the compliment with a slight nod. "Let's go over a few things. I'm assuming that none of these guys were the same as the ones that jumped you in Heidelberg."

"Right. These were Italians."

"You mean they *spoke* Italian."

"No, they *were* Italian. I don't understand the language, but a native speaker—"

Lau held up his hand. "Okay, I forgot. We've been through this before. Speech rhythms and so forth."

"Right."

Lau bowed his head in mock defeat. "All right. What about the one that showed up at the end, the one who apparently saved you? You told the shore patrol he looked familiar. Was *he* one of them?"

"One of the ones from Heidelberg?" For a moment Gideon wasn't sure. *Could* he have been the ferret-faced man? The man on the bridge had seemed to move in the same spare, powerful, dangerous way. No, Ferret-face had been more compact, more coiled.

"I don't think so," he said. "No, definitely not. In fact, I assumed he was with the shore patrol, but they told me no."

"But he spoke like an American?"

"Yes, he did—I think. This time I'm not completely sure. I wasn't concentrating too well at the time."

"Doc, if you could try to remember where you'd seen him, it could make a big difference."

"You're telling me. I've thought about it so much, I'm not sure anymore that he *was* familiar. John, go back a minute; why would you think that one of those bastards from Heidelberg would be saving my life now?"

"Well, are we really sure he was trying to help you? You were pretty groggy at the time, and you didn't see how it ended."

Gideon absent-mindedly tongued another nodule of pudding. "Still, it wouldn't make sense. . . ."

"No, I don't think so either. I'm just trying to find the connection between the two incidents."

"Then you think there is one?"

"Sure, no doubt in my mind. These kinds of things don't happen to people in real life. Once is strange enough, but twice—uh-uh, something's going on."

"God, I'm glad to hear you say that. I was starting to think I was getting paranoid."

The nurse came in to take Gideon's tray. *"Mes compliments au chef,"* he said. *"Formidable."*

"Don't be smart. Doctor's going to be very disappointed when I tell him you didn't eat up all your gunk."

"Do you suppose I could get some hot tea, Sue? I need something to dissolve that stuff."

"Sure." She turned to John. "Coffee?"

"That'd be great. Thanks."

"John," Gideon said, as the door swung closed, "am I suspected of anything? Some kind of involvement in . . . all this? Dope or something?"

"Look, Doc, I don't know what's going on myself, so I'm not ruling anything out. But I don't think anyone seriously suspects you of anything. Least of all me."

"Thank you. I appreciate your saying that."

The tea and coffee were wordlessly brought by a shy, pretty candy-striper who left quickly, and the two men sipped in silence for a few minutes. Gideon was feeling very relaxed, and the tea was soothing. He drank and watched the dust motes floating in the shafts of strong Sicilian sunshine that filled the hospital room.

With a start, he realized he was dozing and looked up to see the policeman smiling at him, his coffee finished.

"I know I'm not the world's greatest interrogator," John said, "but I don't usually put 'em to sleep."

"I'm sorry—"

"No, you look like you can use it. If you're up to it tomorrow, there are some pictures I'd like you to look at in the Security Office. I'll come by about eleven."

"Pictures . . .?" Before he could complete the thought, Gideon was asleep again. He was awakened for a dinner of stewed chicken and vegetables, ate hungrily, and slept soundly until morning.

"Nothing, huh?"

"Not a thing." Gideon pushed himself away from the table, rubbed the nape of his neck, and leaned back in his chair. He had been leafing through photographs for an hour. "Where did you get all these characters?"

"Local bad guys," John said. "Mafia, gangsters, a few others. Anybody I thought might be a good bet."

"But you didn't really think they'd turn up."

"No."

They sat, quiet and a little depressed, John's fingers gently tapping the table. A clerk came to the doorway and motioned at him. "Telephone."

When he came back, he said, "They've got the car."

"Who? What car?"

"The guys who ambushed you. They found their car on the road to Taormina, near Mangano."

"How do they know it's the right car? I couldn't describe it to the shore patrol."

"No, but they analyzed some paint they found on the bumper where you rammed it; it matches the paint on your car. There isn't any question about it."

"Great. What else?"

"Not much. Apparently it was doing about a hundred, ran off

the road, exploded, and burned so badly you could hardly tell it was a car. They pieced together enough to identify it as a Lancia that was stolen from a garage in Catania on Thursday, but that's about it. Somebody was still in it, but burnt to a crisp. The *carabinieri* flew out an expert, a forensic pathologist from Rome. All he could say was that it was definitely human. He couldn't even tell for sure if it was a man or a woman. There's nothing but a few bones."

"Bones?" Gideon was suddenly excited. "Damn it, John, I don't care what shape they're in I could tell more than that from them. I've got to see them."

"Believe me, you couldn't—"

"John, you seem utterly determined to forget that I am a physical anthropologist by profession." In response to John's tolerant smile, he went on. "And a damned good one."

"Relax, Doc, relax. I've seen the stuff. A few finger bones and stuff, all cracked and burned. You could put them all in a coffee cup and still have room for a cup of coffee."

"You've *seen* them? And you didn't tell me? I thought they just found it!"

"No, they found it Friday, the day after the ambush."

"Well, why the hell didn't you tell me before?"

"Will you calm down? I didn't know for sure it was the right car till just now."

"Yes, but—"

"And you didn't look that terrific yesterday. It didn't seem like such a great idea to mention it."

"Sure, but—"

"Hey, Doc!" John's tone had changed. He was getting angry. Gideon closed his mouth in mid-sentence and sank back against his chair, exasperated.

John glowered and stabbed a forefinger at him. "You don't have to be told everything, you know. *I'm* the cop. All you are is the lousy victim." Then his frown dissolved into merry creases as he burst into his sudden child's laugh.

"All right," Gideon said, "but I'd still like to see those bones, Mr. Cop, sir."

"That's better. They're at police headquarters in Catania. I'll drive you over later, if you want. Hey, how about some lunch? I'm starving."

John had wanted to go to the base cafeteria for hamburgers, but Gideon, trading on his weakened condition, talked him into going to a clean, modest little trattoria a few miles down the road. There John ordered a full meal; Gideon had soup and pasta with fresh sardines and a little butter.

"You know," John said—and then had to stop while he chewed the last chunk of a thin, tough steak pizzaiola, which he had ordered contrary to Gideon's advice and was consuming with evident relish—"you know—" a gulp of red wine sent the mouthful down—"you know, I'm not so sure that the two attacks are related after all."

"Come on, John," said Gideon, "you said yourself it would be a pretty wild coincidence for two things like that to just happen."

"Right, but wild coincidences *do* happen. The situations are too different. In Heidelberg you were assaulted and searched by two guys who knew exactly what they were looking for. Here in Sicily they were trying to kill you outright—no more, no less."

"How can you know that for sure? How do we know they weren't looking for it, too—whatever it is—and that killing me wasn't just the easy way to get it?"

"Because they put a car in your way across a fast road on a dark night. The chances were damn good they'd blow you and your car to shreds. So what were they going to search? Uh uh, they wanted you dead."

Gideon poked morosely at his last sardine and pushed the plate away. "I don't know. It doesn't make any sense either way."

When the waiter brought the fruit and cheese, Gideon took only a little Bel Paese; his mouth didn't feel up to dealing with apples or pears. John reached for the largest, reddest apple and bit into it with powerful incisors.

Suddenly an image came back to Gideon. "Hey! The guy on the bridge. I remember him! I saw him in a restaurant, in Aci Trezza! He was watching me! He was eating an apple!"

"What did he look like?" John was excited.

"I don't remember. Tough-looking. He was with another guy. But he was eating an apple—with his mouth."

"What apple?" shouted John. "What do you mean, with his mouth? Who gives a shit about an apple?" He had half-risen from his chair.

"The way he was eating it—it means he was an American."

"Oh God," John said, falling back into his chair, his enthusiasm gone. "Another anthropology theory." He bit into the apple again with a resounding crunch.

"No, John, now listen. "You just took a bite of it, right? Europeans don't do that, you know that—especially Italians. They peel it with a knife, and they cut it into little pieces, and they eat them with a fork."

"Oh, come on, Doc."

Gideon glanced around the crowded little restaurant. "Look over there, for example." Two tables away, a solemn, bespectacled man in a black suit was surgically incising the skin of a banana, preparing to remove its contents with his fork. "See?"

"I know, I know; Europeans mostly eat fruit that way, Americans mostly don't. Doc, *mostly* isn't *always*. It's not exactly proof."

Gideon was a little piqued. It had been a first-rate deduction, he thought. "At this point we don't need proof; we need some clues. Don't forget I thought he sounded like an American when he yelled at them to drop their guns."

"All right, let's say you're right. What does that tell us that we didn't know before?"

"Hell, I don't know. You're the cop; I'm just the lousy victim. Aren't *you* supposed to put it all together?"

"Oh oh, now I've made him mad. All I meant was, I thought you had some theory about it."

Gideon's energy seemed suddenly exhausted. His ankle had begun to throb. It would be good to lie down and get his foot raised. Maybe three hours out were enough for the first day.

"No theory, John," he said, "I don't know what it proves. I think you're right; it's probably not important."

There was silence for a while. Gideon rolled a little cheese into a ball between his thumb and forefinger. "I think maybe I ought to get back to the hospital."

"All right, you want to let the bones go till tomorrow? Or just forget about them?"

The bones. He'd forgotten. His ankle stopped aching, and his energy came back with a rush.

8

IN THE BASEMENT LABORATORY of police head-quarters in Catania, they waited at a table covered with a large piece of butcher paper. John's pidgin-English conversation with a portly police captain had been comical and confused, and Gideon had only been able to help a little with his rudimentary Italian. At first the captain, with lavish gestures, had refused them entrance to the laboratory. Then he had told John they could come in now but that they couldn't see the remains. "*No, no, no, no, no. Impossible, signore. Lei scherza!*"

In the end, without the use of a single word, but with the most extraordinary series of gestures Gideon had ever seen—involving individually raised eyebrows, pursed lips, cocked head, and a wonderful accompaniment of arm, hand, and finger motions—he had managed to communicate, with almost word-for-word exactitude: Ah, but I did not understand! If you are the Americans we have been expecting, then of course—of *course*—you may see them. My apologies; I am so stupid."

A little later a thin, dark policeman brought them a manila envelope on a plastic, cafeteria-style tray. John undid the metal clasp. "I'm telling you, you're not going to be able to make much out of this."

"I *am* an anthropologist, you know."

"So you keep telling me." He gently shook the contents onto the butcher paper.

It was true, Gideon thought; they didn't look like much. Seven or eight fragments, ashy and fire-bleached, not a whole bone among them. . . . Upper end of a right tibia—an adult, that could be seen from the union of the epiphysis with the shaft; it was one of the last of the long bone fusions to occur. . . . A piece of mandible with two teeth in place—on the small side—Marco's perhaps. . . . A few shards of scapula too burnt to tell him anything. . . . A piece of occipital bone. . . . And some splinters of wood that the "expert" from Rome had apparently thought to be bone.

"John, can I borrow some paper and a pen? And do you suppose you could see if there's a pair of calipers around this place, or a ruler, anyway? And if you could dig up a cup of coffee, that would be nice."

John was smiling his crinkly-eyed smile.

"What's so funny?" Gideon asked.

"You are. You just look like a professor all of a sudden. You really look like you're in your element. All you need is a magnifying glass and a Sherlock Holmes pipe and a white coat."

"Great idea. A magnifying glass would be very helpful, thanks." He grinned. "Skip the pipe and the coat."

When he had gone, Gideon realized how correct John had been. He *was* in his element. Sitting in front of a pile of bones to play detective, patiently unlocking their secrets one by one; there was nothing more absorbing, nothing more satisfying, nothing he'd rather be doing. At least there hadn't been for two years now. A shiver worked slowly down his spine. How much he used to delight in sharing with Nora the little osteological deductions he'd made. She'd pick him up at the lab, and he'd go over them with her, step by step. ("I was really puzzled until I noticed that the crack in the left parietal had partially healed. That established two things beyond doubt: that the blow to the head had been delivered while he was still alive, and that he had lived no more than three or four weeks more. Therefore . . . .")

And she would ooh and aah.

When she had died, he had come near to killing himself, the only time in his life he'd ever thought about it. He hadn't known how he could possibly live without her. He did, somehow, but even now he wouldn't let himself think of her, except when he awakened sometimes in the night and dreamed, drifting back . . . .

So what was he doing now, chin cupped in his hands, elbows

on the table, staring glassily at nothing? There were things to be done. He reached for the mandible and blew off its coating of powdery ash. It was the left rear corner of the jaw, where the ascending ramus joins the basilar segment. He ran his index finger lightly over it. No, it wasn't Marco. The face that had covered this jaw had been more heavily muscled. You could tell from the rough ridges where the powerful masseter muscle had been attached. It was a male for sure; too rough for a female.

He touched the fragment of occiput; yes, a thick, raised superior nuchal crest, evidence of a massive trapezius muscle. The man had been heavy-jawed, thick necked, and broad-shouldered. It wasn't Marco, and it wasn't the one with the Etonian accent either; he had been too slender. It must be the other, then, the one who had been about to shoot him. He had been muscular and big-boned. . . . No, that wasn't right either. These bones were strong and bulky, but not large. The jawbone was definitely on the small side, in fact.

What was more . . . he looked at it again to make sure . . . yes, he was right! It wasn't Caucasian; it was Mongoloid. Even though much of the corner had crumbled away in the fire, you could see where it showed signs of flaring widely at the mandibular angle. That was typical of Mongoloid skulls; it was one of the things that gave an Oriental face its broad, flat appearance. The signs of powerful musculature supported a Mongoloid hypothesis too. The flaring wasn't pronounced enough to be an American Indian, but more than you'd expect in a Chinese. Japanese, most probably.

So far so good. The teeth, now. There were two of them still in place: second and third molars. The third molar was perfectly and fully erupted, not always the case with a wisdom tooth, and further evidence that the person had been an adult. There seemed to be some evidence of differential wear on them, which might help him to pinpoint the age, but the fire had cracked them both and made it hard to tell. . . . Damn, where was John with that magnifying glass?

Impatiently, he looked over his shoulder toward the doorway and started violently when he saw John standing only two or three feet behind him.

"Whew, John! Don't *do* that! How long have you been standing there?"

"You were so deep in thought, I didn't want to interrupt." John set down two paper coffee cups. His own was already emptied; he must have drunk it while watching. "With the great Italian coffee they brew here, I don't know why anybody drinks this lousy instant, but that's all there is. Here's a magnifying glass. Do you still want calipers? So far I haven't been able to figure out sign language for them."

"No, a ruler would be fine."

"Okay, back in a minute."

Gideon took a swig of the coffee without tasting it, and put the mandible under the glass. Yes, he had been right. The cusps of the second molar were definitely worn down. The third molar showed less attrition—just a little abrading of the cusp tips and the tooth edges. It was impossible, of course, to make a reliable age estimate based on tooth wear unless you knew what sort of food had been habitually consumed. Diet could make all the difference in the world. The *relative* wear of different teeth did provide some useful information, however.

His educated eye studied the two teeth. The second molar was roughly twice as worn as the third. Now, assuming that the second had erupted at twelve and the third at, say, twenty (here plain guesswork took over, third molar eruption time being notoriously variable), then—assuming that the teeth had been wearing down at the same rate ever since they had come up— what age would the person have been when the second molar had been chewing away for twice as long as the first and was therefore twice as worn?

It was like a Sunday paper riddle. He took another sip of the coffee, tasted this one, and grimaced. Then he made a simple matrix on one of the sheets of paper that John had carefully torn from his notebook, and filled it in.

Twenty-eight. At twenty-eight the second molar would have been masticating for sixteen years, the third for eight. But twenty-eight seemed young for these bones. What if the third molar had erupted late, at twenty-five? Then he would have been . . . thirty-eight, at which time the second molar would have been grinding away for twenty-six years, and the third molar for thirteen years. Thirty-eight looked about right for these remains. He wasn't sure just how he knew that, but he had long ago learned to trust his instincts when it came to bones. Anyway, they weren't instincts; they were intuitive responses to subliminal but well-learned cues. Yes, he'd bet on thirty-eight, plus or minus a couple of years.

What had he learned so far, then? He knew the envelope held what was left of a male, about thirty-eight, short and muscular, Oriental, and definitely not one of his attackers—at least not one that he'd seen. Who was it then? What had he been doing in the car?

Suddenly realizing that he'd been leaning stiffly forward in absolute concentration for fifteen minutes, he slumped back in his chair and finished the last of the coffee, satisfied and aware that he was enjoying himself very much. He picked up the mandible again. There was something else about the tooth-wear pattern, something that rang a bell. . . .

John returned with a metal ruler. "Hey—" Gideon held up his hand and John stopped obediently, nailed to the floor.

It was the second molar that was bothering him—the oddly eroded, concave depression on the anterobuccal edge. He had seen something like that before; where was it?

With startling clarity, it came back to him. It had been one of the great triumphs of his graduate years at Wisconsin. He and the great, the studiedly eccentric, Professor Campbell had been in the laboratory studying a cranium and mandible that had been plowed up by a farmer and then turned over to the university's physical anthropology laboratory by the Madison police, for help with identification. It was a routine occurrence. Usually such bones turned out to be remnants of centuries-old Indian burials, but this one hadn't.

They had already identified the cranium as that of a Caucasian in his fifties, buried between ten and thirty years before. Professor Campbell had puffed away at his pipe, chewing audibly on the stem, his thick, carefully combed eyebrows arched high. He had muttered to himself about the remarkable, saucer-shaped depressions in the first and second molars. "Hmm," he said (puff), "hmm. What do you think, Oliver? What could it be (puff-puff), what could have done it? Hm?"

Gideon, a second-year doctoral student, had sat, shy and deferential, waiting for the great man to answer his own question.

"Just don't know," Professor Campbell said, through a veil of fragrant smoke. "What could do that? Never seen it before." The celebrated eyebrows frowned in defeat.

Gideon cleared his throat. "Sir," he said, "could it be from a pipe? Would smoking a pipe for maybe decades do it?"

The professor had been delighted. He whooped, pushed his massive body from his chair, and shambled to his desk, rummaging in drawers until he came up with a dental mirror. Together they had explored his own right lower molars. Gideon was embarrassed and delighted by the intimacy, and they had quickly found it: the same depression in the same place.

"Oliver," the professor said, "that's splendid, splendid!"

After nearly twenty years, Gideon could still bask in the glow. There was even a little more. "Professor," he had said, made bolder by success, "do you think we could hypothesize that he was right-handed? Don't most pipe smokers hold their pipes in their dominant hands? And don't—"

"Of course! Excellent! People who hold their pipes in their right hands generally put them into the right sides of their mouths. Wonderful! The police will never understand it. To determine handedness from a mandible! They'll be talking about it for years!"

Gideon had checked that same afternoon on a sample of fifty pipe smokers in Sterling Hall (smoking pipes had been *de rigueur* for serious graduate students in 1963) and had found that forty-four of them habitually put their pipes into their mouths on the same side on which they held them in their hands, and that forty habitually held them in their dominant hands. Months later, when the police had definitely established the identity of the remains—the victim of a mass murder in the 1940s—his pipe-smoking and right-handedness had been confirmed.

And now here it was again, the same depression in the second molar. The man had smoked a pipe, and in all probability he'd been left-handed. Now—

"Uh, Doc," John said, "do you mind if I watch?"

"Of course not," said Gideon.

"Could you explain to me as you go along? That is, if I could understand it?" He was a little shy; Gideon was touched.

"Sure," he said. "It's not complicated, really. What I'm going to do is estimate the height."

"You can tell how tall the guy was from *these*?"

"I can make a rough guess."

"So can I, but that doesn't make it right." John said it aggressively, provocatively, but Gideon was beginning to understand his style. In a second he would burst into laughter.

He did, and Gideon laughed too. "Well, that's the difference between a professor and a cop," Gideon said. Look, it *is* pretty iffy, but it's a place to start. This is the tibia, the proximal part of it, anyway. That's your leg bone, from the knee down. It's the only one of all these pieces we can use to estimate height. You can only do it from the long bones. The idea's simple enough; people with long tibias usually have long femurs—thigh bones—and if they have long thigh bones they probably have long vertebral columns, and so on. The same relationships hold true for short people. So if you can get a measurement on *one* of the long bones, you can project the others, and total height too.

"But not all tall people have long legs." John was sounding genuinely interested, like one of Gideon's own anthropology students.

"Right, only *most* do. If I had a hundred tibias here, I'd feel confident in estimating the average total height. The few tall ones with short legs would balance out the few short ones with long legs. But with only one, how do I know I don't have one of the oddballs? I don't, but the odds are on my side."

"Fair enough."

"Okay. We can shortcut the calculations a little. If I remember correctly, we can get the approximate total height from the tibia by multiplying tibial length by ten, dividing in half, and subtracting about five percent. The taller a person is, the less reliable that becomes, but I think this guy's short. Anyway, let's measure it."

John sat, childlike in his concentration on the fragment in Gideon's hand. When Gideon didn't do anything for a long time, he finally asked, "What's the matter?"

"You've got the ruler.'

John chuckled delightedly and handed it over. Gideon realized he was beginning to like John Lau very much.

The tibial fragment was 113 millimeters long. "All right," Gideon said, "time for a major leap of faith. I'll guess that we've got about a third of the total bone here—you can tell from the popliteal line, this ridge on the back. That would make the total length . . . 339 millimeters, say 340."

He jotted a few numbers on a piece of paper. "Total height, 1615 millimeters," he said. More jotting. "About five-four."

"All you have to do is know the formula? That's all there is to it?"

"That's what Watson was always saying to Holmes . . . after the fact."

"Except that Sherlock Holmes was always right." The enthralled student was giving way to the skeptical cop. "No offense, Doc, but you sure made a lot of unverifiable assumptions there. Maybe they're okay when you're measuring ten-thousand-year-old Neanderthals. Who could prove you were right or wrong? But this stuff would never hold up in court."

John was quite right, Gideon knew. He'd often had similar thoughts about prehistoric finds. But he also knew somehow that his estimate was accurate. "I may be an inch or two off, but no more. You can count on it." Pettishly he added, "And the Neanderthalers are a lot closer to a hundred thousand years old than to ten."

"Okay, Doc, you're the expert. Only I'm still not convinced. But what are you suggesting? That it's the little one, Marco?"

"Marco?" Gideon had forgotten that John wasn't aware of the rest of his findings. "No, it's not Marco. Marco was about twenty. This one was nearly forty. And Japanese. And built like a wrestler, say 145 pounds."

All this was put rather more confidently than the data warranted, but a strong front seemed appropriate. Then the coup de grace:

"And, if it's of any interest, he was left-handed and he smoked a pipe."

The effect was more than Gideon had hoped for. John's mouth dropped open and he actually stammered. "You're telling me you know all that from . . . some . . . some skull bones and a . . . a piece of leg bone? You don't have any hand bones—any, any arm bones! How can you know he's left-handed?" John was chopping at the air with both hands, his quirky temper on the rise.

"Gently, John. I'm not pulling your leg."

Slowly, simply, Gideon began explaining his conclusions. John was testy, however, and querulous, arguing every point. Gideon didn't have the energy for it. After a few minutes his enthusiasm had drained away. "The hell with it, John; I don't give a damn if you buy it or not. Solve it all yourself. Look, could we go back? I'm really bushed." He could feel the torn muscles in his cheek sagging, blurring his speech. His ankle had begun to throb again, and it felt grossly swollen.

"Fine," John said, sounding as if he didn't give a damn either. "If it's all right with you, we'll stop at the Security Office on the way in to see if anything new has come in."

Gideon didn't answer. It wasn't a question.

In the car, he sulked most of the way. John was silent and fidgety. As they neared the base, John suddenly said, "Look, Doc, I know you know a lot of things about bones. If this was some old fossil skeleton, I wouldn't argue with you. What do I know? But I can't just blindly accept what you're telling me. What am I supposed to put in my report? 'Professor looked at burned piece of jawbone and identified victim as five-foot-four-inch male Japanese with a birthmark on his left ear and a pimple on his ass'?"

Gideon's eyes were closed. He opened them. "Five-four was wrong," he said slowly. "That formula was for male Caucasians.

This guy was Mongoloid—he'd have a shorter leg length relative to total body size. That means I underestimated. He's probably about five-five. And change his weight to one-fifty."

"Come on, Doc—!"

"John, don't worry about it, will you? I'm just talking to myself. Believe whatever you want."

He was quiet again for a while, dozing a little in the late afternoon sun. Then, after the brightly smiling Italian guards had waved them through the base gate, he said, "John, I have a favor to ask. Nobody else calls me Doc. Nobody *ever* called me Doc. Nobody calls *anybody* Doc. My name's Gideon."

John lit up. "Okay, you're on, Gid."

"*Gid?* Oh God, *please.* If we have to choose between Gid and Doc, I'll take Doc." He shook his head. "Gid! Jesus Christ!"

"What a prima donna," John said. They both laughed, glad to be friends again.

"If I have to choose between Doc and Gideon, I'll stick with Doc. Takes less time to say."

"So be it," Gideon said. "I'm resigned."

At the Security Office, John left Gideon in the car while he went into the white frame building. A moment later he returned and leaned into Gideon's window.

"Nothing new. There's a telephone call for you from Heidelberg. Do you want to go in and call back?"

"Heidelberg? Gosh, I forgot!" Dr. Rufus had called him two days before, full of avuncular concern and reassurance. Gideon was not to worry about the Heidelberg lectures that week; when news of Gideon's "accident" had reached them, they had contracted with a German professor from Heidelberg University to deliver them through an interpreter. "Not quite the Oliver éclat," Dr. Rufus had said, "but adequate."

As for the following week's lectures in Madrid, they would take care of those, too, if necessary. Gideon was to concentrate only on getting well at his own pace.

Gideon, however, did not intend to spend the next couple of weeks in a hospital bed. Putting what little verve he had into his voice, he had told Dr. Rufus he'd be ready to fly to Madrid by the next weekend, but that he'd call in a day or two to confirm. Then he'd forgotten all about it.

John handed the message to Gideon. A routing slip stapled to it showed that the call had come in to the Education Center yesterday. The message had been forwarded to the hospital and then to Security. It was from Eric Bozzini, not Dr. Rufus, and it said "Pls call back. Impt." For a moment he couldn't place Eric Bozzini. When he did, he wondered why the laid-back Californian should be telephoning him—with an Impt. Call, no less.

Even using his cane, he needed a steadying hand from John to get out of the car, up the three steps, and into the office.

"My God, I feel like I'm a hundred years old," he muttered as he fell into a chair behind a battered wooden desk with a telephone on it.

John went to talk with the shore patrol personnel while Gideon telephoned. To his surprise he got through on the first try.

"Hello, Eric, this is Gideon Oliver."

"Hey, Gid!" shouted Eric. Gideon raised his eyes ceilingward, but said nothing. "What do you say, man? Hey man, what's happening? You had an accident, huh? You okay now?"

"Yeah, Eric, I'm fine. What's up?"

"You know, I was in Sig on Friday," Eric said. "Tried to see you, but they said no visitors."

"I'm a lot better now. What's up?"

"Rufe said to check with you about whether you were going to do the Spanish gig." Gideon almost laughed. Eric was laid back farther than ever.

"Sure, Eric. I'm sorry I wasn't able to call back earlier."

"Fantastic, man. We figured you'd say that. Like, the show must go on, right? Well, I've been working on your logistics—I don't know if you knew Cindy Poretzky had to go back to the States, so I've been made acting logistics director?"

"Uh huh," said Gideon, although he had no idea what Eric was talking about. He began to be sorry he hadn't waited until tomorrow to return the call.

"So I've been working on your logistics. Believe it or not, the easiest way for you to get from Sicily to Spain is to fly back to Germany and take a direct shot from Rhein-Main to Torrejón. So—"

"Wait, I'm getting mixed up. I thought I was going to Madrid. Where's Torrejón?"

"Torrejón's the name of the base you're going to. Twenty miles from Madrid. Groovy place. Fantastic chicks." Amazing, Gideon thought; he must get his vocabulary from 1950s movies.

"Yeah, man," Eric said, with a leer Gideon could feel over the wire. "Get all the Spanish pussy you want."

Change that to 1970s movies, Gideon thought. "Fine," he said. "What do I do?"

"Well, if you're able to fly tomorrow, we got you a special dispensation for a military flight out of Sig to Rhein-Main. Then come on down to Heidelberg for a couple of days—we got you a BOQ reservation at Patrick Henry. Then on Sunday you fly commercial out of Frankfurt to Madrid. Air force bus'll leave for Torrejón an hour after you get there, and we've already set you up in the BOQ."

Gideon was impressed in spite of himself. "That's really helpful, Eric, thanks. I hadn't even thought about how I'd get there."

"We got our act together here, man. Service is our motto, right? Look, I hear John Lau from NSD is out there on something. Can you connect with him?"

Gideon smiled. "I believe so."

"Okay, get a hold of him and let him set it up for you to come back with him. It'll save you a lot of paperwork."

"Will do, Eric. Thanks again."

"Take it easy, man. See you in Heidelberg."

Gideon hung up and swiveled around in his chair to see John sitting on the edge of a desk in the midst of a group of shore patrol men, looking at him with an oddly calculating expression. Without asking, John took a sheet of paper, some form, from the hand of the man sitting behind the desk and walked over to Gideon, never changing his expression. Silently, he held the form out.

It gave Gideon a nervous, guilty feeling. "What is this, John? What's the matter?"

"Read it." Gideon half-expected him to toss the paper at him, but he laid it carefully on the desk.

The form was unfamiliar. Gideon shifted in his chair to ease the pain in his ankle. "Is this a missing person's report?"

John nodded, still watching him with that peculiar expression. "One of the base cafeteria workers. Been missing since last Friday."

"John, I'm not up to fooling around. Will you tell me what's going on, please?"

"Read this part." He put his forefinger a third of the way down the page. "Read it out loud."

Gideon was annoyed with the game-playing. He read it silently: *Name* Kenneth Ito; *Height* 5'5" *Weight* 148. . . . At that point he couldn't keep from shouting. "*Race* Asian! That's the guy!" Under circumstances that were less grim, he would have whooped with triumph.

John nodded. "It's him," he said in an almost comically respectful tone. "Shore patrol tells me he worked nightshift and took the Dump Road home. They must have killed him, planted him in the car, and then burned it. So the police would think the driver was still in it and not bother to search for him." He shook his head. "Goddamn, Doc, that's really something."

Gideon read further: *Age* 38; *Handedness* Left. The guesses had all been right, remarkably right. "This *Distinguishing Characteristics* section," he said. "They forgot to say he smoked a pipe."

John turned and called to the shore patrol. "Hey, did this guy smoke a pipe, do you know?"

One of them shouted back, "That's right, I forgot. He always had his metal pipe, one of those air-cooled jobs, stuck in his mouth! Hey, how the hell did you know?"

John turned back to Gideon. "That is really something," he said again. "I never saw anything like it. I owe you an apology." He shook his head. "I can hardly believe it. From those little pieces of bone. Doc, how *do* you know he smoked? How can you tell he was left-handed?"

Gideon smiled. "You know my methods, Watson."

"No, seriously."

"Oh no," Gideon said. "I tried to explain it once before, and you gave me nothing but a hard time. I think I'll just keep a few tricks up my sleeve."

"Hey, don't be like that." John suddenly smiled. "Anyway, you were two pounds off on his weight."

Gideon frowned. "Hmm," he said, "that's impossible. He pretended to scrutinize the form worriedly. "Ah, here," he said with feigned relief, "this explains it. He had thinning hair. When I said one-fifty I was assuming he had a full head of hair. No way I could tell otherwise. Allow a couple of pounds for hair and you get one-forty-eight." He handed the form to John.

John's dumbfounded expression was the most delightful thing Gideon had seen all day. "Does hair weigh that much? Doc, are you kidding me?"

"Would I kid you?" Gideon said.

Book 3: Heidelberg

9

THE TRIP TO HEIDELBERG was smooth and easy. They left Sigonella at 11:00 A.M.; at 5:00 John was back at his office and Gideon was in the lobby of the Bachelor Officers' Quarters, trying to reach Tom Marks by telephone. He had quite a few questions to ask him, and John had advised him to go ahead and ask, although he doubted that he'd get any answers.

Mr. Marks was not in, Frau Stetten informed him. Perhaps Dr. Oliver could come the following day? The following day was Saturday, Gideon said. Was Mr. Marks at his office on Saturdays?

"We work when we must," was the lofty Teutonic response, and across Gideon's mind there flashed an image of the wrought-iron *Arbeit macht frei* that once greeted newcomers to Dachau. "We will say nine o'clock, yes?"

"Fine," Gideon said. "Thank you very much." Silently he added, "Heil Hitler."

He had hung up the telephone and was standing there frowning at himself for being subject to such groundless, stereotypical thinking when he became aware that Janet Feller, smiling warmly and looking tall and clean and lovely, had been observing him for some time.

"Sorry, I didn't mean to wake you up," she said. "You look like the World's Original Absent-Minded Professor."

The words, spoken so often by Nora, made his heart turn over, and while he fumbled witlessly for something to say, he was further flustered by the soft light that suddenly suffused her face. No one had looked at him like that for a very long time. For an irrational instant it seemed that Nora was back again, that the past had somehow changed, that time had bent.

She reached a hand toward his cheek and stopped with her fingertips a few inches away.

"You've really been through it, haven't you?" she said, with something in her voice that hadn't been there at the dinner party the week before.

It finally occurred to Gideon that she was reacting to his face. He had forgotten how damaged it was. "It was nothing," he said stupidly, watching her.

Janet dropped her hand back to her side. "Nothing?" she said. "You sure look like hell."

"So people have been telling me. But it's nowhere near as bad as it looks." His voice sounded appropriately calm in his ears, but his heart was beating rapidly. For the first few months after Nora's death, of course, he was always seeing her in the street or on campus, or getting on a bus. But it hadn't happened for at least a year.

"I sure hope not," she said. "I see you're using a cane."

"Only for another day or two. Really, I'm all right." He paused and cleared his throat. Asking for a date was something that came no more easily to him at thirty-eight than it had at eighteen, and he had to lower his eyes to do it. "I don't suppose you're busy for dinner tonight?"

She laughed. "Thanks a *lot*."

Gideon was confused at first. Then he laughed, too. "I mean, I don't suppose you're *free* tonight? I thought we might have dinner."

"Sounds swell," she said.

"Fine. Where shall I get you?" He stepped back a little, afraid she could hear his heart thumping.

"Get me? I live here."

"You live in the BOQ?"

"Certainly. Why not? Cheapest place in town and a sink in every room. I'm in Twenty-one. Come by in an hour."

*   *   *

Heidelberg is one of the very few German cities that was never bombed during World War II. As a result it has an Old World quality more authentic and pervasive than most of Germany's other ancient cities. In the Old Town, housed in a baroque palace, is the Kurpfälziches Museum. On his first day in Heidelberg, Gideon had gone there to see the exhibit of *Homo erectus heidelbergensis*, the famed 360,000-year-old jawbone that had rocked the scientific world seventy years before. He was disappointed to see that the display contained only a plaster cast of the bone, but was pleased to find an elegant restaurant tucked into one corner of the courtyard. He hadn't eaten there then, but had marked it as a place to come another time. It was here he took Janet.

Over veal steaks with cream sauce accompanied by an excellent Beilsteiner Mosel, she listened pensively, almost tenderly, to his description of the attack in Sicily. Relishing her attention, he milked the story for as much sympathy as he could, then sighed and sat back in his chair with a suitably noble expression on his battered countenance.

"But why did they do it?" Janet asked. "What was it about?"

Gideon came close to revealing his involvement with NSD but changed his mind. The less she knew, the better for her. My God, he thought; the need-to-know principle. He was starting to think like them. "The police have no idea," he said. "They figure it was a Mafia thing, that I was mistaken for someone else."

"Do you buy that? It doesn't sound like the Mafia."

He was suddenly alert. "What do you mean?"

She shrugged and held out her glass. He filled it. "Janet," he said, "what really happened to those other two visiting fellows?"

"You think there's a connection?" She sipped and then delicately licked the fruity wine from her lips.

With an effort, Gideon kept his mind on the conversation. "Well," he said, "do these sorts of things happen to the regular faculty?"

"No," Janet said. "It's odd, now that you mention it. As far as I know, no USOC prof has ever been killed here or even seriously hurt, except that other fellow and now you."

"What about the Econ fellow you and Eric were talking about last week?"

"Oh, Pete?" She searched for his last name. "Pete Berger? I didn't know him all that well. Nobody did. He was kind of a strange bird; awkward, shy, hard to talk to, never mingled much. I know he had a bad reputation for missing classes, and Dr. Rufus was thinking about firing him. But he never got hurt, as far as I know. He just disappeared for good one day and never showed up again. . . . Oh, I see what you mean. Yes, it *is* peculiar, isn't it?"

"Yes, isn't it? Where was he when he disappeared?"

"Up north somewhere. Bremerhaven, I think. I wish I could tell you more."

"What about the other one?"

"The guy that got killed? I never met him. I just heard his car ran off the road in Italy."

They paused while the waiter brought them each a cup of coffee.

"Janet," said Gideon, stirring a little sugar into the strong, fragrant brew, "when you were telling me some of this last week at the dinner, Eric tried to shush you up, remember? Why did he do that?"

He studied her face. She looked at him with open, innocent eyes. Lovely eyes, really, with clear, beautiful hazel irises.

"Oh, I think he just didn't want to frighten you off. But we. were all pretty sloshed, as I recall." She sipped her coffee and put the cup carefully in its saucer. "What are you suggesting by all the questions? That there was foul play involved?"

"I don't know what I'm suggesting. I'm just trying to make sense out of it." He waited until he caught her eye again. "You don't suppose they were involved in undercover work, some kind of espionage, or—?"

"Espionage? *Spies?* Are you serious?" Her incredulity told him one thing he wanted to know; recruiting of faculty by NSD was not routine. Janet, at least, had not been approached by them.

For a while they drank their coffee in silence. It was three times as expensive as it would have been in an American restaurant and there were no refills, but it was delicious. Gideon

85

was comfortable with Janet, and the veal sat well inside him. He listened to the splashing of the fountain in the courtyard and watched Janet frowning thoughtfully at her coffee. She was very beautiful, more so than Nora had been, really, and although the memory of her spluttering wine across the table during that alcoholic tête-à-tête with Eric still put him off a little, who was he to criticize? As she said, he had been pretty well sloshed himself.

"How about a walk?" he said. "It's a pretty night, and it would do my ankle some good."

"I'd love it," Janet said, and sounded like she meant it.

Gideon paid the bill, pleased when she didn't demand to share it.

They walked slowly down the Haupstrasse, Gideon leaning on his cane, past busy sidewalk cafés and restaurants. For four hundred years the Haupstrasse had been the main street of Heidelberg; now it was open only to foot traffic, filled with strollers on this mild fall night, most of whom munched bratwurst or pastries purchased from sidewalk vendors. The smells of sausage and coffee, and the sounds of German conversation, oddly enough, seemed homey and warm. When Janet put her arm through his, Gideon trembled a little and glowed, and tried to look like a Heidelberger out for a *spaziergang* with his *Fräulein*.

"*Sehr gemütlich, nicht wahr?*" he said, patting the hand that lay in the crook of his elbow.

"*Jawohl,*" she answered, and squeezed his arm.

He bought them a sack of almond and chocolate pastries at a *Konditorei*, and they munched along like everyone else, smiling at passersby and murmuring "*Guten Abend.*"

Janet, more at ease with him than she had been before, told him about the dissertation on which she was working: a history of women book collectors in the nineteenth-century American Midwest.

Gideon made sympathetic noises and asked interested questions, but in his heart he sighed a quiet "Oh no." He liked women, really liked them, more than men, and respected them at least as much. In his own field, the cultural anthropologists

86

whom he most respected were Margaret Mead and Ruth Benedict. Yet feminists often bored and sometimes irritated him with their grim, contentious rhetoric. He hoped that wouldn't happen with Janet.

"What are you going to call it?" he asked between bites of pastry.

" 'Keepers of the Written Word: A Study of Oppression, Sexism, and Bibliophily.' "

She delivered the cumbrous words so ponderously, notwithstanding a mouthful of nuts and chocolate, that he thought she was joking. He laughed.

It was a mistake. She leaned on his arm to make him stop walking and face her. "You find that funny?" Her eyes were cool and serious.

Gideon winced and even drew a tiny breath between clenched teeth in an effort to make her think that she had inadvertently hurt his ankle but that he was stoically trying to keep it from her. It was a cheap trick, of course, intended primarily to head her off and secondarily to rekindle in her that warm sympathy in which he'd been basking until those damn female book collectors came up. He thought he carried it off fairly well, but perhaps he had been too subtle; her face was without pity.

"What is it that's so humorous about it?" she said. "Do you think women bibliophiles have *not* been oppressed? Can you even grasp what it was like to be a female intellectual in a society that was dominated by—"

"Janet, don't go all polemic on me. All I was laughing about was, well, was how all serious titles have to have a colon in them nowadays. They used to have subtitles. Now it's all one title with colons. I don't know why, but it strikes me funny."

It was so wonderfully irrelevant that it served as a much-needed non sequitur. After a sharp glance at him, Janet seemed to decide he was being truthful. She opened her mouth to speak and then closed it.

"Do you know," Gideon asked as he moved them gently along, "I haven't yet been to one of the student taverns. Isn't the Red Ox near here? How about a beer?"

"I don't think you're the type," Janet said, still ready to fight. Gideon smiled innocently at her, although under other circumstances he might have asked her what she meant.

She smiled suddenly, and the warmth came back into her eyes. "Well," she said, "I suppose one can't come to Heidelberg without hoisting a stein at the Red Ox. What would Sigmund Romberg think?"

When they walked into the smoky, noisy Restaurant Zum Roten Ochsen, he found that she was right. He didn't like it at all. The age-blackened ceiling of the big tavern rang with lusty male voices raised in martial-sounding songs, and with the clank of beer steins beating time on old oak tables. It was all very jolly and picturesque, but it depressed him.

He knew these songs had been sung in this room for nearly three hundred years. He knew that images from *The Student Prince* were supposed to leap to the mind of the visitor. They didn't. What he saw instead was an ominous scene out of the 1930s: flushed, sweating faces, glazed and fervent eyes. . . . It wasn't for him; maybe another time.

"You're right," he shouted over the singing. "Let's go someplace else."

They turned to leave and were almost bowled over by a husky, perspiring serving wench who might have stepped out of a Frans Hals painting: rosy cheeks, cherubic smile, peekaboo seventeenth-century bodice and all. Arms aloft, she banked as she charged toward them, apparently taking advantage of centrifugal force to keep the four liter-sized steins of beer she carried in each red hand from spilling.

Janet ducked under one brawny forearm, Gideon under the other, and they emerged laughing and hand-in-hand into the street, where Gideon ran directly into a smallish man standing on the sidewalk at the entrance. His first reaction was one of concern. They had been moving with considerable impetus, and Gideon weighed nearly two hundred pounds. The man in the street, he was sure, was going to be knocked sprawling. Automatically, he reached out to steady him.

Gideon's second reaction, following closely on the first, was amazement. Running into the motionless figure was like running into a two-ton statue. Not only did he not go flying; he didn't budge. It was Gideon who was nearly knocked off his feet.

His third reaction was a mixture of alarm and fury, just barely in that order. It was the ferret-faced man, staring at him with an expression closer to disgust than menace. The man began to turn away.

"Hey!" Gideon cried. "You! Wait!" He thrust out his cane to block the man's path. Calmly, the smaller man seized it and pulled it across his chest, jerking Gideon toward him and spinning him half-around. Then, with an expert, economical motion, like a martial-arts instructor demonstrating before a class, he lifted his foot and brought down the sole on the calf of Gideon's left leg. Gideon's knee buckled like cardboard, and he fell to the ground, writhing desperately to keep his weight off the injured ankle. The cane was wrenched from his grasp and sent clattering into the street.

As a boxer in college, Gideon had learned to anticipate an opponent's movements by watching his eyes. Now, even as he landed heavily on his back, he looked up into the face above him and was stunned by a blazing look of surpassing contempt, theatrical in its intensity.

The man blinked, and a little of the glittering danger left his eyes. Then he pivoted abruptly, as if forcing himself to leave, and began to walk firmly away.

"Wait a minute, you—" Janet cried, stepping slightly forward. Gideon's arm went out to warn her off, but she stepped back on her own when the man stopped, rotated his snaky neck, and fixed her with those fierce eyes. Turning a little further, he looked at Gideon one more time with a glare that said he was considering whether he might not rather come back and kill him after all. Apparently deciding against it, at least then and there, he turned once more and disappeared quickly into the darkness.

The entire episode had taken about ten seconds, not enough time for a crowd to collect, but four or five nearby people were watching intently.

Gideon picked himself up self-consciously, brushing off Janet's offered help. Gingerly, he tested his left ankle; amazingly, it was no worse than it had been before. Janet, also looking self-conscious, began to dust him off with her hands.

With a surly gesture, he shrugged off her attentions, then apologized at once.

"I'm sorry." He reached for the hand he had just brushed away.

"I know," she said, squeezing Gideon's hand. "Hey, how'd you like to come up to my place to see my dissertation notes?" She wiggled her eyebrows roguishly, but Gideon could feel her hand trembling in his. He found it strangely affecting. Vulnerability was a side of her he hadn't seen before. Of course, he thought it might be *his* hand that was doing the trembling; his heart was pounding hard enough.

A wide-eyed, rosy-cheeked adolescent wordlessly handed Gideon his cane. He took it with a nod of thanks, and they began to walk back down the Haupstrasse.

Janet took his arm again. "What was that about, Gideon? It happened so fast I hardly saw it. Who was that creep?"

"He was one of the ones in my room at the Ballman; the one with the knife. He was following us." Gideon could hear the irascibility in his own voice. He was annoyed with Janet, but he didn't know why.

A little uncertainly, Janet laughed. It didn't improve his temper. "I think you're becoming paranoid," she said. "Or melodramatic is more like it. If he was following us, he wasn't very good at it. He was standing right out in the middle of the street gawking at the Red Ox like anyone else."

Gideon didn't think so. Ferret-face didn't strike him as a gawker. "No," he said impatiently. "I think we surprised him by coming back out almost as soon as we went in, that's all."

Janet thought about it. "Could be." She thought about it some more. "You know, I never saw anyone move quite like that. He had you flat on your back so fast I could hardly follow it."

"Well, hell, Janet," he said, his voice rising, "I've got a bunged-up ankle, and this damn cane throws me off balance. . . . What the hell is so funny?"

She was laughing again, easily now, and with an affection that put a chink in his petulance. *"You're* funny," she said. "You sound exactly like a twelve-year-old that just got beat up by the neighborhood bully in front of his girl."

"God damn it, Janet—" he began, and then realized she was absolutely right. "You're absolutely right," he said. "That's exactly what I've been doing." He stopped walking and faced her squarely; it seemed important to get this right. "Janet, I've been acting like an immature boob. I had no call to snap at you like that. I'm sorry."

She smiled at him—a wide, warm smile. "Professor Oliver, you're a very likable man." She hugged his arm to her, and he felt the back of it brush her breasts, first one and then the other. He shivered, knowing from the change in her eyes that she had felt him tremble.

"Now," she said, "what about those dissertation notes?"

"Can I trust you?" he asked.

"What do you think?" She wiggled her eyebrows again.

"I hope not. Let's go."

10

TO GET TO HER room in the BOQ, they had to walk past Gideon's door. He paused there to take a long look at the floor around it, even using his cane to probe the strands of the nearly nonexistent carpet nap. There were no toothpick slivers. (He had switched from paper clips to toothpick pieces; they were easier to break off and much less likely to be spotted by intruders. He had also taken to putting one at each side of the door for insurance.)

When Janet asked what he was doing, he explained and added, "I suppose you're going to say this is paranoid too."

"Even paranoiacs have enemies," she said seriously.

Janet's room was a replica of his, except for the mess.

Janet took a slip and blouse from the green plastic-covered armchair and tossed them on one of the beds. *"Setzen Sie sich,"* she said. "I'll make some drinks."

After rummaging first in a desk drawer and then in the closet, she located a bottle of Scotch and poured some into a couple of paper cups. She gave Gideon his drink, kicked off her shoes, and sat on one of the beds, her back propped against the white metal bars at its head. As she drew her legs up, Gideon caught a glimpse of long, tawny thighs. Suddenly, he was both excited and shy. He looked down into his cup and swirled the liquid around.

"So tell me," Janet said, "how do you like teaching for USOC?"

"It's okay, but it's been pretty dull so far."

Janet laughed as she brought the drink to her lips, spluttering the Scotch a little. When she had done that over wine with Eric, it had been an annoying mannerism, contrivedly girlish. Now it seemed spontaneous and charming.

"Janet Feller," he said. "Nice name. Right out of a teenage romance. Do you know I don't know anything about you?"

"Ah, you *would* like to hear more about the dissertation, then? Excellent. Let me read you the first two hundred pages—"

"No, I mean about *you*."

She told him. For over an hour, through three cups of Scotch, she told him how she'd been raised in Illinois; how at eighteen, on a trip to Athens with her parents, she'd fallen in love with a Greek truck driver; how she'd married him against the wishes of both families and then lived two hellish years in his mother's house in Piraeus, never managing to learn the language. Somehow, her father, an elementary-school principal, had managed to engineer a divorce and bring her back to Champaign, where she had lived at home while working on her B.A. in history. Her father's graduation present was a trip to New York. There she promptly met and married another truck driver. That had lasted two months.

This was all vaguely unsettling to Gideon. Janet was full of surprises. Every time he thought he had her fitted into a niche, she came up with something new.

"Hmm," he said, "you seem to fixate on truck drivers, don't you? I wonder if there's a name for that. Truckerphilia, maybe."

As soon as he said it, he was sorry. He had meant to be entertaining, but it had come out flip.

Janet, however, appeared to be amused. "It does seem that way, doesn't it?" she said as she got up to pour their fourth drinks. "Truckerphilia. Sounds naughty. Say, you don't by chance happen to drive a truck, do you?"

"I could learn," he said, feeling loose and happy. "I don't see why it should be difficult. I'm super-competent in a Rabbit, except for parking and backing up, and turns give me a little trouble." He sipped his Scotch, enjoying her laughter. "Go ahead, what happened after that marriage?" As she hopped back onto the bed, Gideon watched her smooth thighs more openly.

"Nothing; that's all there is. I put in four years of graduate work at the University of Chicago, came to USOC three years ago, and I've been teaching and trying to write my damn dissertation ever since. Oh, and I never got married again, and I'm thirty-one."

Thirty-one was what he'd guessed. "Astounding," he said. "Quite well preserved, in my opinion."

"So I assumed from all that leering and heavy breathing."

"Sorry. I didn't mean to be so obvious."

"Like hell you didn't. I gather you're a leg man. A legophiliac." She smiled sweetly. "Or did I just forget to put on any pants?"

Gideon's cheeks turned hot. Women had changed a lot in the decade since he'd been in active pursuit. He'd had little practice at the new banter and, try as he did, no witty response came to mind. Angry with himself for being a prude, he bent over his empty cup, trying to hide the fact that he was blushing.

Janet leaned forward and clasped her arms around her knees. "Hey, Gid," she said softly. Coming from her, in that tone, "Gid" didn't sound so bad. "That was crude, wasn't it? I've had too many Scotches. Now I'm embarrassed. Look, how about telling me something about you? You know everything about me."

"There isn't much to tell," he began, but then he found there was. At first he talked about his childhood in Los Angeles, about how he'd wanted to be an anthropologist before he even knew there was such a thing, about how he'd supported himself through his Ph.D. at Wisconsin with a host of part-time jobs: waiting tables, being a night watchman, delivering cigarettes to vending machines. ("Did you drive a truck?" asked Janet. "Only a little one," Gideon said, "a panel truck." "Oh," she said, with a make-believe pout, "that doesn't count.")

He told her, too, about how he'd boxed at local fight clubs for fifty dollars a fight when part-time jobs dried up. Once, calling on a talent he hadn't known he possessed, he had lived for two months on his takings as a ping-pong shark in the Student Union. They were both laughing, and he was feeling relaxed again. But suddenly he found himself in the dangerous region, the region he'd never shared with anyone. He told her about Nora and what she'd meant to him, and even—at least to the extent that words could do it—about what it had been like when she had died.

When he was done, she came over to him and knelt between his legs, laying her head against his chest and embracing him with unexpected strength. It made Gideon's entire body tingle. Bending his head, he kissed her soft, fresh-smelling hair, then turned up her face and kissed her gently on the lips. Their faint raspberry taste was a surprise, an exciting one.

When he released her head, Janet remained looking into his face for a long moment, then hugged him even harder. With nearly unbearable pleasure Gideon could feel her breasts against him, her body pressed hard between his legs. He ran his hands through her hair and over her face. Catching one of his hands, she brought it to her lips and kissed it.

"You're a nice man, Gideon. I like you *very* much," she said, with her head against his chest. Her voice had a throaty quality that hadn't been there before.

"Um," said Gideon, his own voice a little unsteady, "I appreciate the warm and no-doubt sisterly intent of all this, but I have to confess that my own feelings are becoming rather, um, amatory."

Janet shifted her knees to snuggle in even closer. Her fingertips played gently over his thighs. "I'm aware of that, my friend. I'm not wearing a suit of armor, you know. However, I think 'erotic' would be more accurate than 'amatory.' In fact, I'm positive," she said as her hands continued to explore him. "And if you think I'm being sisterly, you sure got a funny family."

Gideon was breathless. He had forgotten the way it could be. "Janet, Janet, come and lie down with me," he said.

She led him to the bed and began to unbutton her blouse. He stopped her, though, and with trembling, reverent fingers, undid the buttons one by one, slowly and with care.

"Hm?" he said drowsily. He was lying on his back, not sure if he was awake or asleep. Janet's head was tucked into his shoulder, her body pressed against his side, her leg thrown over his.

"What?" she replied, her voice muffled by his chest.

"No, I asked you what *you* said." On its own, his hand moved slowly down her side into the deep valley of her waist, up and over the big, delicious, roller-coaster curve of her hip.

"Mmm. How do you expect me to concentrate when you do that?" she said, her voice becoming interested. "Hey, are you in the mood for a little more . . . ?" The arm that had been lying across his chest shifted, and her hand began its way down his belly.

Laughing, he caught and held it. "No, wait, have a heart. Believe me, I've shot my wad."

"Gideon, what a gross expression. I'm surprised at you."

"It's not gross at all. The phrase stems from how you fired a cannon in the nineteenth century. You take a wad of—"

"I *know* what it stems from. I mean that the use of that particular metaphor under these particular circumstances is somewhat coarse. Wouldn't you say so?" Her hand broke free and moved on down him. "Besides, it feels to me like the old cannon's getting ready to shoot another wad."

"Now *that's* gross," he said, catching her hand again and moving it away. "Come on, hold off a minute and tell me what it was you said."

She pulled her hand free and poked him in the side. "Oho, so that's the way it is, is it? The old story. First it's all tender supplications, but now that he's had his way with her, it's 'hold off a minute,' is it? You nasty . . . man!" She punctuated the last word with another jab in the side.

"Ouch!" Laughing, he leaned over and pinned both her wrists

to the bed. "I'm pushing forty, you know. I can't do this sort of thing all night. Now what was it you said?"

"All right. I don't know what you *think* I said that was so important, but all I said was that I'm glad you're stopping in Heidelberg. Is that such a surprise?"

"That wasn't what you said. You said you were glad I didn't go the usual route directly from Sigonella to Torrejón."

"So what's the difference? Gideon, you're hurting my wrists."

He let go at once, and she immediately grabbed for him again. They rolled over, wrestling and laughing, and ended up in a long, sweet kiss that quieted them both and almost made Gideon lose the thread he was trying to follow. Lying in Janet's arms, pressed against her from face to toe, he made a last effort.

"The difference is, Janet, that Eric told me there *wasn't* a direct route; that the only way to get from Sigonella to Torrejón was by coming through Frankfurt."

"That's crazy. Since you were flying military anyway, you could easily have gone just to Naples and then to Torrejón, or maybe even on a direct flight. Or you could have flown commercial from Catania to Rome, then to Madrid. There's no reason to come back to Germany."

"Are you sure?"

"Well, I think so. I work part-time in the Logistics Office, and I make up a lot of the itineraries."

"You work with Eric?" There was a slight chill in his voice.

"Oh, for gosh sake, don't go all green-eyed monster on me. A lady has to support herself, you know."

She kissed him briskly. Then she turned on the lamp near the bed and propped herself up on one elbow. Gideon rolled over on his back, his hands behind his neck.

"This oddball routing," Janet said, "do you think it has something to do with the funny stuff that's been happening to you?"

"I sure wouldn't be surprised. Obviously, my ferret-faced friend was aware that I was back." He paused, chewing his lip. "Maybe I was even brought back so he could do whatever it is he had in mind. Or has in mind."

"But what could Eric possibly have to do with that?"

"I don't know, but I intend to find out." He turned toward her again. She was still on one elbow, one round breast swaying gently, inches from his face.

"My God, Janet," he said softly, "how beautiful you are." He cupped the mysterious heaviness of one lovely globe in his hand and moved it toward his lips.

"Be serious, now, Gideon; don't do that," she said, but Gideon noted that she didn't pull away. "This stuff scares me. Do you think you're in danger? Is Eric involved? What could the point possibly be?"

"Mmm," said Gideon.

"Gideon, don't do that," she said again, but her voice was husky. She began to stroke his hair.

"Mmmmmmmm," he said.

Deep in the night, he had a childish nightmare. A glaring monster—an old movie-style zombie with outstretched arms, but with features that were familiar—pursued him. He couldn't run; his feet were caught in gluelike mud. He must have cried out because he was awakened by Janet caressing his cheek.

"Sh, sh," she said. "It's all right, I'm here. Shh."

When he was free of the dream, she said, "Do you want to talk about it? Did it have to do with the little rat in the Haupstrasse?"

As soon as she said it, he knew to whom the features had belonged.

"Yes," he said. "You know, the way that guy looked at me tonight . . . as if I were a . . . a. . . ."

"A fat green worm he found in his soup."

"Ugh. Yes. Like that. That's what bothers me the most. That man detests me, absolutely despises me—and I don't even know who he is. It's so—"

Janet placed her fingers on his mouth and then gently cupped his face. "Sh," she said again. "Four a.m.'s a rotten time to try to think anything through. We'll talk about it in the morning. Hug me, please."

But when he jumped out of bed four hours later, Janet merely opened one eye. "Eek," she said. "There's a naked man in my room." She chortled and went back to sleep.

Gideon put on enough of his clothes to walk down the hallway to his room. The check of the carpet, almost habitual by now, revealed no toothpick slivers. Entering the room, he found it pleasantly austere, almost monklike, after Janet's clutter. Not that he was complaining. A little clutter wasn't the worst thing in the world.

While he shaved and showered, his mind kept drifting happily over the previous night, although he knew he should have been framing questions for Marks. Certainly he wasn't in love with Janet; he doubted if he would ever really love anyone again. But she was surely the best thing that had happened to him since Nora. Cautiously, he probed his mind for traces of guilt or disloyalty, but none were there. He had crossed a big barrier last night. Things were definitely looking up.

By the time he finished dressing, he was whistling. It was 8:25. If he didn't dawdle, there'd be time for a cup of coffee and a roll at the Officers' Club before heading downtown.

At the door to his room, he paused to search for the toothpick slivers so he could reinsert them. They would fall out, of course, whenever he opened the door, and he usually picked them up on entering. When he'd returned from Janet's room, however, he'd had a cane in one hand and some clothes in the other, so he hadn't bothered.

Or had he? They weren't on the floor. A panicky sort of alarm went through him as he searched his memory. No, he was sure he hadn't picked them up. Opening the door wide, he checked to see if they had somehow lodged in the jamb or the hinges and failed to drop the floor. That hadn't happened, of course. The wood splinters were simply gone.

Closing the door again, he stood with his back against it, his mind working jumpily. Could he have forgotten to place them before he went out with Janet last night? He wasn't sure. He couldn't remember doing it, but he couldn't remember *not* doing it either. No, he thought, he *must* have; there was no way he would have forgotten to do that. Someone must have been in his room, then—perhaps during the night, perhaps earlier when he'd been out with Janet. His check of the carpet when they'd returned hadn't meant anything one way or the other.

In the back of a notebook, he found the list of articles he had made in Sicily and began to move around the room checking things off. It still didn't seem possible that anyone had been there; it might mean that someone had seen the two tiny splinters fall to the floor when the door opened, and had simply removed them. Gideon just couldn't accept that. Each sliver was the pointed end of a toothpick, less than a sixteenth of an inch long. Unless you knew what you were looking for, they would be invisible against the mottled beige carpet. No, it was impossible. No one could have seen them.

But someone had. On top of his desk, in the exact middle, lay a sheet of white paper he hadn't noticed before, its edges neatly aligned with the borders of the desk. In the middle of the paper, a heavy black circle had been drawn with a marking pen. And in the middle of the circle, neatly parallel to each other, lay the two minute fragments of wood.

With a spurt of energy, Gideon hurried through his list. Nothing was missing. There was no sign of anyone having been there, as far as he could tell, except for the paper on the desk. Going back to the desk, he stood looking down at the slivers, trying to analyze what he was feeling. There was the now-familiar sense of privacy invaded, of vulnerability; he had felt that in both Heidelberg and Sicily, when he'd found that someone had been in his room. But now there was something different. Then, fear had been a prominent emotion. Not now. He wasn't even remotely frightened. That ferret-faced son of a bitch had come into his room when he wasn't there, had covered up his tracks without a trace, and then had had the effrontery, the gall, to flaunt the fact that he'd done it, as if Gideon were so stupid he'd never have figured it out for himself. Which happened to be true, but that was beside the point.

What he was feeling was a cold, lucid anger. In the mirror above the desk, he saw his own battered image: red welts from the cuts around his eyes, a livid scar where his cheek had been torn, fading but still-prominent bruises over the rest of his face. What the mirror didn't show was the anxiety he'd been living with since the first time Ferret-face and his friend had skulked into his room and ambushed him two weeks ago.

Well, he was done being a pawn. If NSD, and John Lau for that matter, couldn't protect him, he would protect himself. And he'd settle his own scores. No more of this passively waiting around until the next time he got beaten up.

He crumpled up the paper with the slivers and tossed them into the wastebasket. When he walked to the door, his back felt straighter than it had in a long time. He threw the cane on the bed as he left. He felt very, very fine.

11

THE YOUNG GUARD IN the dreary vestibule was the same one who'd been on duty before. He looked sourly at the ID that Gideon held up before the thick glass.

"I have an appointment with Mr. Marks," Gideon said.

The guard shoved a half-eaten *Oh Henry* candy bar off a typewritten sheet on the counter in front of him, then brushed away peanut and chocolate crumbs with the back of his hand. He studied the sheet for a long time. Finally, with a sigh and a what-the-hell-I-don't-give-a-shit shrug, he said, "Go ahead."

Gideon was in the mood for a fight, but not with a churlish adolescent who didn't even know he was being rude. He walked down the seedy hallway to Marks's office, where he found Frau Stetten looming steeply over her typewriter. Without stopping her typing, she glanced up at Gideon and cocked her head at the door to the inner office.

"Thank you and good morning to you too," Gideon said.

As usual, being snide gave him an immediate rotten feeling. Catching her eye as he walked past her, he smiled at her as pleasantly as he could. In return she bestowed a highly perfunctory lip contraction that made him sorry he hadn't left well enough alone.

Marks was half-sitting on the windowsill in a pensive, judicial pose, arms folded and head inclined, with the earpiece of his horn-rimmed glasses between pursed lips.

The man of a thousand roles, thought Gideon. Had he been posing like that since nine o'clock, or had he leapt there upon some secret signal from Frau Stetten? Maybe there'd been warning of Gideon's approach from the guard. All of the possibilities were in keeping with what he'd seen of Marks so far.

"Sit down, Dr. Oliver," he said without moving. "Just thinking through a tricky little problem here."

With an affable smile, Gideon sat down in a metal side chair. The desk top was littered with the remains of an earlier meeting: half a glass pot of coffee, three or four styrofoam cups, and three doughnuts, two of them untouched.

Gideon gestured at them with his chin. "No chance for breakfast this morning. Do you mind?"

"What?" said Marks abstractedly from the labyrinthine corridors of profound thought. "Yes, certainly. I mean, no, of course not."

Gideon wolfed down a vanilla-iced doughnut. It was delicious. The coffee was lukewarm, so he poured what was left of the milk from a metal creamer into a cup and drank that. Inasmuch as Marks was still chewing his spectacles, Gideon went cheerfully on to the next doughnut, a jelly-filled one. Besides tasting good, his impromptu breakfast seemed to throw Marks off his stride, which was fine. Gideon needed a lot of information from him, and if he were rattled, so much the better.

Marks took his glasses out of his mouth and sat down behind his desk with an "Ah, well. . . ." that announced he was regretfully now back in the mundane world represented by Gideon Oliver. He lit a cigarette while watching Gideon lick the last of the jelly from his fingers.

"I thought we had a nine o'clock appointment," Marks said.

"Sorry. Someone broke into my room last night. It held me up."

"Is that right? Don't tell me the Sock Bandit of Sicily has struck again?"

"Is that supposed to be funny? Look, Mr. Marks—"

"Oliver, let's stop fooling around. It's not working. We picked the wrong man. Let's forget the whole thing." He dragged deeply on his cigarette.

Gideon was so surprised that all he could do was echo Marks stupidly: "Forget the whole thing?"

"That's right. Consider yourself fired. Without prejudice, of course."

"Fired? Hell, you never *hired* me!" The anger Gideon had been carrying around went from a simmer to a boil. It felt good. "Now let's get a few things straight. A couple of weeks ago, you asked me to take on an assignment—for the cause of peace, if I remember correctly. There wasn't going to be any danger to me, virtually none, as you put it—"

"Monsieur Delvaux."

"What?"

"*Le directeur* said that, not me."

Gideon looked sharply at him. The stare was blandly returned through a haze of cigarette smoke. Marks wasn't quite the clown he'd been last time.

"Since then," Gideon went on, "I've been beaten up twice, I've been attacked by an armed gang, my room's been broken into at least two times—"

"Not quite right; you've only been beaten up once. The first time you were beaten up was *before* you took the assignment. Remember, we talked to you Friday, the day after—"

"God damn it, Marks, don't fuck around with me!" He clamped his mouth shut; this wouldn't do. Using profanity was rare with him, a sure sign that he had slipped from the cool, rational anger with which he'd walked in, into the sort of loutish tantrum he despised. It was he, not Marks, who was off his stride. He took a long, slow breath.

Marks put his hands behind his head and leaned back lazily, eyes narrowed against the smoke of the cigarette dangling from his mouth.

"A little while ago, you said you'd picked the wrong man," said Gideon more quietly. "I'd appreciate knowing what you think I did wrong."

Marks raised his right eyebrow above his horn-rimmed glasses in a gesture that must have taken hours of mirror practice. "Look, Oliver, you're just not the type. Our people have to be unobtrusive. You seem to have a way of getting into violent situations. To be perfectly frank, we think there's something unstable about you, and we can't risk it."

"Unstable?" Gideon couldn't sit still any longer. He jumped to his feet. "I can't believe this! You're actually blaming *me* for what's been happening?"

"You get into altercations on the *street*, for God's sake! Like last night on the Haupstrasse . . . just because someone bumps into you . . . I mean, really—"

"Bumps into me! Marks, that wasn't *someone*! That was the man who tried to kill me a couple of weeks ago. He was following me—" Gideon stopped himself, aware of how emotional he was and how melodramatic he sounded. A sudden thought hit him. "Wait a minute. How did you know about that? Are you people following me around?" He sank back into his chair.

"We've been keeping an eye on you, yes. We wouldn't just turn you loose without protection. And it's been more trouble than we can afford."

"Protection!" Gideon said. He knew he kept repeating Marks, but he couldn't help himself. Somehow, Marks had taken control, and every statement he made was so newly outrageous that it threw Gideon into fresh confusion. "If that's the way you protect your people, no wonder the free world's in trouble."

"Is that right?" For the first time, Marks's voice had an angry edge. "Just who do you think got you out of that ditch in Sicily?"

"The man on the bridge? That was one of your men? Then you must know who those . . . goons were."

"Forget it. I already told you more than I should have."

"Marks, I have a right to know. I came awfully close to being killed."

"We don't operate on right-to-know. We operate on need-to-know, remember? And you don't need to know."

"Marks—"

"Oliver, there's no point in continuing this. I'll be as honest as I can." He lit another cigarette from the stub of the old one and inhaled deeply. "We are terminating our relationship with you because it's not doing any good. That's all I'm at liberty to tell you." He reached for a manila folder on the desk and opened it. "Now, I have a lot of important things to do." Once again Gideon was being dismissed.

"At liberty, hell," Gideon said. "You don't know any more than I do about this, do you? I don't know why I'm wasting my time talking to Delvaux's errand boy." He got up again.

As simple as it was, it worked. Marks was still Marks. Two red spots appeared on the sides of his throat. He slammed the folder closed. "The Russians needed something from Sigonella; they got it. They needed something from Rhein-Main; they got it. They got it without having to go to you." As he spoke, smoke dribbled from his mouth as if his tongue were on fire. "They don't need you. They're obviously getting what they need some other way. So you're not doing them—or us—any good. What's more, you're one hell of a lot of trouble. So thanks for all your help, and good-bye. You're no longer involved." He opened the folder again.

Gideon put his hands on the desk and leaned over Marks. "It's not that simple. There's something about being run off the road, and shot at, and garroted, and having a knife waved in your face that's highly involving—engrossing, even. Whether NSD likes it or not, I'm involved, and I intend to stay involved."

Marks looked up at Gideon, his hands flat on the folder. "It's not *that* simple either. I'm having your schedule changed again. You won't be going to any more sensitive bases, I'm afraid. So there won't be much chance for involvement."

"What do you mean, 'again'?" It *was* you who got Dr. Rufus to change my schedule in the first place?"

"What?" said Marks with mock surprise. "You mean the learned professor didn't have that figured out? Yes, of course it was us, and we intend to do it again. You can kiss romantic Torrejón off, Doctor. On Monday you'll be off to Frankfurt."

"Oh no," said Gideon with more confidence than he felt. "No way. I'm a teacher; I don't work for NSD. I agreed to go to

Torrejón, and that's where I'm going. I've put too many hours into preparing my lectures to have the schedule changed with one day's notice." This wasn't strictly true, but it wouldn't hurt.

Taking the cigarette from his mouth, Marks stifled a fake yawn. "We'll see," he said.

In his mind Gideon drew a comic-strip balloon with dotted lines. "Screw you," he wrote in it. (Imaginary profanity didn't count.) Aloud he said, "Well, thanks for your time." As he was leaving, he smiled again at Frau Stetten, receiving in return an aloof and virginal nod.

"Puffed wheat," said Dr. Rufus from behind him.

"Pardon?" Gideon said, turning in his chair and beginning to rise.

"No, stay where you are, my boy," said Dr. Rufus, coming up to Gideon and pounding him on the shoulder. "I said that the object you are holding in your hand and studying so carefully is a kernel of puffed wheat."

He had come looking for Dr. Rufus a few minutes earlier, straight from NSD headquarters. The chancellor's secretary had said he was somewhere in the building and had shown Gideon into his office to wait. He had taken a thickly upholstered chair in a grouping by the window, and his attention had been caught at once by the large glass bowl on the coffee table nearby. He had thought it was full of lentils or pebbles until, sticking a finger in, he had found them hollow. He had just picked one up to smell it when Dr. Rufus came in.

With a sigh, the chancellor plumped his bearlike body down in the sofa opposite Gideon. "Ah, yes, puffed wheat, couldn't live without it. Finest snack in the world. Munch 'em all day long and never gain an ounce. Why, the whole bowl probably doesn't contain ten ounces. Of course, you have to get the good kind, not the ones in the plastic bags; those are two-thirds sediment."

He settled back and crossed one chubby thigh over the other. "Well, well, well, you've had quite a harrowing adventure, I hear. I hope you're all right now?" His face sagged as he took his first good look at Gideon. "Oh my! You've really been hurt, haven't you? I had no idea. . . ."

Gideon smiled, something he could do with no pain at all now. "You should have seen me last week. I'm fine now, and they tell me it won't be long before I·look myself, or at least before I'm predominantly flesh-colored again."

"I'm certain of it. Still, I just had no idea. . . ." Dr. Rufus slowly shook his head back and forth.

The commiseration was making Gideon uneasy. Until then he had been rather pleased with the improvement in his appearance. "Sir," he said, "I've just come from NSD. Tom Marks told me that the reason you changed my schedule a few weeks ago was so that they could use me as an informant at Sigonella and Torrejón. Is that true?"

"Well," said Dr. Rufus, frowning and reaching into the puffed wheat, "well now—"

"Dr. Rufus, I've been through a lot since I came to USOC. I'd certainly appreciate the truth."

Dr. Rufus absent-mindedly popped a kernel into his mouth. "All right, Gideon, I agree with you." He was still frowning, and Gideon could see little beads of sweat glistening on his pink forehead. "I'm just not sure how much I'm allowed. . . ." He wiped his brow, snorted forcefully, and appeared to come to a decision.

"All right," he said, looking extremely uncomfortable. "About a week before the new faculty came to Heidelberg, Mr. Marks called me. He had a list of, oh, three or four of you. There was you, and Dr. Kyle, and, um, Mr. Morgan, I think. Mr. Marks asked me if I could assign any of you to both Sigonella and Torrejón, as a favor to the NATO Security Directorate. Ah, no, it wasn't Mr. Morgan, it was Dr. Gordon. I remember because—"

"You mean he would have taken any of us? He didn't want *me*, specifically?"

"You, specifically? Oh, no, no. They ran checks of the incoming faculty, and the three of you—you know, I think it *was*

Morgan—were found to be entirely trustworthy; 'clean' was the way Mr. Marks put it. Choosing *you*, I'm afraid, was my doing."

"Why *did* you pick me?"

"Well, Dr. Kyle teaches physics, you see, and Torrejón had just had physics last semester; and Mr. Morgan—yes, it *was* Morgan, I'm sure of it—teaches only undergraduate courses, and Sigonella needed a graduate offering. You, on the other hand—"

". . . got into this incredible situation because I happen to teach graduate anthropology."

Dr. Rufus looked contrite. "I'm afraid that's right. I can't tell you how sorry I am that it's resulted in so much trouble for you. If I'd had any idea you'd be hurt. . . ." He spread his hands, palms upward, in an impotent gesture of sympathy.

"Dr. Rufus," said Gideon, "forgive me, but just what sort of thing did you think NSD had in mind?"

The chancellor shook his head woefully. "I suppose I didn't think. Mr. Marks assured me there wouldn't be any risk. And I, well, I felt it was USOC's duty to provide assistance to NATO, as long as it didn't interfere with our plans."

"Well, it sure interfered with my personal plans."

Abstractedly, Dr. Rufus ate some more puffed wheat. "Of course," he said, "I don't know what it is Marks asked you to do; I never do. But are you certain that your, ah—" he gestured at Gideon's scarred face—"is a result of your . . . um, association with NSD?"

Gideon ignored the question. "What do you mean, you *never* do? Has Marks asked you to do this before?"

"What?" In his surprise at the question, Dr. Rufus put back into the bowl a kernel he had been about to eat. "Well, yes, certainly, of course. Didn't I say that? Nearly every semester. There's always some small schedule rearrangement or program change they'd like us to make. If we can, we do. If we can't, that's the end of it. But nothing like this has happened before. . . . Sicilian gangsters shooting at you. . . ."

"What about the two previous visiting fellows?"

"Oh no, surely you don't think . . . why, I can't really

recall. . . . Mr. Marks asks us not to keep records of that sort of thing. . . . But look, Dr. Dee wasn't attacked; he was killed in an automobile accident in Italy."

"And so would I have been, if I hadn't been able to brake in time. Dr. Rufus, I can't believe you've allowed your faculty to be used like this."

The chancellor's remorseful expression made him relent a little. "Of course," Gideon went on, "I understand why you'd want to help NATO. I feel the same way. But to simply do whatever they want without asking any questions, and to put your staff into situations of danger without their even knowing it. . . ." Feeling unpleasantly sanctimonious, he let the sentence trail away. Dr. Rufus hadn't put him into his situation; he'd done it himself. If he hadn't wanted to go along with NSD, he'd had his chance to say so to Marks and Delvaux.

Dr. Rufus mopped the back of his neck and put his handkerchief in his pocket. He was done with sweating, the gesture seemed to say. He sat up straight, his hands on his knees. "You're entirely right," he said. "I've always been ambivalent about this sort of thing, you know. I should never have allowed it. My God, to think I might be responsible. . . . My boy, we'll cancel your Torrejón assignment, of course. Where would you like to deliver your lectures instead? I'll personally arrange it anywhere we have an education office. We certainly owe that much to you. Rome? Athens? How about Istanbul? Berlin?"

"Torrejón."

Dr. Rufus looked at him with his mouth open. Gideon had an urge to toss in a puffed wheat kernel.

"Yes, Torrejón. Now that I'm in it, I want to stay in it. There are too many loose ends for me to just give it up."

"But my boy, my boy, you've already been nearly killed. Oh, I could never let you . . . oh no, it's out of the question. I'd never forgive myself. . . ." The handkerchief was out and at work again. "Besides, Mr. Marks, Mr. Delvaux. . . . They'd never permit it—"

"Are you saying that, as chancellor, you have to get *their* permission to assign your own faculty?"

"Well, in a case like this. . . . Why, I think I should. . . . After all. . . ."

"Dr. Rufus, I've nearly been killed twice. I've got thirty-some stitches in my face. I've been driven to hurting other people, maybe killing one. My privacy's been repeatedly violated. And," he said, realizing for the first time what the heart of it was, "I've been made to feel like a puppet, a pawn . . . a fool. I'm not out for vengeance; at least I don't think I am. But I can't just walk away from it now and let it ferment for the rest of my life." Embarrassed and a little surprised by his vehemence, he stopped.

Dr. Rufus looked at Gideon with a mixture of pride and concern, as a father might watch a son going off to war. "Very well, my dear boy, I understand, more than you think I do." He patted Gideon's knee. "Torrejón it is. Mr. Marks can go to hell. But you will be careful, won't you? If there's any help I can give you. . . ."

"Thanks, sir; John Lau's already being very helpful. In fact," he said, standing up, "I'm supposed to meet him for lunch in half an hour. Then I've got a few business stops to make back here."

The chancellor rose and walked with Gideon across the office. "Ah, yes, you'll have to pick up your travel orders and tickets and things. And be sure and stop by the library. Bruce has been holding onto some new books for you."

"I will. I have to return some to him, anyway."

"Fine." Placing his hand on Gideon's arm to stop him at the door, he spoke in a low, earnest voice. His honest face, close to Gideon's, was redolent of after-shave lotion and puffed wheat. "Gideon, are you sure you're doing the right thing? Shouldn't this be left to the professionals? My boy, if anything were to happen to you. . . ."

"Don't worry, Dr. Rufus. I know exactly what I'm doing," said Gideon, wishing mightily that he did.

12

HE HAD ARRANGED TO meet John in a small café on the Marktplatz. He was fifteen minutes early, so he ordered a beer and sat back at an outdoor table, enjoying the view of the old church a hundred feet away. Like the castle above, it had managed to survive the seventeenth-century Orleans War and fires. But the slow depredations of time, which had made of the castle a striking dowager, mysterious and alluring, had turned the Heilig-Geist-Kirche into a frowsy slattern. In a sense, though, thought Gideon, the castle was dead and embalmed, a museum piece; the church was still alive. Crude wooden stalls stood between its late Gothic buttresses, just as they had in the Middle Ages. Once they must have displayed venison and oil and rough beer. Now it was newspapers and magazines, and key chains that said "Olde Heidelberg."

A misty rain began to fall, the first precipitation Gideon had seen since coming to Europe. The tourists in the square melted away, and the merchants began to close up their closetlike stalls or to cover them with green canvas. Gideon remained outside, however, protected by a red-and-white table umbrella advertising Grenzquell beer, and enjoying the wet-clay smell of the rain. As a northern Californian, he had come to love the fog and rain, preferring stormy days to sunny ones. Here in Heidelberg he found himself enchanted by the mist that now obscured part of the castle and by the rain that glistened on the antique cobblestones of the square.

How nice it would be if Janet were sitting with him, he thought. His heart contracted suddenly; he had thought of *Janet*, not Nora. He felt . . . how? Guilty? Sad, because he was finally saying good-bye to Nora? Hopeful, because the despair might finally be at an end?

He shook his head to clear it. Addicted as he was to it, he knew that introspection of one's emotions was pointless. Psychiatric

110

dogma to the contrary, one's emotions would work out their own problems or they wouldn't; thinking about them wouldn't help.

Ten minutes later John came up, protected by a trench coat and a big black umbrella, and looking cold.

"Hey, Doc! What are you sitting outside for?"

"Hi, John. It's beautiful in the rain."

"Not to me. I'm not going to sit out here. What are you, crazy?"

"Okay," said Gideon. He picked up his beer and, under the protection of John's umbrella, they both went inside. Finding a corner table they ordered *Nürnbergerstadtwurst* and *weinkraut*.

"Hey, where's the cane?" John said.

"I left it at home. The ankle felt pretty good this morning. Haven't missed it yet."

"That's great," said John with such genuine warmth that Gideon was moved. "I'm sorry I was late. I've been finding out lots of good stuff."

"Like what?" Gideon said.

"First tell me what you got from Marks."

"Not much." Over their plates of pungent little sausages and cooked, sweet cabbage, he told John what he had learned from Marks and Dr. Rufus. He also told John that he had no real evidence that any of it was true.

"Uh uh," said John, chewing his *wurst*, "I think it's true all right. It fits in with what I've found out."

"But it doesn't make sense. Why would they have sent that guy all the way down to Sicily just to protect me? I didn't have any real kind of assignment, and I was apparently just one of a string of USOC'rs they used. Certainly they can't have enough men to give that kind of protection to all their informants. Or do they?"

"Yes, they do. Look, whatever else you might think about Marks and the rest of the Intelligence outfit, they don't just use people callously. If they thought there was a chance you could get in trouble, yes, you bet they'd have protection for you. Sometimes they use Safety people. I've had that kind of assignment."

"Is that what you were doing in Sicily last week?"

"No, I came as part of my regular job—protecting USOC life and limb."

John, who had done more listening than talking, had finished his meal. For a while he nursed his beer, watching Gideon eat.

"Doc," he said finally, "I hate to admit it, but you were right about the apple."

"Come again?"

"The guy on the bridge. You said he was an American because he ate an apple with his mouth."

Gideon had forgotten. "Right!" he said excitedly, with his mouth full of sausage. "He *was* an American?"

"Yup."

"Ha! You see what scientific ratiocination can do? Who was he?"

"Come on, I can't tell you that. You want me to compromise—"

"I know, the need-to-know principle. I didn't mean *who* is he, I meant *what* is he?. . . . Where is he from?"

"From where Marks told you. He's an American, an NSD intelligence agent, and his assignment was to watch out for you."

"Well, I wish he'd watched out a little earlier."

The policeman showed a sudden flash of temper. "You're lucky he got there when he did. And that he was brave enough to risk his life for you."

Gideon accepted the rebuke. "You're right. He saved my life. He wasn't hurt, was he?"

"Yes, he was hurt," said John, still angry.

"I'm sorry to hear that. Not seriously, I hope."

"Bad enough," John muttered into the nearly empty stein. "About like you. Lacerations, contusions, broken collarbone." He was showing the concern, universal and understandable, of the policeman for his brother. Gideon kept forgetting he was very much a cop.

"Look, John, I'm sorry for what I said about him getting there earlier. I meant it to be funny and it wasn't. If our positions had been reversed, I don't know if I would have had the courage to stop and shoot it out with those guys. I owe him my life. I'd like to thank him for it some time." It was easy for Gideon to put conviction into his words; he meant every one.

John seemed mollified. "Not much chance of that. I only know his code name myself. What happened was that the searchlight got shot out and the bad guys managed to get to their car. Our guy chased them for a while, but finally wound up going off the road outside of Catania. That's where he got hurt."

"Did you know this when we were in Sicily?"

"No, I just found out. I'm breaking all kinds of rules to get the information I'm getting, let alone telling you. But I think NSD has put you in hot water, and I'm not so sure Marks knows what he's doing. And you sure as hell don't."

"Thanks a lot. I appreciate your confidence."

John smiled. "You know about bones and about languages; I give you that. But you're operating in a different world—with different rules and very nasty people."

"I know it, John. Believe me, I'll take all the help I can get."

"Are you going to have another beer?" John said.

Gideon shook his head. "I've already had two."

John signaled for a beer and then waited for the waiter to deliver it and leave before he began. "You know the questions you keep asking? If we don't know what it is that the Russians are trying to find out, and we don't know why they want to know it, what makes us think they're looking for anything?"

Gideon nodded. "And why," he said, "do we think they'd look for it at Sigonella and Torrejón, as opposed to a hundred other bases?"

"Right," John said. "The answers are pretty simple, it turns out. NSD has been intercepting KGB messages for months that say just that."

"That they don't know what they're looking for, either?"

"No, that they need 'X' information from certain bases like Torrejón and Sigonella. It's the 'X' that's the problem. The messages are in cipher, and the ciphers change all the time. We—that is, our Intelligence cryptographers—have been able to get the gist of most of the messages—*where* the information is; *when* it's needed by. But not the most crucial parts, not the 'X.'

113

The Russians seem to be using some sort of special codes for those. It could be they don't want their own field personnel to know what they're looking for."

"Wait a minute, John. That doesn't make sense. How can you look for something if you don't know what it is? How would you know when you've found it?"

"You'd know when some person you were waiting for—your source, I think they call it—handed you an envelope or a package, or maybe even just gave you some code word or number that you had to transmit back. You wouldn't have to know what it meant."

"I'm not following you."

"That's because I haven't given you the kicker yet. Doc, you sure you don't want another beer?"

"Am I going to need one?"

John's eyes twinkled momentarily in his familiar smile, then turned sober. "No, you can handle it. The kicker is that there's somebody from USOC involved."

"On *their* side?"

"Yup. The source—the guy that gets the information from the base and passes it on to the Russians—he's a USOC'r."

"Holy moley," said Gideon. "This is beginning to sound like a movie. Maybe I will have that beer."

Again they waited for the waiter to leave before they continued.

"Who is it?" Gideon asked.

"Don't know. Or at least that's what my contact tells me. Apparently the Russians refer to him only by code name. But I guess there's no doubt about him being from USOC."

"John, let me get this straight. Are you telling me that someone on the USOC faculty is a Russian spy?"

"Well, an American traitor. It amounts to the same thing. Whatever they're looking for, a USOC'r gets it and passes it on to them."

"You mean Marks doesn't have any leads? I mean, it doesn't sound that difficult. If they know the bases the stuff is gotten from, and when it's needed, all they have to do is find out which

USOC person has been at all the right bases at the right times, and it has to be him."

"Very good; you're starting to think like a cop. The problem is that this has been going on for a long time, a year or more. At least ten bases have been involved. We still haven't figured out what the first seven were—never broke the codes. Then the codes changed or something—this is out of my line, remember—but we were still only able to figure out the last three the Russians needed: Rhein-Main, Sigonella, and Torrejón. Now only Torrejón is left. If they get what they need there. . . ." John had been leaning forward with his elbows on the table. He sat back and moved his glass in slow circles on the table. ". . . . if they get what they need there, then they'll have everything they need . . . for whatever purpose they need it. And nobody on our side knows what that is. Or who the leak is. Hey, Doc, you haven't touched your beer."

Gideon thought he saw where the discussion was leading, and it made him uncomfortable. "I don't really want it. What I'd really like is to take a walk in the rain. How about it? You have a raincoat, and that monster umbrella of yours will cover us both."

"Out in that rain? Brr. . . . But okay, you've had it tough; I'll humor you."

After the stuffiness of the restaurant, the moist, cool air renewed Gideon's strength. Even the sound of the rain hissing on the paving stones was refreshing. They walked a block to the river, each in his own thoughts, and found themselves at the foot of the Alte Brücke, the oldest of Heidelberg's three bridges across the Neckar. For a while they stood looking at the twin towers that marked the entrance, each one topped by a "German helmet" that gleamed wetly.

"There's a cell in one of those towers, did you know?" Gideon said.

"Fascinating," said John.

"Yes, the left one. Or maybe the right, I'm not sure. There was a pope imprisoned there in the thirteenth or fourteenth century. Or the twelfth. Maybe it was a bishop, not a pope." He paused. "I think I better go back to the guidebook."

115

They walked across most of the deserted bridge in silence. Then Gideon finally said what was on his mind. "As far as the last two bases go—Rhein-Main, Sigonella—there *is* one person from USOC who was at both."

"Yes," said John, "you. You landed at Rhein-Main from the States."

"Yes. Does Marks suspect me?" He stopped walking suddenly, struck with a thought that should have been obvious. John continued on for a step, and the soft rain fell on Gideon's face. He hurried to catch up.

"No, he couldn't," he said, answering his own question. "Marks is the one who *sent* me to Sigonella."

"That's right. Anyway, Marks isn't involved in this part of it. His job is to flush out the KGB agent. Finding the USOC'r, the traitor, that's Bureau Four's responsibility. And they and Marks don't share their information."

"The need-to-know principle in action. That's really insane, isn't it?"

"No, to tell the truth, I think it makes sense. You couldn't do ordinary police work—the kind I do—that way . . . separate investigations, completely separate systems. But espionage is a different thing. It took us a long time to figure out that you can't let even your own agents in on other agents' secrets—"

"Come on, John, really—"

"No, it's true. That's why the British have MI-5 and MI-6. The Russians have their separate departments too, but they keep changing the names. Even the U.S., for that matter, has the FBI and the CIA. A Russian spy in Texas, that's FBI business; the same spy goes over the border to Mexico, it's the CIA's affair."

"All right, I buy it . . . I don't, really . . . but if Marks doesn't tell this Bureau Four the reason I was in Sigonella, won't *they* suspect me?"

"Marks *has* told them. They *do* communicate when they have to. They're on the same side, you know. They just don't do it any more than they absolutely must."

At the far end of the bridge, they turned left along the path that followed the bank of the Neckar. The rain had subsided to a mist;

Gideon stepped away from John's umbrella to enjoy the feel of it moistening his face and collecting in his hair.

"You're crazy," John said. "You really enjoy getting wet, don't you? You're going to catch one hell of a cold."

"You don't—"

"You don't catch colds from the rain. I knew you were going to say that." John was slightly annoyed. "Colds are caused by getting wet and tired," he went on. "Goddamit, just because you're a professor doesn't mean you know everything about everything. Why the hell do you want to take chances? You just came out of the damn hospital."

John's tone was exactly that of an anxious mother scolding a five-year-old who had gone into the rain without galoshes. He was not so much angry as worried, Gideon realized with a stab of guilt.

Gideon moved back under the umbrella's shelter. "You're right," he said.

"It's stupid to take chances."

"You're right," Gideon said again.

When they reached the modern Theodore Heuss Brücke, they turned back. The rain had stopped, and blue sky was visible.

"John," Gideon said after a while, "it just occurred to me that there's someone else from USOC who was at Sigonella. Does Bureau Four know that?"

"Who?"

"Do you know Eric Bozzini?"

"I think so. Middle-aged surfer type?"

"Yes. When I telephoned him from Sigonella, he told me that he'd been there a few days before. Friday, I think he said. That'd be the day after I was ambushed."

"Do you know why he was there?" It was a professional question. John wasn't impressed.

"Can't remember. Whatever it was, it sounded legitimate at the time."

"It probably was. He's Logistics. Has to visit a lot of bases. So do some of the other administrators: Dr. Rufus, Mrs. Swinnerton—"

"Still, it seems worth getting the information to Bureau Four, doesn't it?"

"All right," John said without enthusiasm. "I'll mention it to my contact, and they'll hear about it if they don't already know. But I can't just go up to Bureau Four and say, 'Here's some information I have on this super-secret case I'm not supposed to know about.' I wouldn't even know who to talk to, and I don't want to know."

Fine. If John didn't think it was worth fighting the bureaucracy, then Gideon would follow it up with Eric himself. In a way he was pleased. It gave him a direction, a place to start. Not that he believed Eric could be a spy or—appalling word—a traitor. But then, could Bruce Danzig, or Janet, or Dr. Rufus, or anyone else he'd met at USOC?

"I'm still a little puzzled," Gideon said.

"Only a little? Then you're in better shape than I am. What's your problem?"

"I can't figure out what a USOC'r's role would be. We just have low-level clearance; we wouldn't have access to secret materials or high-security areas. What could any of us do for the Russians?"

"That's true," John said. "Hmm."

They had reached the Alte Brücke again and began to walk back across it to the Old Town. Now that the weather had cleared, cars were zipping down the narrow center, so they had to keep to the walkway along one side.

"Hmm," said John again.

Gratified to have come up with a question that hadn't occurred to the policeman, Gideon tried to answer it. "Is it possible that the USOC'r is a go-between? That somebody who works on the base gets the information and passes it on to him, and he passes it on to a KGB agent?"

It seemed absurd to Gideon as he said it. Talking about KGB agents so matter-of-factly was preposterous, like play-acting.

But John was excited by the idea. "Yeah, yeah! That's right! Maybe." As always when he was excited, his speech turned vehement, ejaculatory. "Somebody on the base gets the information. He gives it to the USOC'r. A live drop, they call it. The USOC'r leaves whenever he wants, and passes it on, probably in another country. Sure! Makes sense. Hey, good thinking!"

He banged Gideon on the back so hard that he almost propelled him off the curb into the oncoming traffic, then pulled him back with the same motion. They both laughed.

"I'm glad you think it's so brilliant," Gideon said, "but it's full of holes. If a base employee can get the stuff, whatever it is, why doesn't he just pass it on to the KGB agent himself? Why complicate things with a middleman?"

"Because a Russian agent would try to avoid having direct contact with someone with access to secret NATO information. It would make it too easy for us to figure things out. But what's suspicious about some Sigonella employee—who works with computer flight-planning programs, say—talking to a USOC instructor or counselor? And why should NSD be suspicious when the same USOC'r happens to share a table with a stranger in Vienna a month later? Why would NSD even be watching him?"

"I suppose so," Gideon said doubtfully. "But—"

"In fact," John said, chopping at the air with his hand, "they wouldn't have to meet at all! They could use dead drops! The base employee just leaves the information at some predetermined place on the base, and the USOC'r picks it up later. Then the USOC'r uses another drop to get it to the KGB, maybe a thousand miles away. What's wrong with that?"

"It's too complicated, that's what," Gideon said. "If they use . . . dead drops, then they don't need the USOC'r, do they? You're always telling me that the fewer people there are involved, the better. Why couldn't the base employee just drop it off in Vienna himself? No one would ever see him meet the KGB man."

"He couldn't do that, because he'd never get off the base with it in the first place," said John. "Somebody who works in a top-secret area of the base gets pretty thoroughly shaken down when he leaves. At least I think he does. But a guy like you just gets waved through, right?"

119

"Well, yes, but now look; if all this is so important, why don't they just check out everyone who leaves the base? They do it when they have alerts."

"A brilliant question," said John. "I asked it myself. And the answer is that we don't want the Russians to know that *we* know they're up to something. If we put the bases on alert, they'd know we were onto them, and that might precipitate whatever it is that they're planning to do. Which is exactly what we're trying to avoid. Simple, yes?"

Gideon shook his head. "My God, this is like listening to someone read an IRS tax manual."

They were back in the vicinity of the Marktplatz. John gestured at a gray Volkswagen. "Going back to USOC Administration? Can I give you a lift? You look too confused to use the *strassenbahn.*"

They didn't speak while John concentrated on driving through the narrow, busy streets of the Old Town. Even a Volkswagen beetle has difficulty with two-way streets designed to permit the passage of a single horse-drawn coach. John drove expertly, however, as quickly and confidently as the Germans themselves. Within a few minutes they were on the fast Friedrich-Ebert-Anlage, and then heading smoothly out on Rohrstrasse.

"John," Gideon said. "No offense, but do you really know what you're talking about? Or are you making all this up?"

John threw back his head and laughed delightedly. "The answers are 'no' and 'no.' I'm not making any of it up, but I don't know what I'm talking about, either." He paused, looking hesitant. "Look, Doc," he said slowly, staring at his hands on the wheel, "I understand why you're going through with this Torrejón thing, and I admire you for it, but, well. . . ."

"John, if you were in my place, you'd do the same thing," Gideon said with sudden heat. "I can't just walk away from it as if it never happened to me. I need to find out what it's about."

"Sure, but what are you going to *do?*"

"What do you mean, do?"

"What do you mean, what do I mean? I mean *do.*" John was excited, too, chopping at the air again. "*How* are you going to find out what it's about? Wait for somebody to try to kill you again?"

"No. I'm going to check and see if any other USOC'rs show up, or if any have been there recently, and uh . . . I don't exactly have a plan, do I?"

"You sure as hell don't."

"Okay, so what would *you* do?"

"Me? If I were you, I'd ask me to come down and help you out."

"Are you serious? Would you really come? Why didn't you say so before?"

"I was waiting for you to ask me. You're kind of funny about this; I thought maybe you wanted to do it all by yourself."

"Heck, no. I'd *love* to have you down there, John."

"Good. I can't do this officially, you understand, but I have lots of leave time and nothing else doing right now. If I get a military flight to Torrejón tomorrow afternoon, I'll get there a few hours after you."

"Great, and who knows? Maybe I'll get knifed or shot or run off the road, and then you can stay down there officially and wrap it up."

"Sure," John said. "We can always hope." They both laughed.

"I've gotta go, Doc. I'll see you down there tomorrow." Awkwardly, he put out his hand. Gideon took it. "It's been a good day, Doc. I think we're getting someplace."

Returning John's wave as the big policeman drove off, Gideon wasn't sure he agreed. Certainly, it was marvelous about John's coming down, and it was nice to have some cogent if convoluted ideas about what the Russians were up to, but he didn't feel any closer to answering the most compelling questions of all: What did it all have to do with *him*? Why was anybody trying to kill him? Why had his room been broken into three times—at least three times—in two weeks? What did anyone want with three pairs of his socks? And why was he being stalked by the ferret-faced man?

Just possibly, Eric Bozzini might provide some answers.

13

"I CAN'T TALK TO you now, man. It has really hit the fan." His desk a jumble of papers, Eric spoke through a ball-point pen clamped between his teeth, while one hand picked up the telephone receiver and the other moved to dial. His laid-back image was showing signs of strain. Even his carefully teased hair looked dispirited, the strands having separated at a crucial point to reveal a large expanse of bare, gleaming scalp beneath.

"I don't have time to come back later," Gideon said. "I need to talk to you now." He sat down.

"Come on, man. The teaching schedules are all screwed up. Half the bases are on exercises; there are alerts all over the place—"

"What about my schedule? Is it being changed?"

"Where you supposed to go? Torrejón?"

"Yes."

"Forget it, man. I don't know where you're going, but you ain't going to Torrejón." He shuffled among the papers and folders on his desk. "What?" he said, staring at the paper he had dug out. He passed it to Gideon.

The heading said, *Spain, Oct-Dec 1981. Upper Division and Graduate.* The rest of the sheet consisted of a single column showing NATO bases and course offerings. Most of the courses had been crossed out in pen.

Zaragoza: All courses crossed out.

Rota: All crossed out.

Torrejón: Among several other listings was *ANTH 242 Emergence of Man OLIVER.* Like the others, it had been crossed out. Unlike them, however, a red circle has been drawn around it and a marginal note written, also in red: *HOLD CLASS AS SCHEDULED. FRR, 5/10.*

FRR. That would be Frederick R. Rufus; 5/10 was October 5, European-style. Today's date.

"Sonofagun," Eric said. "I *know* that wasn't there this morning. Huh." He sat staring at the paper.

Dr. Rufus must have gone in and checked the schedules right after he had talked with Gideon, then, and made sure his Torrejón request was put into effect.

Eric got up and went to a file cabinet, where he stood with his back to Gideon, going through some manila folders. A Western-style shirt accentuated the soft bulge that spilled over his belt in back. If anything, he had gotten a little puffier in the last two weeks.

"Yeah, here it is, man," he said, turning. "Got your packet all ready; never got around to canceling it. Train ticket to Frankfurt, Lufthansa to Madrid. Bus schedule to Torrejón. BOQ reservations, too." He handed the packet to Gideon. His forehead glistened with an oily, unhealthy sheen. "You'll love it; fantastic chicks."

"So you said. Eric, why did you route me through Heidelberg to get me to Madrid?"

"What do you mean?"

"Why not direct from Sigonella to Torrejón? Or through Rome? Why all the way back up to Germany?"

Eric bristled. His hand went nervously to his hair. "Hell, I don't remember why I got your particular itinerary. Maybe all the direct flights were booked. It happens all the time. The instructors usually like to stop off in Heidelberg anyway; use the library, see some people. I thought I was doing you a favor."

"I appreciate that, Eric. It's just that it does seem the long way around."

"Hey, look, man, I got forty fucking itineraries to worry about." With the back of his hand, he made an irritated swipe at the papers on his desk. "You know how much work that is? Shit, I've been on the phone to the airlines for eight hours a day for two weeks. There's tourists all over the goddamn place. Shit." He plopped back into his chair; the cushion emitted a sympathetic, whistling sigh.

"I don't know, Eric—"

"Hell, I talked it over with Rufe; he thought it was okay."

123

"With Dr. Rufus? Does he get involved in that kind of detail?"

"Yeah, sometimes. Especially with you. You're the visiting fellow, which is such a big deal." His expression implied a differing opinion. "Besides, you were getting beat up every time you turned around. He was just checking to see you were getting treated right. He didn't beef, and I don't see what you're complaining about. Christ, sometimes I gotta route people through Oslo to get them to Spain."

Gideon sighed. "Let me ask you another question, Eric—"

"Look, man, can't you give me a phone call next week? I'm up to my armpits right now." He slapped the arms of his chair. "Ah, what the hell. You want some coffee?"

Gideon shook his head. Going to a messy table at the side of the room, Eric poured water from a pot on a one-ring hot plate, then added instant coffee, stirring it with a plastic spoon. He took a sip, made a face, added sugar with the same spoon, and returned to his chair.

"So what are the questions?" He tossed back a slug of coffee as if it were a shot of bourbon.

"I was wondering what you were doing in Sigonella last week."

"I was making my Italian round. Logistics checks out every one of our bases at least once every two years. Looks over the accommodations, settles complaints, makes new contracts, that kind of stuff." He frowned. "Why?"

"Just sorry I missed you," Gideon said. "If you're going to be down at Torrejón next week, let's have dinner."

Eric tossed down another slug of coffee, peering suspiciously at Gideon over the rim of the cup. "All right, I just might be there."

"Oh?" said Gideon, feeling his breath quicken.

"Yeah, I'm scheduled to hit Spain and Greece in the next few weeks. Of course, with all the alerts, I don't know. I'll give you a call."

As hard as it was to believe, then, everything was beginning to point to this harried, laid-back, not very intelligent administrator. He had been at Sigonella at the right time, and he was going to be at Torrejón at the right time.

Eric drained the last of his coffee and made another face. "Yuck."

Then they sat and looked at each other for a long time. Gideon attempted to read Eric's expression. Was he trying to stare him down, or did those half-closed, dull eyes reflect no more than a bovine resignation to Gideon's continued presence? Gideon couldn't tell.

Finally Eric frowned with the expression of a man who had something to say. He closed his eyes and belched—a remarkably deep, resonant sound, around which he managed to enunciate with great clarity the word "barf."

In the hallway, Gideon's anticipated elation did not material-ize. As telling as Eric's presence at Sigonella was, as well as his planned trip to Torrejón, Gideon couldn't bring himself to believe the Californian was a spy. If ubiquity were evidence of spying, then Gideon was a proven spy, too. Interesting thought; in spite of John's reassurance, it was still possible that NSD's Bureau Four suspected him, on the same grounds that he suspected Eric. And when they found out—if they didn't know already—that Gideon was going to be at Torrejón upon his own insistence, and for not terribly cogent reasons, he was going to be even more suspect.

No, the only difference between Eric and him was that Gideon knew *he* wasn't a spy, which left Eric as the only other USOC'r, as far as he was aware, to be at the crucial bases at the right times. And yet, Eric just didn't feel right as a spy. Could spies be that fatuous, that transparent? Moreover, his explanation of Gideon's routing through Heidelberg had the ring of truth.

All the same, he'd see that the information about Eric got back to Bureau Four if he could. He'd have to do it through John and his "contact." How absurd that he was unable to talk to them himself, but he didn't know who or where they were, and they weren't on formal speaking terms with Marks. Ridiculous. It was no way to run a cold war.

"Well, well, *Gideon Oliver*, talking to himself like a USOC veteran, and after just three weeks. My, my."

Without realizing it, he had entered the faculty library. At a desk behind the counter sat Bruce Danzig, regarding him from beneath eyebrows facetiously raised, lips set in a prim little smirk.

Gideon got quickly to the point. "Hello, Bruce. I wanted to return the books I borrowed before I went to Sicily." He placed the two slim texts on the counter. "I understand you've been saving some new ones for me."

"My, aren't we businesslike today?" Danzig said. Then he deepened his voice in imitation of Gideon's. "Yes, sir, Professor Oliver, sir!" His chin, never very prominent, disappeared into his collar as he delivered a punctilious mock salute.

Gideon unenthusiastically returned it with a brief, pro forma smile. "If you have the books available, I'd appreciate seeing them."

The frivolity left Danzing's expression; his voice turned glacial. "I'm afraid I'm not sure to what you're referring. Did you ask me to hold some books for you?"

Oh Christ, now I've hurt his feelings, thought Gideon. He hadn't meant to; he simply wasn't in the mood to deal with Danzig's finical little witticisms. He tried to sound more friendly. "No, but Dr. Rufus mentioned to me that you'd been kind enough to find some books you thought I might use."

"Oh yes, I recall. It was Dr. Rufus, not I." He sniffed; a gesture of disdain, Gideon supposed. "We were looking over the new arrivals, and he—not I—noted some for which he thought you might have some use. Inasmuch as you showed so little interest in our collection before, I must admit I haven't personally made any great attempt to search out resources for you."

"I think you've developed an excellent collection, Bruce. It was simply that I didn't need anything last time. But now, with this 'Emergence of Man' series, I need all the help I can get."

The little librarian was not won over. He continued to watch Gideon coldly.

The hell with it, Gideon thought. "Look, do you want to let me see them . . .?"

"Of course." With a series of meticulous movements—push the desk drawer closed, delicately move back the chair, swivel to the right—Danzig arose and went to the shelves behind the counter. He found the four books at once and brought them to Gideon with a viperous little smile.

For no reason he could think of, a sudden thought struck Gideon. "I don't suppose you're going to be in Torrejón next week?"

"Torrejón? No, why? What would I go to Torrejón for?"

"Oh, I just thought we might get together. Didn't I hear you were in Sigonella last week or the week before? I missed you then."

"I, in Sigonella? No, you're confusing me with Bozzini, heaven forbid. Fortunately, my job doesn't require me to travel. Besides, I detest the Mediterranean. Did you want these books or not?"

Too bad, Gideon thought. Danzig would have made a more satisfactory spy. Glancing briefly at the books, he saw that two were revised editions of old introductory texts, but the third was Campbell's excellent *Human Evolution*, and the fourth was a reprint of Weidenreich's thirty-year-old *Skull of Sinanthropus Pekinensis*, one of those classics he'd somehow never gotten around to.

"I'll take these two," he said, signing the cards. "Thanks, Bruce. I'll see you next week."

"I wait with bated breath."

When Gideon got back to the BOQ at 4:30, Janet hadn't returned from the Heidelberg University Library yet. He left a note on her door, asking her to stop by, and went to his room. He hadn't left any slivers or paper clips or hairs in the door that morning—what was the point now?—but he looked carefully through the room, list of articles in hand. Everything seemed as he had left it.

Seemed. He knew, however, that he was dealing with an antagonist more subtle and expert than he had previously thought. Why he had an antagonist at all was the real question. If he knew why Ferret-face was dogging him, why he looked at him with such hatred . . . but he didn't know, and it was too late in a long day to do any serious speculation about it.

He poured himself a little Scotch, found three hoary ice cubes in a tiny compartment in the refrigerator, and sat down with the

Campbell text—it was good to get the weight off that ankle—for a different sort of speculation. He was, after all, an anthropologist, not a spy, and was soon engrossed in Campbell's elegant theories on the evolution of bipedal locomotion.

Janet knocked on his door a little before six. His heart gave a little jump when he saw her. Women book collectors or not, she was the most attractive woman he'd seen in a long time. The only one, really.

"Good day at *der Bibliothek*?" he asked, surprised by a slight thickening of his voice.

She was standing in the doorway, oddly hesitant.

"Come on in," he said. "Have a drink. I might even be able to dig up some more ice."

"I can't, Gideon. I don't have much time."

"Why, what's the matter?"

"Well, I have a date."

"A date?" He stood there with the drink in his hand. "With someone else?" he added stupidly.

"Yes, why not? What's so amazing about that?" When he didn't say anything, she went on irritably. "Did you think I was just going to come in and say 'Take me, I'm yours?' Listen, Gideon, you just walked into my life yesterday, and you're going away again tomorrow. I'm not going to sit around pining away just because I went to bed with you last night."

"Who do you have a date with?" It was all he could think of to say.

"I don't see why that's any concern of yours." Gideon wondered what she had to be angry about.

"Yes, you're quite right," he said. "I guess my male chauvinistic value system ran away with me. Enjoy your date. Thank you for last night. I'll drop you a line from Torrejón."

To his surprise, her eyes brimmed suddenly with tears. In her annoyance with them, she stamped her foot like a little girl. Gideon wanted very much to take her in his arms and kiss the moisture that shone on her soft cheek. He held back, however, half in what he knew was childish retaliation, half because he wasn't sure how she would react.

"That's what I hate about women," she said. "Damn it. We cry

128

at the drop of a hat. It doesn't mean anything. Our glands are different." He was sure she wanted to brush the tears away, but she let them stay. "All right, it's with Eric. It's just a stupid dinner at some stupid Heidelberg professor's house."

Janet with Eric—gross, fat Eric. Gideon suppressed the images that sprang quickly to his mind.

"Have a wonderful time," he said. "It's been very pleasant knowing you. Perhaps I'll see you again when I come back to Heidelberg."

"Damn you, Gideon, if you wanted to see me tonight, you could have asked me this morning, instead of assuming you owned me like some caveman. You stupid man!" She glared at him through her tears, looking wondrously huggable. "Stupid *man!*"

His mood was ambivalent as he watched her stride down the hall. On the one hand, he was very sorry indeed that he wouldn't be spending the evening in her company and (another male chauvinist assumption) the night in her arms. But there was also an unmistakable if somewhat wistful sense of reprieve; clearly, he had narrowly missed becoming enmeshed in a Meaningful Relationship. He sighed. Maybe later on he'd be ready to try that. In the meantime, he would have been happy to settle for a Meaningful Experience or even a Moderately Significant Relationship. A Good Lay wouldn't have been so bad, either.

He poured himself another Scotch and settled down to spend the evening grappling with the intricacies of simian brachiation.

A little after midnight, he heard her voice at the door.

"Gideon!"

Without putting on a robe and almost without waking up, he jumped from the bed and opened the door a few inches.

"Yes?" he said, blinking at her in the glare of the lit hallway. She smelled of the cool night, and when she laughed softly at him, he shivered with . . . lust? Love? He wasn't sure.

"What are you laughing at?" he said.

"You. Look at your hair. You look as if you've just come out of six-month hibernation. Open the door some more. I bet you're not wearing anything."

As he knew she would, she suddenly pushed at the door. He offered resistance of the most token sort, and she was quickly inside, turning on the light as he took her into his arms and pressed his lips against the soft, clear skin of her cheek, just where he had wanted to kiss her earlier. The roughness of her wool suit against his bare skin and the slipperiness of the slip under her skirt excited him at once.

"Eek," she said. "Just as I thought. There's a naked man in *here*, too. Good heavens, this place is full of them."

"Mmm," he said, nuzzling at her faintly perfumed throat.. "How was dinner?"

"Lousy. I couldn't wait to get back here to say something to you."

Her seriousness brought his face up, but he didn't let her go. "What is it?"

"Well . . . ," she said, laying her head on his shoulder, wanting to be coaxed.

"Come on, tell Papa," Gideon said, his naked skin jumping where her long hair lay over it.

"Well . . . just . . . take me, I'm yours." She raised her eyes to his. "If you want me."

Without warning, his eyes filled.

"Gideon," she said, startled, "what's this?" A tentative finger explored his wet cheek.

Gideon pretended a gruff embarrassment. "So, I'm crying. Contrary to your theory, lachrymal glands are not sexually specific organs. Males have them, too."

"How poetically you put things," she said. "It's lovely."

He kissed her on the lips—a lingering, eyes-closed kiss, inhaling the peachlike fragrance of her breath.

When he came up for air, she said, "You know, I feel somewhat overdressed for the occasion."

"I see what you mean," Gideon said, his fingers already at the buckle of her belt. "Why don't we lie down and discuss it?"

In the morning he made it a point to request the pleasure of her company when he returned the following week.

Book 4:
Torrejón/Torralba

14

WHEN YOU ENTER MADRID from the east, on the highway from Zaragoza and Torrejón de Ardoz, you watch the clean, rocky countryside with its occasional flocks of sheep give way first to blank-faced factories lining the roadway, and then to block upon block of dreary, high-rise apartments that make the heart sink. The air, especially in the hot summer and fall, turns gray-brown and choking; the noise of honking horns and backfiring motor scooters becomes nearly unbearable; and the traffic snarls reach extremities worthy of Rome or Paris. By the time you reach a downtown parking garage, the only thing that keeps you from turning around and driving right back out is the thought of going through all that traffic again.

And then you walk out onto the Paseo del Prado.

It is one of the world's great avenues. Grand proportions, long rows of green trees, cool, bubbling fountains, and elegant, restful sidewalk cafés create a refuge of quiet and repose in the midst of the mind-jarring hubbub. As soon as Gideon saw it, his jaw muscles, which had knotted during the hot hour-and-a-half drive, relaxed.

He stopped at the first outdoor café they came to. "I have to have something cold right now, right here," he said to John.

"I'm for that," John said. "Anything to put off the Prado." They sat at a table in the shade of a tree and signaled for two beers. John leaned the back of his chair against the wide tree trunk.

"It's beautiful here," Gideon said. "God, it's great to be out."

"Come on, Doc, you make Torrejón sound like Devil's Island."

"It is, when you only have five days in Spain and you spend three of them on an air base that looks, feels, and sounds like it's in the middle of Oklahoma. And smells like it, too."

"You ever been to Oklahoma?"

"No."

"That's what I thought."

They were both depressed, disappointed with three days of effort that had produced nothing. The old leads had evaporated, and there were no new ones. Following John's suggestion, they had taken adjacent rooms in the BOQ, and John had remained inside, on his side of the thin wall, whenever Gideon had gone out, but no one had ever come. At other times, Gideon stayed in John's room while John checked with Security on all the ID cards and temporary passes that had been issued during the previous two months; the only USOC'r that had been there before Gideon was a "local" business management instructor, an American woman who lived and taught in Spain. She had left several weeks ago at the end of the summer session.

The only exciting moment had come when Gideon, lurking on John's side of the wall, had heard an intruder in his own room. Ignoring John's instructions, he had dashed through the connecting bathroom and burst wildly in upon an elderly Spanish maid who had screamed and hit him with a pillow.

Eric Bozzini had come late Monday morning and had left at four in the afternoon. John had found out the time of his arrival, and Gideon met him with the rented car for the mile-and-a-half drive to the Officer's Club for lunch. He also drove him back at the end of the day and spent several tedious hours with him in between. Eric was garrulous and good-humored, seemingly not in the least anxious to shake him off. When Gideon wasn't with him, John shadowed him from a distance. The net result was a certainty that Eric had conducted nothing but Logistics business at Torrejón. What he might have done had they not been there,

132

they had no way of knowing, but Gideon was more convinced than ever that Eric was not the mysterious USOC'r of the Russian messages.

American NATO bases are among the least exotic, most humdrum places in the world. After two days at Torrejón, Gideon, growing restive, had begun to wonder if he'd deluded himself into expecting a nonexistent adventure. Why was he so sure the things that had happened to him were not simply coincidences? Coincidences *did* happen, after all, and were they not, by definition, unlikely sets of causally unrelated events? With NSD cutting its ties to him, what made him think he'd still be of interest to the Russians, if indeed he ever had been? How did he know they hadn't already gotten whatever it was they were after at Torrejón? After all he'd been through, he still didn't know who or what he was looking for. Nor was he very clear on his wheres or whens. That left whys and hows; not so hot there either.

On Tuesday night, at their regular after-class meeting in John's room, John had told him that he had been ordered back to Heidelberg and had to fly out of Torrejón late the following afternoon.

With less difficulty than he had anticipated, Gideon had convinced him that they should give up the hunt and go see something of Madrid on John's final day. John had grumbled a bit about it being unsafe for Gideon off the base, but hadn't taken long to agree to a trip to the Prado; he was as frustrated and bored as Gideon.

Now that they were finally out, the beer, the food, and the Paseo were all beginning to raise their spirits. With a try at jauntiness, John banged his empty glass on the table. "I'm still not ready for all those paintings. How about some more shrimp? And let's split another bottle of beer."

Both men relaxed with their refreshed beers and let their eyes rove about the scene around them. Gideon looked with pleasure at the eighteenth-century colonnade of the Prado and at the long rows of narrow windows. Three weeks in Europe had hardly diminished his I-can't-believe-I'm-really-here-seeing-all-these-wonderful-places attitude. John, however, was looking from face to face of diners and passersby with more than casual interest.

"Looking for anyone in particular?" Gideon asked.

"No," John replied, his eyes continuing to move. "Cop's habit, I guess. Just seeing if there's anyone watching us, or anybody else who looks like a cop or an agent. Anybody who doesn't quite belong."

"I understand how you'd spot a cop—he'd have his back to a tree or a wall, the way you do—but how do you tell agents?"

"You learn. It's part of the job."

"Are you finding anything?"

"Probably not," John said, smiling as he peeled a shrimp with his fingers. "There are a few people who don't look Spanish. I was just wondering if one of them could be a Russian. The blond guy leaning against the fountain—the one studying the guide-book so hard."

Gideon sipped his beer and looked at the tall young man over the rim of his glass for a few moments. "Nope," he said.

"Nope, what?"

"Nope, he's not a Russian."

"If you mean he's reading a German guidebook, I can see that, too, but that doesn't prove anything."

"Of course not; I was looking at him from an anthropometric perspective."

"Oh boy," John said.

"Oh boy, what?"

"Oh boy, I'm about to get bullshitted."

"How can you say that?" said Gideon, keeping his face straight with an effort. "I was just going to point out that he's a classic model of Nordic subrace characteristics: extremely dolicocepha-lic—cranial index of no more than seventy-five; leptorrhine nasal index. Why, look at the compressed alae and malars. Just look at those gonial angles!"

"See? I can always tell when it's coming. So, if he's not Russian, what is he?"

"Swedish, or maybe from the Norwegian uplands, or even northern Germany or England. But definitely not Russian."

"What would he look like if he was Russian?"

"If he were Russian, he might be one of several anthropomorphic types, or a composite. First, he—"

"I'm already sorry I asked," muttered John.

"—could be an East Baltic brachycephal, or he might be a Dinaric acrocephalic brachycephal, or an Armenoid—" Gideon couldn't help bursting into laughter at John's disgusted expression. "You're not doubting me, are you?"

"Doc, I never know whether you're kidding when you do that. Jesus Christ, acrybrachyphallic. . . . "

Gideon finished his beer and wiped his lips with the cloth napkin; he was feeling much better. "Anyway," he said, "I'd still bet that guy's a Scandinavian."

"But—"

"What's the difference, anyway? You don't have to be a Russian to be a Russian spy. And he could come from Scandinavian parents but be a Russian himself. No way to tell that from cranial conformation. But how can you be thinking about spies on a day like this in a place like this?"

"That isn't the point. You just finished telling me—"

"In any event, it's moot." Gideon gestured with his head, and they both watched the tall young man walking away from them toward El Retiro Park, his head still buried in the guidebook.

John sighed in mock exasperation. "You know, you're the only guy in the whole world I never win any arguments with."

"That's because I am a Ph.D. and therefore know all kinds of smart stuff."

John nodded soberly and sighed again, like a man resigned to his fate. "I think I'm ready for the Prado now."

John was a good sport about it, but it was obvious that the endless galleries severely tested his endurance. He expressed considerably more appreciation for several of the women visitors than for any of the works of art, and was always a few steps ahead

135

of Gideon, pulling him on to the next painting, the next room. Gideon quickly gave up on John's art education and concentrated on enjoying the paintings himself.

After three hours in the museum, he had had enough. Promising the long-suffering John no more than a ten-minute detour, he led them back to the Velazquez rooms for one more look at *Las Meninas*. At the entrance to the Great Rotunda, Gideon stopped.

"Now *there* you are," he said, pointing at a hulking man with shaggy, dark hair who stood in front of a portrait of Philip IV mounted uneasily upon a horse. "*That* is an absolutely classic Armenoid composite. Acrocephalic, mesorrhine, cephalic index of at least eighty-five, everted lower lip—"

"Are you saying he's Russian?"

"Maybe. More like Balkan—Rumanian, Yugoslavian, Bulgarian. . . ."

John looked keenly at the man, watching him move slowly to a second portrait of the ungainly Philip and bend close to examine the ornate frame.

"Don't get excited, John. What would an agent be doing here?"

"It's not that. I just think you're wrong. I say he's English."

"English! That guy doesn't have an English gene in his entire body. He's pure Balkan."

"A famous professor once told me there's no pure anything."

"So much for famous professors," Gideon said.

"How much do you want to bet?"

A disapproving guard approached with outstretched palms and frowning brow. "*Señores . . . por favor. . . .*" They apologized and moved out of the entrance way.

"I'll bet you dinner at the Zum Ritter when we get back to Heidelberg," Gideon said in a whisper.

"You're on," John said. "I say he's English; you say he's Rumanian or something. What if he's neither, or both?"

"If he's not eastern European, or his family isn't, I'll buy. But how are we supposed to find out?"

"Let's go ask him."

Gideon, shy with strangers, quailed slightly. "You can't just walk up to him and ask him where he's from."

"Why not? How about if we just say 'good afternoon' to him in English and see how he answers? I think that will settle it right there."

As they started forward, Gideon touched John's arm. "But what the heck makes you so sure he's an Englishman?"

John smiled broadly and tapped his temple with a forefinger. "Who else would carry a big black umbrella on a day like this?"

Gideon saw the craziness in his eyes as soon as the man turned toward them. John didn't.

"Good afternoon," John said jauntily. "Lovely paintings, aren't—"

With a cry that was part shriek, part snarl, the man flailed at John with the umbrella. Catching him off balance as he ducked, the blows struck him on the shoulder with surprisingly solid thuds, sending him reeling backwards and finally depositing him on the floor in a sitting position. A quick look at his face told Gideon he was more surprised than hurt. The man lifted the umbrella again.

The room seemed to explode away from the upraised umbrella. People ran for the exits or fell back against the walls. Several women screamed, and some of the men dropped to the floor. Gideon, emerging from the momentary paralysis into which he had been shocked, jumped for the umbrella, concerned almost as much for *The Surrender at Breda*, which hung inches from the waving metal point of the umbrella, as for John. He managed to get his hand around the shaft and drag it sharply downwards, away from the canvas. The man, twisting as his arm was wrenched, stepped forward just as the umbrella came down, so that the point struck him on his left foot. Gideon heard a distinct, sharp click, and assumed that blow must have cracked a metatarsal.

The effect on the man was extraordinary. With a shuddering gasp, he sprang back a step and clasped the umbrella tightly to his body. His eyes, panicky and crazed an instant before, pierced

Gideon with a look so laden with despair that Gideon instinctively stepped forward to help. For a second the big man stood there, his eyes rolling ceilingward, like the St. Sebastian of Zurbarán come suddenly to life, embracing an umbrella instead of a cross in his twentieth-century Passion.

Gideon's hesitant touch galvanized him, and with a choked cry the man brushed him aside and ran for the exit, scattering the people in his way. John, in the act of rising from the floor, launched himself at the rushing figure but couldn't reach him, so that he hung outstretched and suspended for a long moment, like a stop-action frame of a diver, before he fell to the floor with a crash.

At the exit, the guard who had earlier asked them to be quiet made a half-hearted attempt to block the doorway, but then dropped back against the wall, ashen-faced, before the charging man's onslaught. The man disappeared toward the exit at a full run.

As the room's shocked stillness gave way to a sudden babble, Gideon went to John and helped him up.

"Are you all right?" Gideon asked.

"Except for my pride."

"There wasn't anything you could do. It happened too fast. I was just standing there with my mouth open through most of it, myself."

"And all I did was keep falling on my face."

"Not always your face," Gideon said. "John, do you have any idea what that was about?"

John shrugged and winced as he rubbed his shoulder. "Damn heavy umbrella. No, I don't know what it was about. We just picked a crazy Englishman to talk to, I guess."

"I suppose so," Gideon said, smiling. He paused while they looked each other in the eye. "Do you really believe that? That it was just another coincidence?"

"Of course not. What do you make of it?"

They walked from the Great Rotunda under the awestruck scrutiny of the crowd, quiet again as they watched them go. The guard at the door, still pale, hesitantly moved toward them as if

138

he were about to speak, but thought better of it and let them pass unmolested.

"I really don't know," Gideon said. "It's one more crazy event that doesn't seem to connect with anything else, but it must. Whatever it was, something about you scared that guy witless."

"Or something about you."

By the time they had turned off he highway at Torrejón, they had exhausted all the theories that were even remotely plausible, and Gideon was musing and abstracted as they walked through the base terminal toward John's plane. "Did you see what happened when the umbrella punched him on the foot?" he said. "It was as if he was a big inflated doll and the point of the umbrella punctured him and let all the air out. Or that his big toe was his Achilles' heel"—Gideon grimaced at his metaphor, but John didn't notice—"and that hitting him there meant his end. and he knew it."

"Doc," John said gravely at the gate to his flight, "you're trying to make sense of a lot of puzzling things that nobody's been able to figure out, so I can't blame you for wanting to fit them together. But you only know a little part of the espionage picture, and I don't know much more. Don't lead yourself into thinking that you're the center of everything that's going on, or that everyone's after you, or that you can save the world."

Gideon grinned wryly. "You've just given a textbook description of the classic paranoiac psychosis: delusions of persecution, delusions of grandeur, and the construction of an elaborate, internally logical system to account for everything." He paused. "You could be right."

15

THE THREE OLD MEN sat side by side on the ancient wrought-iron bench, looking like octogenarian triplets identically dressed and posed by a doting centenarian mother with a turn for the grotesque. On each head a shapeless black beret sat squarely, pulled down to the ears. The patched frock coats of rusty black, equally shapeless, might have been cut from a single bolt of cloth. And each gray, sparsely whiskered chin was propped upon a knobby pair of hands clasped over the handle of a wooden cane as scuffed and scarred as the men themselves. Their eyes followed the group of strangers—foreigners, city people—who had left their cars along the roadside just outside the little village and now approached the dusty plaza, self-conscious and out of place.

"Is that your professor and his students, Ignacio?" asked one of the three without turning his head. "They are grown-ups, not children. I can't tell which is the professor. Do you think it's them?"

"How should I know?" said the one on the left, with appropriate unconcern. Actually, he knew that they were, and he knew the others knew. Who else could they be? Not tourists, certainly. There weren't any tourists in Torralba

When the authorities had built the ugly little *museo* in the hills outside the village, they had said there would be hordes of tourists coming to see the elephant bones that had been dug up, and that they would stop at the village to buy food and soda pop and hats to wear in the sun. But Ignacio Montes hadn't believed them, of course, and neither had anyone else. And naturally there weren't any hordes of tourists.

For one thing, why would anyone travel all the way from Madrid or Zaragoza just to see some old bones? Now, if they had some old saint's little-finger bone, that would be different. But these were just elephants' bones, or so they said.

Only Ignacio knew there weren't any elephant bones there, no matter what the authorities said. If those things were elephant bones, what had they been doing under the ground? Who could bury an elephant in that soil? He had been in that little building a thousand times, and he should know. Once he had borrowed Joaquin's hammer to chip off a piece, and had satisfied himself that it was made of stone.

Besides that, everyone knew there weren't any elephants

140

around Torralba, and there never had been any. Elephants came from China. Even he, who couldn't read and had never been to school, knew that. And even if there *had* been elephants, and even if those stones *were* bones, why would anyone want to see them when they could see real, live elephants—from China—in the zoo in Barcelona, only a few hours down the road? Last year, the schoolchildren had gone to Barcelona on a big bus, and they had gone to the zoo and seen living elephants tied with chains on their legs.

And as for those rocks the authorities said were cavemen's tools, that was the most foolish of all. Was every chipped rock you could hold in your hand a tool? Then the authorities were welcome to come and dig all they wanted out of the wheat fields every year. That would make everyone happy.

Still, when he had been mayor four years ago and they had offered him the "honor" of being custodian of the *museo*, he had accepted, and he had quietly kept the post, although he was no longer the mayor. Putting aside the tremendous glory of it, if they were crazy enough to give him 500 pesetas a month for sweeping out the dust once a week (more or less) and for opening it up to the crazy professors who came to see it, why should he object? And then, of course, there were the *propinas*—the tips. If Rafael or Joaquin knew about those, they'd be fighting for the job.

Already today he had gotten a *propina* of 500 pesetas—a month's salary—from the ugly man with the fierce eyes. He hadn't liked the man, hadn't liked his looks—a small, angry man with the body of a monkey and the cunning face of a weasel. And the eyes! Brr, a bad man. But he had paid good money, and all he had wanted was the key to the *museo* and Ignacio's promise to let no one else in that day, even this professor and his students. And on top of it all, Ignacio had been promised *another* 500 pesetas afterwards. He doubted that he would really get it, but who knew? In any case, he would certainly follow his instructions. The weasel-faced man was not one he would care to make angry.

But the professor was going to be angry. He had already sent Ignacio a telegram two days ago—to receive his first telegram, he

141

had had to live for eighty-two years—saying he was coming with his students to see the site. Well, let him be angry. Ignacio would claim he never received it. How was the professor to know?

Across the square, one of them spoke hesitantly to old Vicente, who pointed toward Ignacio. The man thanked old Vicente courteously and began to come across the square, followed by the others. So that was the professor. A big man, but with a soft smile. Better to make him angry than the other one.

Ignacio would have no trouble pulling the wool over his eyes. In his mind, he rehearsed what he would say: Telegram, señor? To *me*? Surely not, never in my life. And I am extremely sorry, but the *museo* is closed on Thursdays. Perhaps tomorrow? For a small deposit I can reserve it entirely for you. . . .

Being denied admission to the little museum had been a severe disappointment for Gideon, so much so that he had angrily accused the old man of lying. At once ashamed of himself— although he was sure he was right—he had tipped him ten pesetas and then walked with the class up to the site to see if the day could be salvaged.

He found that it could indeed. For Gideon, it was enough just to be there, standing on the very site itself, delivering the lecture of a lifetime, the lecture of an anthropology professor's dreams.

They stood in the middle of a flat depression a few hundred feet in diameter, at the foot of an arid, steep hill. In the distance, small, parched wheat fields ran irregularly up a broad, sloping hillside. Aside from those, the only sign of man was the squat little concrete-block museum at the edge of the depression. Five hundred feet away, a line of delicate trees marked the all-but-dry bed of the Ambrona River and provided the only relief in a scorched, shimmering landscape of dun, beige, and ochre. The sky was covered by a thin, gray-white cloud-sheet that muted the sun's brilliance but offered no protection against its heat.

Around him was a semicircle of fifteen rapt students, so enthralled that note-taking was forgotten.

Professor Gideon Oliver was giving it his all: "It was on the spot on which we stand, then, that *Homo erectus* ceased to be a scavenging animal that moved in straggling, starving bands. It was here that man was born. It was here that mankind began, here that the first seeds of civilization were sown . . . three hundred thousand years ago . . . ten thousand generations."

The rich words, describing an unimaginable expanse of time, thrilled him as much as they did the students, and his voice vibrated and soared with emotion.

"It would have been this time of year, during the fall migration to the lowlands. Thirty of them—*Elephas antiquus*, the huge straight-tusked elephant—would have come screaming and trumpeting over this hill from the northwest." Fifteen heads swiveled to follow his pointing finger; fifteen pairs of eyes peered anxiously up the parched hillside, as if the long-extinct monsters were about to come pounding down upon them.

"Where we are now was a bog; this barren hillside was covered with trees and long grasses. Driving the elephants was a gigantic grass fire. The wind was blowing toward the southeast, and the elephants were swept down the hillside into the bog. Over there"—he pointed again, this time toward the trickling river— "other fires had been set to prevent them from crossing to solid ground."

Gideon paused and took a deep breath, savoring the struggle that was as alive as the twentieth century for him. "And so here they stayed," he said in a deeper, quieter voice, "panicked and stumbling in the deep mud; giant males, females . . . infants. At the edge of the bog stood the hunters, the fire-setters. They had only to wait—and they were patient—for the mired elephants to become helpless. Then, one by one, they were killed with stones and wooden spears. The next day they were butchered. It was the earliest known evidence of such an enterprise in the entire history of the world."

Gideon breathed deeply again. He was tired. The site held deep meaning for his conception of man, and he had tried his best to convey it for thirty minutes. From the glazed, worn looks of the students, he had been successful.

"To sum it up then," he said a little wearily, "what makes Torralba epochal in the history of mankind is that here, for the

143

first time, a project was undertaken that required two, or maybe even three family groups of twenty or thirty individuals to *cooperate*—to trust each other, to take risks. It was the beginning of everything—language, mathematics, laws. Here we took that first tentative step from caring only for blood kin toward being members of a society of man."

The beginnings of a breeze ruffled their hair and made a soft sound in the dry brush on the hill. For perhaps twenty seconds, a respectful silence endured. Gideon's words echoed in his own mind, as he knew they did in the minds of his students. Two or three of them bent toward the gravelly ground and contemplatively picked at embedded fragments with their fingers. Gideon knew exactly what they were wondering: Is this stone right here in my hand one of the rocks they threw at the elephants so long ago? Has it lain here undisturbed for three thousand centuries, until I, here and now, picked it up? Was the last person to touch it a naked, savage ape-man?

It was precisely the kind of near-mystic musing that had first attracted Gideon to anthropology, and it still sent chills down his spine.

The mood was broken by one of the less receptive students, a glib, bearded civilian from the personnel office.

"A couple of questions, Dr. Oliver." From his tone, Gideon knew they would be arguments, not questions. He steeled himself. "One, from what you say, was this the start of civilization, or wasn't it really the start of our rape of the environment? Just what do we mean by 'civilization'?—The ability to kill animals by the hundreds?"

Gideon glowered at him, to no effect.

"And I keep wondering about the anthropologist's usage of 'man' and 'mankind.' Shouldn't it be 'people' and 'personkind'? Were there only cavemen? Weren't there any cavewomen?" He looked quickly around the circle for approval but got only bleak stares.

Gideon was half-heartedly putting together his response when one of the women, a uniformed lieutenant down on her knees in the dirt, saved him.

"Oh, for Christ's sake, Dennis, I don't want to deal with that crap now."

There were several muttered "Right on's." Mentally, Gideon applauded. He couldn't have said it better. Dennis opened his mouth to speak, but the lieutenant cut him off.

"Dr. Oliver, what kinds of things would we have seen in the museum if we'd gotten in?"

"I'm not really sure, Donna," Gideon said. "Possibly, some of the elephant bones *in situ*. There wouldn't be any human bones, because none were found. Probably some of the stone tools from the site. Maybe some spear fragments; the oldest known weapons in the world were found here, you know."

"Now, you see, that's my point," said Dennis, warming up for a speech. Again he was interrupted, this time by a shout from a student who had wandered over to the squat building.

"Hey, the museum's unlocked!"

With the others, Gideon walked over to the structure. When they had first arrived, several of the men had stood on each other's shoulders to peer through the high windows into the dark interior, but no one had thought of trying the door. Now Gideon could see that there was no padlock on the rusty hasp. The student who had called out had pushed the green metal door open an inch or two and was looking at Gideon for approval to open it all the way.

Instinctively law-abiding, Gideon hesitated for a moment, but only for a moment. This was Torralba, and he might never come this way again. Besides, the incident with the old caretaker had brought out his refractory side. He nodded, and the student pushed the door farther open.

"Something's blocking it," the student said, leaning his body against it. Suddenly, he stiffened and jumped back. "Hey, there's a guy in there!"

The door remained about three-quarters open. Spotlighted in the shaft of soft sunlight that streamed through it, a body lay on its left side on the earthen floor, its back toward the doorway. Its legs were bent at the knees so that the feet prevented the door from opening completely. It was a dark-haired man wearing a tan

145

windbreaker. Where his right ear should have been was a hideous mess of torn flesh and sinew. A great, red-brown stain glistened dully on the jacket's back and had discolored the pale earth around the man's shoulders and head.

Two of the students, a man and a woman, dropped to the ground and put their heads between their knees. The others stared in dumb, greedy shock. Gideon's courage failed him. He felt an overpowering sense of onrushing doom, an urge to turn and run, to leave undisturbed whatever lay within.

"Well, let's see what this is about," he heard himself saying quietly.

The students wordlessly parted for him. At the entrance he was caught by a terrific smell of blood, a slaughterhouse stench. He steadied himself momentarily with a hand on each side of the doorway, closed his eyes, and willed himself not to be sick. The warm perspiration on his body had turned cold; an icy globule ran freezing from his armpit down his side. He forced himself to breathe in the fetid atmosphere. Then he stepped over the body, carefully avoiding the blood, and turned firmly to look at the man's face.

It wasn't John.

Until then, he hadn't even realized what the irrational fear had been, but now the flood of relief dropped him to his knees, heedless of the blood and the gaping students. He closed his eyes again and thanked the ancient primitive gods that had hovered there since mankind's dawn.

But behind his lowered eyelids a flicker of recognition sprang up, an uneasy memory. . . .

To his mind came a long-forgotten anecdote of Sartre's in *Being and Nothingness:* You are late for an appointment with your friend Pierre in a café. You are not sure if he has waited for you. As you come in, you quickly scan all the customers in the crowded room, and you see that he is not there. But what exactly have you seen? Would you know any of the hundred customers if you were to see them again? No. You have not really seen them. You know they are not-Pierres, that is all. Only when you have given up the search for Pierre will they become recognizable entities in their own right, foreground rather than background. . . .

So it was with the maimed thing by which he kneeled. At first he knew only that it wasn't John. Now he knew who it was. He opened his eyes and looked.

Ferret-face. With pity and revulsion, but also with the sense of a great load lifting from his shoulders, he studied the dead man. There was little remaining of the right side of his face. Through shreds of red muscle and gleaming ligament, Gideon could see the round yellow condyle of the shattered mandible. One eye was half-open, one was closed, and the lower part of the face was queerly askew because of the broken jaw. Even so, and even with the drying blood that covered the features, it was unmistakably Ferret-face.

The hunter had himself been hunted down. But by whom? Almost indifferently, Gideon turned the question over in his mind, but he couldn't concentrate. He was more absorbed by a glow of triumph—vicious, but undeniably satisfying. I am still here, alive, his thoughts ran, and you are dead. I've won; you've lost. With an effort, he put aside the ugly thoughts and looked up at the students clustered around the door.

"Well, he's certainly dead," Gideon said, his voice echoing in the cool concrete structure. His words jogged a young, crew-cut student out of his stupefaction.

"You better not touch anything, Professor." When Gideon looked up at him, he blushed and added self-consciously, "I'm in the military police. We'll have to inform the *Guardia Civil*." Again, a self-important, embarrassed pause. "This looks like homicide."

Gideon resisted a strange urge to laugh. *Looks* like homicide. What did he think—that a heart attack had blown away half the man's head? He rose to a standing position, conscious of the bloody stains on the knees of his beige trousers.

"You're right, of course," he said. "Maybe there's a telephone in the village."

The MP came forward and offered Gideon his hand to assist him in stepping over the corpse and the blood-soaked ground. As

Gideon took it and came back through the door, the boy stiffened and froze, eyes wide with dismay.

"Jesus Christ, there's another one!"

Gideon spun and looked within. At the far end of the narrow twenty-foot-long aisle that bisected the building lay what could have been a discarded, life-sized puppet. It was on its back in the gloom, its arms akimbo, its legs outflung, and its head and shoulders propped against the base of the concrete wall.

It was the man from the Prado: the man with the umbrella.

16

GIDEON TOOK ANOTHER LONG swallow, and the warmth and relaxation finally began to spread outwards from his stomach. It was his second bourbon, and he was drinking it in the dim cocktail-lounge atmosphere of the Officers' Club bar on the base. A dull ache at the back of his neck reminded him that he had been sitting rigidly erect since he came in, and he let himself sink back with a sigh against the booth's black plastic upholstery.

Since he had found the second dead man, his mind had been working in a kind of otherworldly fervor, agitated and darting, turning in upon itself, questioning, testing, doubting—yet it had produced nothing of consequence, and little in the way of logical thinking. Gideon had given up trying to direct his racing thoughts hours ago and now sat there like an observer, watching his own mind go where it would. The bourbon seemed to be helping, however. He signaled the waitress for another.

The first thing he'd done when he'd gotten back from Torralba had been to telephone John in Heidelberg from the lobby of the BOQ, but John had been out of the office. Rather than trying to get another line to call him at home, he had asked to talk to Marks. He had been connected at once and had briefly described what had happened. Marks had instructed him not to return to his room but to go to the Officers' Club and wait there for the telephone to ring in the booth just outside the bar.

Gideon had been reassured by Marks's brisk efficiency and by the fact that he was familiar with details such as the location of a telephone booth at Torrejón. He had, however, defied orders and returned to his room to shower and change his bloody clothes.

When the telephone rang, Gideon took his drink with him to the booth.

"Hello?" Gideon said.

"Who is this?" It was Marks.

"For Christ's sake, it's me. Gideon Oliver."

"Are you alone?"

"No, I have eleven pals from the KGB in the booth with me. Look, Marks—"

"All right. Hold your horses. Now listen. You're not to go back to your room under any circumstance. We have a place for you—"

"Why not?" Gideon asked.

"Don't get excited. You're to go—"

"I'm not excited. You just told me not to go back to my room. I want to know why not."

"Don't give me a hard time, Oliver. You've already caused a lot more trouble than you're worth."

Gideon very nearly hung up on him. Instead, he took a long, slow sip of his drink and mentally drew a dotted-line balloon. But he couldn't think of anything to write in it.

Marks apparently heard the tinkling of the ice in the glass. "You're not drinking, are you? That won't do. I'm not going to have you—"

"Let me remind you," said Gideon, steadied by the alcohol and by Marks's familiar offensiveness, "that I don't work for you. I was fired, remember?" Marks began to interrupt, but Gideon talked over him. "I'll give you thirty seconds to say what you want to say, and then I'm hanging up. Go."

"You stupid—"

Gideon hung up and waited there for the telephone to ring again. He knew that he was being more cocksure than was good for him, but slamming down the receiver was an impulse not to be denied. Just as he began to worry that Marks might not call him back, the telephone rang again. He let it ring five times before picking it up.

Marks's voice came from the earpiece. "Who is speaking, please?"

"This is Tom Marks, calling to speak to Gideon Oliver," said Gideon.

There was silence at the other end. After a few seconds, Marks spoke, suppressed anger obvious in the soft, distinct words: "Oliver, we're not sure whether you're in any danger or not, but we don't want to take any chances. If they don't know where you are, you'll be safer. Stay away from your room."

"Who's 'they'?"

"Who's 'they'? The KGB."

"Do you think the KGB is after me, then? Why?" Despite the grisly events of the day, Gideon was beginning to feel a certain jauntiness. Being pursued by the KGB was not without its élan.

"I'm not at liberty to discuss that," said Marks predictably. "Now listen, please. We've arranged for you to spend the night in on-base housing. We've gotten a two-bedroom house for you. You're to go to the Security Office and ask for the keys that are being held for Colonel Wellman."

"What if they ask for identification? Besides, some of the Security people know me."

"Don't worry about it; it's arranged. Stay in the house and wait for us to call. We'll get back to you tonight or early in the morning. Don't go out. Just wait for our call."

"I'm scheduled to leave for Heidelberg tomorrow, you know."

"We know; tomorrow afternoon. You'll hear from us long before that."

"All right," said Gideon. He hung up, and finished his bourbon sitting in the telephone booth.

The call came at 7:00 A.M. Gideon had just awakened and was lying quietly in the first supraliminal moment, aware that something unpleasant had happened, but not remembering what it was. He waited with some anxiety for full consciousness to return and was somewhat relieved when he remembered the previous day. Of his entire life, the worst moments had been during the three or four months after Nora had died, when he'd awakened to the heart-constricting knowledge that she wasn't there anymore. Since then, nothing had seemed too bad.

He had forgotten to note the telephone's location before he went to bed, and it took him a few seconds to find it in the living room.

"Ah, Dr. Oliver, this is Hilaire Delvaux. Do you remember me?"

"Of course. Good morning."

"Can you meet me in the Officers' Club for breakfast?"

Gideon's sleepy mind processed the question slowly. "You're here in Torrejón?"

"Most certainly."

"I'll be there in twenty minutes."

He was there in ten. With his shaving equipment and tooth-brush still at the BOQ, his toilet was a five-minute affair. Monsieur Delvaux was seated at a small table near the glass wall that looked out on the club's green central patio. If he noted Gideon's unkempt appearance, he gave no sign. But then, Monsieur Delvaux did not appear to be a keen observer of fashion. He was dressed exactly as he had been when Gideon had seen him last: rumpled white shirt with wrinkled collar, and pants belted so absurdly high that Gideon could see the buckle as he looked at him across the tabletop. He was eating toast and drinking coffee. As soon as he saw Gideon, he wiped his mouth and jumped up, still chewing.

"Ah, Dr. Oliver," he said, his French accent very pronounced: Docteur Oh-le-*vair.* "Will you have something to eat?"

"No, I don't think I could eat anything. But you go ahead, please."

"Yes," said Delvaux, "you must be very disturbed. Not pre-cisely a quiet professor's life you're leading. I assure you, I sympathize." He sounded rather gay. "You were surprised to find me here, yes?" he said, biting into the bread with his stumpy teeth, his blue eyes sparkling.

"Yes, I was," admitted Gideon. "I assumed you were in Heidelberg."

"In *Heidelberg?*" he cried with delight. "At eight o'clock last night I was in Heidelberg. At nine-thirty I was in Belgium. At midnight in Holland. And I have been in Spain since five. A good night's work for an old man, no?"

Gideon was impressed. Delvaux had a distinctly disheveled look, but no more than at their previous meeting. For a man in his late sixties—maybe his seventies—who had spent most of the night in jets and airports, he was very chipper.

"And all because of you," Delvaux continued pleasantly. "Ah, and I have found out many things, many things. I think you will be interested." He chewed his toast and smiled at Gideon, waiting for a response.

"I'm interested," Gideon said.

"First of all, I believe you are familiar with this gentleman." He wiped his fingers carefully, using the napkin as if it were a washcloth, and reached into the wrinkled seersucker jacket that hung on the back of his chair. From a wallet he took a scowling, full-face photograph of Ferret-face. "Do you know who he is?"

"No," Gideon said. "Only that he's been following me. And, of course, that he's dead now."

"Ah, indeed, extremely dead. I viewed the body an hour ago. And the other one as well."

The experience had not affected Delvaux's appetite. Throwing his head back, he drained his coffee with a delicate sound and wiped his lips. Then, looking Gideon directly in the eye, he went on:

"He's one of our agents."

"One of *your* agents. . .!"

"Ho-ho, I thought you would be surprised." Delvaux chuckled expansively, as if he'd just given Gideon a surprise present. "Well, not one of mine, personally, but yes, an NSD agent. He was with Bureau Four. Do you know what that is?"

"I'm afraid I can't keep the bureaus straight. Is that counterespionage?"

"No, no," said Delvaux. "That's the Second Bureau. Bureau Four. . . . Do you mind if I get some more coffee?" Without waiting for Gideon's answer, he beamed at him and went waddling cheerfully to the cafeteria line, cup in hand.

Gideon's mind was back in a confused whirl. Ferret-face was on *their* side . . . *his* side, rather . . . yet he had been stalking Gideon, had glared at him with crushing hatred, had nearly killed him. Now he was dead, murdered, and Delvaux didn't seem disturbed in the least. Quite the opposite.

Delvaux returned to the table with a brimming cup, sat down, and hunched forward. "Now. Bureau Four. Bureau Four is the part of NSD we don't talk about. They are our internal watchdogs, our secret police. They ferret out—I understand you referred to him as Ferret-face; very perceptive—they ferret out security risks within NSD. They also sometimes . . . entrap nationals of NATO countries whom they believe to be collaborating with the Communists."

"Monsieur Delvaux, I get the impression that you don't hold Bureau Four in high regard."

"I hate them. They are like the SS. They go where they want; they do what they want. They are responsible only to their own director. Wherever they go, their wishes outrank the orders of the highest field officer." The sparkle had left his eyes. He sipped his coffee quietly.

"Can you tell me why he was. . . . What was his name? I can't keep calling him Ferret-face."

"Joseph Monkes."

"And was I correct in assuming he was an American who had spent a lot of time in Germany?" It hardly mattered, but Gideon couldn't resist asking.

"Yes, he had been in Europe since 1959. And yes, he had lived in Germany almost all that time. One of your linguistic deductions, I believe? Very clever." At Gideon's surprised expression, he smiled and added, "I spent an hour talking with John Lau last night."

"Joe Monkes," Gideon said. The name fit, somehow. "Can you tell me why he was following me?"

"I can indeed." Delvaux dropped his chin and looked up at Gideon from under bushy, tousled white eyebrows. "Now, you must look at this with a sense of humor, a certain detachment." Gideon, who had been trying to think of who it was that Delvaux looked like, suddenly remembered: Grumpy of the Seven Dwarfs—but a sly, jolly Grumpy.

"I'll try," he said with a smile. "I'm about ready for a laugh."

"*Bien.* He was following you because he thought you were working for the KGB." He held up his hand when Gideon opened his mouth. "And why, you will ask, would he think you were a spy? Because, I will reply"—here his eyes literally twinkled—"because he knew that the KGB's source was someone from USOC, and he very cleverly determined that you were the only one who had been, or would be, at the critical bases—Rhein-Main, Sigonella, and Torrejón—all at approximately the critical times."

Delvaux waited happily for this to sink in and continued, "But, you will say, it was not the Russians who arranged for me to go there; it was NSD itself, in the person of the estimable Mr. Marks. So why, you will say, did Mr. Monkes not know of this? And I, I will answer—"

"—the need-to-know principle."

"Exactly! Bravo! Will you not admit the adventure has its humorous side?"

Gideon smiled crookedly. "I can see a certain element of farce in it, yes." Then he shook his head and laughed. "That's really incredible, you know."

"I agree." Delvaux laughed too. "We used you as bait—forgive me, an unfortunate expression—as an enticement to draw out our quarry. But the Russians would not be drawn out, and neither would the USOC source—who still remains a mystery, by the way. The only ones who—'bit,' I believe you say? . . . were our own people in Bureau Four." He shook his head. "One for the books, one for the books." He sighed with great contentment. "And now I have some more to share with you."

Gideon was suddenly famished, and excused himself to get some breakfast. He came back with a huge plateful of overcooked but nonetheless appetizing scrambled eggs, with bacon, sausages, fried potatoes, biscuits, juice, and coffee, and sat down opposite Delvaux, who had refilled his own cup.

Delvaux looked at the heaped tray with a mixture of admiration and disgust. "*Formidable.* We Europeans cannot eat a breakfast like that. Except the English, of course." His grimace summed up his opinion of English cuisine. "Now, where was I?"

"Before you go on, I have a question. I wasn't the only USOC'r at Sigonella and Torrejón—"

Delvaux nodded. "Eric Bozzini. John Lau told me."

"So why did Monkes think it had to be me? Why not Eric?"

"I don't think he knew about him. Your schedule was arranged in advance. On paper. Eric Bozzini's was not." He smiled. "Incidently, I myself suspect Mr. Bozzini no more than I do you. You, he, and others may have been at the same bases. It is very easy to travel around Europe today. But let us return to the, ah, misunderstanding between you and Mr. Monkes."

While Gideon addressed his meal, Delvaux carried the conversation single-handedly for several minutes. As the chief of a major regional office, he explained, he was in charge of all NSD functions in Germany, except for those of Bureau Four. That bureau's activities were kept secret from his through strict application of need-to-know logic, of which he approved . . . in principle.

Naturally, the possibility of such a mix-up as had occurred had always been considered, and had in fact happened before on a smaller scale—agents of one bureau beginning to compile dossiers on agents of another, for example. For this reason, certain safeguards were built into the system at the highest levels to make sure no irremediable mistake was made. And none had ever been made, until yesterday.

After Gideon's call to Marks the evening before, Delvaux had become suspicious and had immediately called the director of NSD at SHAPE—Supreme Headquarters Allied Powers in Europe—in Mons, Belgium. A series of conference calls to the far-flung outposts of the NSD empire, and face-to-face meetings in Mons and Brunssum, Holland, had brought out the facts.

The dead man was certainly Joe Monkes, and he had definitely been on Gideon's trail since somehow learning about Gideon's schedule at the crucial bases. Even though he had turned up nothing in his search at the Hotel Ballman, he had convinced himself that Gideon was the traitorous USOC source who was turning over vital military secrets to the Soviet Union. Since then, he had been hounding Gideon through three countries.

"Was he behind the attack in Sicily?" Gideon asked.

"No. He was a vicious man, but that he did not do. That I will come to later."

Gideon shook his head slowly as he poured cream into his coffee. "I thought you said there were safeguards against this sort of thing."

"There are, and they are strictly enforced. But Bureau Four agents are different—I told you, like the SS. They are individualists, free thinkers. They do things their own way, and there are not many who dare quarrel with them, including sometimes their own supervisors."

Monsieur Delvaux had finished with his coffee. He gazed thoughtfully at the grass and trees of the patio, then looked directly at Gideon. "His superior believes Monkes was emotionally unstable, that perhaps your resistance to him and his colleague in Heidelberg created a personal hatred toward you that became an obsession."

Gideon could believe it. Again he slowly shook his head. "I'd say your need-to-know principle needs looking at."

Delvaux laughed; he seemed delighted with the phrase. "Yes, needs looking at! It certainly does. And already certain changes are being made so that this can never happen again. In the present case, the principle is being superseded entirely. I have been placed in charge of all aspects of this matter. All." He sat back with a childish pride that Gideon found charming, and waited for Gideon to say something.

"Congratulations, Monsieur Delvaux."

"Thank you, my good friend." He smiled merrily at Gideon. "Have you finished your breakfast? Shall we walk outside? The day seems pleasant."

The day was not pleasant. The unsubstantial clouds of the day before had thickened, so that an unusual gray sultriness enveloped the base. There was, however, a welcome normalcy in the simple white buildings; the neat, wide lawns; and the sounds of plain, homely American speech around them. Delvaux seemed content to walk in companionable silence, his hands clasped behind him. After a while, Gideon spoke.

"What you've been telling me is extremely interesting, of course. . . ."

Delvaux peeked sideways at Gideon from under his wild eyebrows. "I should think so."

"But I don't understand why you've taken the trouble to come here to give me the information. Why *are* you telling me all this?" Gideon stopped walking, to focus the conversation, but Delvaux continued abstractedly. Gideon took a long step to catch up with the smaller man.

"We have caused you a great deal of trouble," Delvaux said. "I felt we owed it to you to explain it. As I had to come to Spain in any case—to examine the bodies, to secure certain effects of Mr. Monkes, and so forth—it was little trouble to take an hour or two with you. Besides," he said, smiling up at Gideon, "obviously, you already know a great deal more about this than you pretend."

"I beg your pardon?"

"Your excellent friend John Lau was very free last night in telling me about the information he has been passing on to you."

Frowning, Gideon halted again. This time Delvaux stopped with him. "Monsieur Delvaux, is John in trouble over this? I can assure you, he didn't give me any . . . sensitive information—"

"—which you would not, in any case, recognize should it bite you on the nose, eh?" Delvaux laughed. "Don't worry. John has been a little indiscreet, but it is to his credit that he realized before the rest of us that you were in danger. It would have been better if he had gone through formal channels . . . but who knows? We probably would not have listened. In any case, I am satisfied that he neither passed on nor obtained—nor tried to obtain—highly sensitive information."

They began to walk again. "In one thing Mr. Monkes was very meticulous, which is to our good fortune," Delvaux said. "Apparently he was taking punctilious care in documenting a case against you."

"Yes, good fortune has always smiled on me."

Delvaux laughed. "He kept a very careful diary. We deciphered enough of it this morning to answer many of our questions."

They had walked several blocks. At Delvaux's suggestion, they seated themselves in the bleachers of a softball field on which six or seven youngsters were playing a desultory game. Delvaux's facetiousness had disappeared. He spoke seriously.

"Monkes watched you or had you watched from the minute you arrived in Torrejón, but he never saw you do anything suspicious. Nevertheless, he was convinced you had somehow obtained the information you were after."

"Whatever it was."

"Whatever it was. He followed you to the Prado. He was convinced that you were going to meet your case officer—your contact—there. He hoped to catch you in the act of turning over the information."

"But John was with me. He must have known John's with NSD. . . ?"

"Well. . . ." Delvaux gave one of his Gallic shrugs. "Perhaps he thought John was also a turncoat. In any case, the moment he saw Sholokov in the museum, he was certain he was correct."

"Spotted whom?"

Delvaux tapped his thigh. "Ah, I forgot. You wouldn't know Victor Sholokov, a senior KGB agent . . . with Department V."

From Delvaux's tone and meaningful look, Gideon knew he should be impressed. He raised his eyebrows questioningly.

Delvaux spoke with mild surprise at Gideon's ignorance. "Department V—that is their assassination and murder unit. And a very effective one."

"Are you suggesting that this Sholokov was there to murder *me*?"

"Certainly. But of course Monkes didn't know that. He thought Sholokov was your contact. And when he saw him attack John with the umbrella—"

"*That* was Sholokov? Was I right then? Was he Balkan?"

Delvaux smiled. "The scientist verifying his theory. Yes, he was a Rumanian. Most impressive, professor."

"Ha!" Gideon said jubilantly. He'd collect that dinner from John yet. Then he frowned. "But wait a minute; this Department V assassinates its victims with *umbrellas?*"

"You're not very far wrong, but I'll come to that in a few moments. In any event, Monkes assumed that Sholokov had spotted him and that the umbrella attack was simply a way to warn you not to carry out the rendezvous with him. Sholokov," he added, seeing Gideon's confused frown. "So Monkes—"

"Wait, please. I'm starting to lose my way. Why *did* this Sholokov attack John? *Was* he trying to kill him?"

"No, no," Delvaux said. "Don't you remember? You and John walked directly up to him to talk to him. Isn't that correct? It's what John told me."

"Yes, it's correct, but I still don't understand."

"It seems quite clear to me," Delvaux said with a touch of impatience. "Sholokov assumed that you and John had somehow found him out and were approaching him to detain or perhaps kill him. Probably he thought the Prado was full of NSD agents. And so he panicked, then ran. At least, that is what we think."

To shake his head perplexedly was not a habitual gesture for Gideon, but he did it for the third time in an hour. The answers he was getting were as complex and paradoxical as the questions. "So I was being hunted by an assassin who thought *I* was hunting *him*, and who *Monkes* thought was *my* accomplice?"

Delvaux guffawed as if he had heard a joke. "Exactly, exactly!" He dabbed at the corner of his mouth with a handkerchief. "After the incident in the Prado, Monkes decided to remain with Sholokov rather than with you. After all, he knew where *you* were staying and could put his hands on you at any time. He followed him to a hotel near Alcalá de Henares and monitored his telephone calls."

Gideon didn't bother to ask how one goes about monitoring telephone calls. He assumed there was a quick, logical, improbable answer.

"As soon as Sholokov got to his room, he called the Education Office here at the base and learned your schedule for the next day; that you were taking your class to Torralba—"

"They *told* him that?"

"Why not? A person calls, identifies himself as a Luxembourgian military officer who needs to speak with you—"

"But didn't he have a Russian accent?"

"Ah, but not everyone has your facility with linguistics. And of those who do, how many know what a Luxembourgian sounds like? Eh?"

Gideon almost shook his head again. Instead he sighed. The boys had stopped playing and had gone, leaving them alone. Gideon suggested that they walk some more and headed them in the general direction of the base shopping center. He wanted people around, Americans engaged in everyday, routine activities.

"So," said Delvaux, walking with his hands again clasped behind his back and his head thrust forward on its short neck, "Monkes drove to Torralba several hours before you were due to be there, with tape recorder and camera, in order to surprise you *in flagrante delicto* with Sholokov—"

" . . . who was actually going to Torralba for another try at killing me?"

"So we assume. What happened then is—"

"Let me guess. When Monkes got to Torralba, he found that the only place he could observe me without being seen was in the museum, so he paid the custodian to let him in and keep anyone else out. Then Sholokov also came early, and *he* found that the museum was the only place with any cover, and . . . what? I suppose they surprised one another, fought, and killed each other?" Gideon spoke matter-of-factly. The continuing talk of spies and murder had worn down the sharp edge of implausibility.

"It's impossible to tell. Monkes's diary does not include the encounter, of course. But we think that is what happened. And so the book is closed."

They had reached the shopping center. Even at nine-thirty

there was a cheerful, gratifying bustle. The hot-dog stand was already open, and Gideon found the aroma irresistible. He wasn't sure if he was still hungry because of missing dinner last night or if he simply needed to bite into a chunk of down-home America. Delvaux merely shuddered when Gideon asked him if he would like a hot dog, so Gideon bought one for himself and painted it with a heavy coat of mustard. They found a nearby bench and sat down. Gideon bit in, savoring the American mustard's clean tang.

Bright blue patches were appearing in the clouds after all, and the sounds and movement in the shopping center were wonderfully humdrum. He began to understand the virtues of military bases that looked like pieces of Oklahoma, no matter in what exotic locale they sat.

"Do you know," said Delvaux brightly, "that smells very nice. I believe I *will* have one."

He marched off to the stand on his stumpy legs, like a soldier going off to battle, and returned with a hot dog gingerly daubed with mustard.

"My fairs' 'uht dohg," he proclaimed in his most atrocious accent. Then he laughed, and Gideon laughed too.

After a few quiet minutes of congenial munching, Delvaux spoke again.

"Ah! I nearly forgot! Do you recognize this?" He placed a battered black umbrella on his lap.

Gideon had vaguely noticed him carrying it on their walk.

"No, should I?"

Monsieur Delvaux popped the last fragment of hot dog into his mouth. "Look here," he said, pointing to one of several dents in the umbrella. "You are an anthropologist. Would you not say that this indentation matches the cranial conformation of Monsieur Lau?"

"This is Sholokov's umbrella?" Gideon said.

Delvaux energetically licked some crumbs from his fingertips, then rubbed his hands together. They made a dry, rustling sound. He unscrewed the metal ferrule at the end of the umbrella, slipped off the black fabric with its underlying struts,

161

and set them aside on the bench. What was left was a conventional handle of artificial bamboo attached to a very unconventional length of aluminum pipe a little over a foot long and an inch in diameter. Two inches down from the handle, something that looked very much like a trigger protruded from the pipe.

"Pull it," said Delvaux.

Gideon did; there was a click and a powerful concussion inside the pipe. Delvaux took the instrument back from him.

"To pull the trigger releases a spring inside," he said. "The spring drives a piston hammer—you know what a piston hammer is?"

"Sort of," Gideon said.

" . . . drives a piston hammer two inches forward. Inside the tube is, or was, a small cylinder of gas that is attached to a hollow needle. Do you follow me so far?"

"More or less. Go ahead."

The piston drives the needle two millimeters into the victim's skin—your skin, let us say—at the same instant as the gas impels a miniscule pellet, less than a millimeter in diameter, into the tiny skin puncture. The needle retracts at once, leaving you with nothing more than a passing pin-prick sensation . . . and an invisible poison pellet lodged under your skin. Ingenious, no?"

Amid the shopping center sounds of normal living, Gideon found it hard to give credence to the device, in fact to the whole conversation. Nearby an eight-year-old and his mother were talking at the mustard dispenser.

"Mom, could Jesus Christ beat up King Kong?"

"Yes," the mother said, not listening.

"If King Kong was after me, I would punch him in the stomach with a karate chop."

"That's right, hon," the mother said.

Gideon picked up the weapon and looked at it. The soldered joints were surprisingly sloppy. "You know, it's hard for me to believe this sort of thing really exists."

Delvaux smiled. "It was used quite successfully in Munich in 1963, in Vienna a few years after that . . . and who knows how many more times? The poison is unknown and nearly undetectable."

"Why didn't he use it this time?"

"I think we can assume he was working his way up to a 'casual' brush against you when—so he thought—you spotted him."

"But why didn't he use it then instead of hitting John over the head with it?"

"The poison is slow-acting. In four hours the victim notices some difficulty in breathing. In twenty-four hours, by which time he has forgotten all about the brief, stinging sensation of the day before, he is dead. Excellent for leisurely assassinations, but not much use for quick getaways, you see."

"I killed him, didn't I?" said Gideon quietly. "In the scuffle. I heard the click."

"It's hard to say," said Delvaux. "He was stabbed several times in the fight with Monkes. But yes, he also had a pellet in his foot. The autopsy has not yet been performed. Probably the pellet would have killed him soon enough."

Delvaux looked into Gideon's face, his eyes suddenly concerned. "My dear friend, you cannot allow yourself to suffer for this. It was not your fault. He was an assassin, a professional killer. It was his own weapon, meant for you. He brought it upon himself."

Gideon wondered what Delvaux was seeing in his face. What he was feeling, if anything, was a detached, mild interest; it was difficult to convince himself that any of it was real, let alone that it involved him. "You've explained why Monkes was after me," he said slowly, "but why Sholokov? Why would the KGB want to kill me?"

"We believe that also is because of a misunderstanding—"

"I'm certainly happy to hear that."

Delvaux smiled, not without friendliness. "Let me go back a little. As you know, we have been aware for some time that a member of your university has been supplying extraordinarily crucial information to the Russians in connection with a mysterious undertaking we know only as Operation Philidor. Our hope in assigning you to Sigonella and Torrejón, the two remaining bases, was to draw this person out. We hoped that he, or perhaps she, feeling hounded and personally endangered, might turn to you, a naive, ignorant newcomer—you understand the sense in which I speak—for help in getting the needed information. We did not think he—or she—would ask you outright, of course, but we thought he might try to use you in some way. And so we sent you to Sigonella, and we watched you very carefully—"

"Yes, I understand all that. But why would they want to *kill* me? If he thought I was being used to trap him, all he had to do was ignore me—"

"Correct, and that is apparently what he did. But we—" here he paused to give his grandest Gallic shrug—"we, in our brilliance, not only fooled completely our own Mr. Monkes, but also the entire, mighty KGB. They have been under the impression that Dr. Gideon Oliver is in reality one of NSD's most formidable and dangerous agents of counterespionage." He began to reassemble the umbrella.

"By association, you mean? They found out that I had been in contact with you?"

"That's the idea, yes. They made, it would seem, the same mistake that Mr. Monkes did. They discovered that you were assigned to go to Sigonella and Torrejón, and that you had already been at Rhein-Main—all at the critical times. They assumed—correctly, in the latter two cases—that these assignments were no mere coincidences. Their deduction? . . . That you must be an NSD agent sent to these bases in an effort to thwart them. I think we may also surmise that they found out you had been to our headquarters in Heidelberg—the building is watched, of course—and so such a conclusion on their part was really quite reasonable."

After a moment Gideon said, "Monsieur Delvaux, does this sort of thing happen every day in your field? Or am I simply fortunate in having been involved in an extraordinarily . . . interesting adventure?"

Monsieur Delvaux laughed with real amusement. "I have been in intelligence for thirty-three years, and I have never—

neh-*vaire*—encountered an affair like this. And you, you lucky devil, walk right into it the first time!" He laughed again. "Do you know, several weeks ago we began intercepting Russian messages referring to an NSD agent who was hot upon their trail—that is the correct phrase? We racked our brains many hours trying to determine who in the world they were talking about. It was only after the terrible attack on you in Sicily that we began to think it might be *you*. That, of course, is the reason we terminated our relationship, or tried to, when you were last in Heidelberg—concern for your life."

"I wish Marks had told me that. I wouldn't have insisted on coming here, believe me."

"Unfortunately, dealing with others is not Mr. Marks's forte. He did what he was told. But I am surprised that Dr. Rufus consented to send you here."

"Did *he* know the Russians were after me, too? Did everybody know it but me?"

"You and Monkes. No, Dr. Rufus didn't know. But he *did* know we didn't want you sent here, and that has been enough for him in the past."

Delvaux's severely pursed lips indicated more than a little displeasure with Dr. Rufus. Gideon was tempted to inquire further into the arrangement between NSD and USOC. Instead, he defended Dr. Rufus.

"He wasn't very keen on my coming. I leaned on him pretty heavily. And I made a point of asking him not to inform you." He wasn't altogether sure about that, but he didn't like the idea of Dr. Rufus, who had been so reluctant about it, having difficulties on his account.

"So," Delvaux said. "Well." He placed both hands on his plump thighs. He was ready to go. The interview was over.

"Before you go," Gideon said, "there is a small matter that worries me just a little. The KGB thinks I'm some kind of super-duper agent who's going to foil their plan to blow up the world or whatever it is. They've tried to kill me twice—at least, two times that we know of. It seems rather probable that those efforts will continue, doesn't it?"

"No, you can stop worrying. They are no longer interested in you. I guarantee it."

"I value your guarantee highly, but it would certainly ease my mind if you could share with me the reason for your confidence."

Delvaux smiled. "I enjoy you, do you know? Not all Americans have so nice a way with words, even in their own language. Here is what we've done. In the past twelve hours, we have sent four secret messages to our agents which make it extremely clear that you are no longer involved with us in any way, and that they are neither to communicate with you nor to accept any communication from you."

"But it's the KGB I have to worry about, isn't it? What good does—" He stopped when Delvaux raised his hand.

"You see, the KGB works very hard at intercepting our messages, just as we do theirs. And we are well aware of certain of our own secret channels that are not quite as secret as they are supposed to be. The new directives concerning you have been routed through several of those rather leaky channels."

"But how can you be positive they'll be picked up by the Russians? It hardly seems certain." He was beginning to understand the way John felt in their anthropological discussions. Every question he asked received an answer that left him maddeningly incredulous and thoroughly convinced at the same time.

"Oh no. We *know*. You see, we are rather good at intercepting *their* messages too. And twenty minutes before I called you this morning, I received word that the KGB has already sent out word that the . . . what was it? the super-duper agent? . . . is no longer a threat and is to be left in peace. They did not name you, of course, but there is no question that it is you. You are in no danger. Period."

Gideon's mind was beginning to turn soggy. It seemed as if NSD had a more reliable communication interchange with the KGB than it did with its own Bureau Four. "But look," he said. "If *you* can send out false messages for the sole purpose of being intercepted by them, what makes you think *they* can't do the same thing? How do you know that this morning's message about me is reliable?"

"Ah, we can be sure about that. When a message is encoded—"

This time it was Gideon who held up his hand. "Stop. I don't want to know. I can't process any more data. I believe you, I believe you."

Delvaux laughed softly. "That's fine." He looked at his watch. "And now I must go. Is there anything else I can tell you?"

"Yes. Why were my socks stolen?"

"Ah, that is a funny one. We don't have any idea. We know that Mr. Monkes was in your room several times looking for information he thought you'd stolen. But the socks, they make no sense whatever. As far as we can tell, the incident has no significance."

"Could it have been the KGB?"

"That stole your socks? Hardly. Now, if they'd been American blue jeans. . . ."

They said good-bye at the terminal. Gideon shook hands with affection, and felt the grip returned.

"Where are you off to now?" Gideon asked.

"Now I go back to Holland, to Brunssum, to confer with Herr Embacher, the director general."

"The head of NSD? This is as important as all that?"

Delvaux shrugged expressively but did not reply.

Gideon's mood was one of reasonable satisfaction as he watched the bus leave. Delvaux had assured him that his personal safety was no longer at risk. The fact that he had received similar assurances two weeks before was of minor concern. More importantly, his scientist's soul was content—or nearly so; Delvaux had fitted almost all of the missing pieces into place. Only a few annoying questions remained: Who was the spy on the USOC staff? What were the Russians really up to?

And somehow most perplexing and bothersome of all in its own niggling way: Why had someone stolen three pairs of his socks?

17

AS SOON AS HE saw the figure at the top of the stairs, Gideon knew there was something odd about him. A slight, dark young man of twenty with flashing black eyes, he looked distinctly out of place in the BOQ. He was certainly no air force officer. He would have seemed more at home on the stage of a flamenco cabaret or with a sword and *muleta* in his hands at the Plaza Monumental. He was an American, though; Gideon's anthropological intuition told him that. He had the graceful slouch of a New Yorker or perhaps an Angeleno; a big-city boy returned as an indifferent GI to the land of his fathers.

What caught Gideon's attention, however, was the boy's hesitant stealth, a furtiveness that was almost appealing in its naiveté: an abrupt, startled stop when he first saw Gideon at the foot of the stairs, then a quick intake of breath for courage, and a patently feigned nonchalance as he descended. He was even whistling tunelessly as he passed Gideon at the middle of the stairway.

He was nearly past when Gideon saw what he was carrying in his hand. Gideon reached behind him and grasped the boy by the upper arm. The biceps was stringy and tough.

"I think that's my radio you have there, isn't it?"

"What?" said the boy. His eyes darted quickly to the side, and Gideon tightened his grip. "Hey, let go of me, man. What the fuck do you think you're doing? You don't let go of me, I kill you!" The words were accompanied by a snarl, but the heart-pounding fear behind them was obvious. He tried to shake off Gideon's hand, and they both bumped roughly into the wall and staggered down a couple of steps.

The orderly stationed at the reception desk, a large, powerful man with huge forearms, came to the foot of the stairs. "Hey, what's going on?" he said.

"This kid was just walking out with my radio," Gideon said.

168

"Like hell," the boy said. "This is my radio, man."

"Suppose we go up to my room and see," Gideon said.

"Sir, do you want me to call the MPs?" The orderly stood in the middle of the stairwell, one gigantic hand on each bannister.

"I think that would be a good idea," said Gideon.

"No, wait, man," the boy said. "Okay, I took the radio, but . . . the door was open. . . . I just saw it there . . . it was stupid. . . . Hey, let me go, man. I never done anything like this before."

Gideon was sorry for the boy, hemmed in by two threatening men who towered over him, but he didn't believe his story.

"What were you doing here?" he asked.

"I'm a courier. I was delivering a message. My name's Manny Pino," he volunteered. "Look, man—"

"To whom?" asked Gideon.

"Huh?"

"To whom were you delivering a message?"

"Major . . . Major Rosen."

Gideon looked at the orderly. The man shook his crew-cut head. No Major Rosen there.

"But," the boy said, "I couldn't find him, he wasn't here, so I—"

"Where's the message?" said Gideon.

The boy began to cry. Gideon kept a firm grip on his arm. "Call the MPs," said Gideon.

The military police had been able to get nothing more from Manny Pino. In the end, they had taken him away snuffling and terrified. They had also taken the radio and had told Gideon to check through his things to see if anything else was missing.

Grumbling, more annoyed than angry, he found the list of his belongings—so well-used that it was beginning to fray along the creases—and quickly checked off the items. As he had somehow expected, nothing else was missing.

He flung himself into the standard-issue green armchair and pondered. He knew why he was so irritated; he was in the dark again. Only a few hours ago, he had considered things pretty well

169

wrapped up. Delvaux had cogently if implausibly explained away almost everything. As far as Gideon had been concerned, the case was closed; he was ready to forget the theft of the socks.

And then he had returned to his room to pack before leaving for the airport, and found everything blown wide open again. Why in the world would anyone take the trouble to break into his room to steal a $14.95 plastic portable radio? The calculator standing there in plain sight was worth five times as much. It made about as much sense as the socks.

He did, however, know a few things for certain. He knew, most comfortingly, that it was definitely not Ferret-face's doing, unless Monkes had arranged for it before he was killed; and he knew that the theft had conveniently occurred during the time Marks had ordered him to stay away from his room. That made it rather likely that whoever was behind it had access to NSD's instructions . . . or was acting *on* NSD's instructions.

Was it possible that Delvaux had not been leveling with him? He pondered some more, frowning blankly at the neat green lawns below.

Book 5: Brunssum

18

BRUNSSUM, HOLLAND, LIES IN the Dutch Alps, a pleasant region of low hills that serves as a vacation destination for flatlanders who cannot afford to go abroad. To the gourmets of the world, Brunssum is known, if at all, as a good place to spend the night when on pilgrimage to the Prinses Juliana Restaurant in Valkenburg a few miles away. To the military, on the other hand, Brunssum is headquarters of AFCENT, Allied Forces Central Europe, its offices situated in the deep caverns of an old mine on the edge of town.

But for those fortunate few who are both gourmets and members of the military, Brunssum holds a secret unknown to Michelin and Fodor and Arthur Frommer: the International Dining Hall in the AFCENT compound. Here is what many claim to be the finest restaurant in the Netherlands; it is indisputably the best bargain.

Hilaire Delvaux, having shown his ID and paid his $1.50 at the door, had moved through the cafeteria line and helped himself to a double portion of dilled shrimp and asparagus salad, and to consommé madrilene. From the T-shirted man behind the counter, he had ordered the hall's renowned Friday Night Special, Beef Wellington, accompanied by fresh slivered green beans and mushrooms.

Now he sat at a marred plastic-topped table, the food in front of him. Elfin and plump, with his small feet barely touching the floor, he made an odd figure among the lean, uniformed soldiers dressed in the blues and greens and browns of seven different armies.

Delvaux had looked forward all day to the Beef Wellington; he had more than once described it as England's sole contribution to the world's cuisine. Since his hot dog with Gideon that morning, he had eaten nothing, in order to conserve his appetite. But now he wasn't hungry. The meat lay cooling on his plate, its crust slowly turning soggy.

The conference with Embacher had gone badly. The director general, never an easy man to get along with, was understandably under pressure to solve the case. He had ranted and desk-pounded even more than usual: *Who* was the Russians' USOC source? *Why* hadn't Delvaux been able to identify him? *What* was the information the Russians were trying to get out of Torrejón? Exactly what were they going to do with it? Had they or hadn't they gotten it? What did Delvaux propose to stop them? Didn't Delvaux understand there were only two days left before Operation Philidor, whatever in God's name that was?

Yes, Delvaux thought, shuffling string beans with his fork, he understood very well. For all anyone knew, Operation Philidor might be a small adventuristic sortie . . . or it might be the start of World War III, the end of European civilization. But couldn't Embacher grasp the kinds of problems he faced? They had doubled his staff of agents to twenty-four, but how could twenty-four men keep track of the forty-four members of the USOC staff? They couldn't—not when one needed at least three men to keep full-time surveillance on a single person, and not when the entire staff had ID cards that would admit them to nearly any base in Europe.

Later on, a massive review of airline and customs records, and of military records as well, might turn up the source. But how much difference would it make later on? As of now, it could be any one of them. Well, not Professor Oliver and probably not Frederick Rufus. But even there, could one be sure?

He pushed himself away from the table and went to get coffee, nearly bumping absentmindedly into two kilted Scots. What he needed was a hundred men; Embacher should have brought in agents from the CIA, from MI-5. Delvaux had suggested that, and Embacher had just raved on and turned a deeper purple. The man would rather see the end of the world than lose face.

172

That's what came of putting political appointees in such positions. Leaving Delvaux with no coherent instructions, he had stomped from the room and run off for an airplane to take him to SHAPE headquarters in Mons.

As he sat down with the coffee, an aide from the director general's office ran breathlessly to his table; there was a top-priority call for him from Spain. Would he come at once?

"Yes, Karl," Delvaux said into the mouthpiece, "I understand. But I wish to hear his exact words. Will you read the transcript to me, please, from the point where he admits what he was doing, or rather, just before?"

Clearly, but crackling and thin, the words came from the agent in Madrid:

Pino: *I ain't no thief, man. I wasn't stealing nothing. I was putting something in the dude's room.*

Crow: *So what were you doing with the radio? Come on, Manny, you better start telling the truth.*

Pino: *I am telling the truth. I was putting some secret information in one of his books.*

Crow: *You want to let me have that again?*

Pino: *Printouts. I copied some stuff off of printouts in the computer room, and I wrote them on a little piece of paper like the guy told me, and I snuck into this guy's room, and stuck them in his book, like he told me.*

Crow: *Who told you? Oliver, the guy whose room it was?*

Pino: *No, I never seen him before. He wasn't supposed to know about it, man. No, this was the guy I met in the bar.*

Crow: *All right, never mind. What was it you copied?*

Pino: *I don't know. The guy told me the code number of the sheet. It was mostly numbers. Uh, deployment, something like that. Yeah, deployment patterns, stuff like that. Tactical fighters or something. I don't remember.*

Crow: *All right. Now listen to me, Manny. You're in a hell of a lot of trouble. You've been spying—*

Pino: *Hey, man, I ain't no—*

Crow:	You've been spying, and that means you could be executed.
Pino:	(Shouted and jumped from chair; forcibly restrained and handcuffed to chair.)
Crow:	Manny, you're only making it worse for yourself. Now either cooperate—
Pino:	Okay, okay, okay.
Crow:	All right, then tell the truth. I mean it.
Pino:	I am telling the truth. Look. I'm in this bar in Madrid on Monday night—
Crow:	What was the name of the bar?
Pino:	Oh, come on, man, I don't know. It was where all those bars are, where they sell those shrimp. All the guys go there.
Crow:	All right, go ahead.
Pino:	So I'm in this bar, and this guy comes up to me, and he's a reporter from the New York Times. Mr. Johnson.
Crow:	Did you see some identification?
Pino:	What, are you kidding? A guy starts talking to me in a bar, I'm supposed to ask for his ID?
Crow:	What did he look like?
Pino:	I don't know—like a reporter, I guess. He was pretty old, fifty or sixty. He seemed like an okay guy.
Crow:	All right, go ahead.
Pino:	So he tells me he's writing this story about the crummy security on American bases. Like a, a . . . .
Crow:	An exposé?
Pino:	Right, right. So he says if I put the stuff in this guy's book, he'll sneak it off the base and then the Times does a big article, and then they'll pass some laws to tighten up security.
Crow:	Go ahead.
Pino:	Well, that's all, man. I know it's dumb, but I done it. I was trying to be patriotic.
Crow:	He gave you money, didn't he?
Pino:	Well, yeah, a hundred dollars, but that's not why I done it. I—

174

Delvaux cut in. "Karl, did you find out how he knew which book to put it in?"

"Yes, he—"

"No, read me the transcript."

For a moment there was no sound but the crackling and humming of the wires. "Here it is," said the agent.

Pino: *The guy in the bar, he told me to put it in the back of a book, just stick it between the pages so it doesn't show.*

Crow: *Just any book?*

Pino: *No, he gave me the name. I wrote it on a piece of paper. Hey, I still got it. It's in my wallet. (Contents of wallet examined. Found cocktail napkin with penciled note: Skull of Sinanthropus Pekinensis, Franz Weidenreich.)*

"Why did he say he took the radio, Karl? Impulse?"

"Uh-uh. Here, let me find it. . . "

"No, no. You can just tell me."

"He says the man in the bar told him to take it. Not the radio, necessarily, just *something*. Pino said the man told him it would be a cover."

"I'm afraid I don't see—"

"Well—this is according to Pino, now—the alleged reporter told him that Oliver had ways of knowing if anyone had been in his room, even if a single book or anything was moved a fraction of an inch. But if something was *missing*, the idea was that Oliver would be bound to think somebody had been in there to steal something; it wouldn't occur to him that somebody had *left* something."

Delvaux laughed drily. "What do you think of all this, Karl?"

"We haven't put Pino on the polygraph yet, but I'd bet he's not lying. I think the whole thing is so crazy that maybe it's true."

"That's precisely what I think. Splendid work, Karl. You've done wonderfully."

Delvaux's breath was shallow with excitement as he replaced the telephone. So Monkes had been correct after all. It *was* Gideon Oliver, but an innocent Gideon Oliver, who was unknowingly carrying tactical aircraft deployment plans from Torrejón. No doubt the Russians had gotten the information in the same way at Sigonella, only then it had been three pairs of socks, not a radio, that had served as cover.

If only he had given credence to Oliver's complaint then and had investigated the theft. . . . But it was too late for that now. Now the only important thing was to find Oliver and the book before the Russians did. How strange to think that the key to an East-West confrontation might lie between the pages of an abstruse text in the care of a brilliant but frighteningly naive professor of anthropology.

But where *was* Oliver? He had been scheduled for a flight from Madrid to Frankfurt that afternoon. He was probably in Germany already, on his way to Heidelberg. My God, was it already too late? There must have been a hundred chances for them to get the information from Oliver: at the airport in Madrid, on the airplane itself, at the Frankfurt airport, at the train station in Frankfurt. . . . No, he told himself. Do not become addle-brained at the moment of success. Be rational.

There was no time to waste on speculation. Oliver had to be found quickly. With Operation Philidor set for Sunday, the Russians would have to get hold of the information within the next twenty-four hours, and that would mean some time tomorrow, no doubt at Heidelberg. Whoever the USOC source was, and however patient, he would be tense with the strain of operating on a timetable that left no room for error. And tense spies were dangerous spies; Oliver's life would be in considerable peril as long as he held the deployment plans.

There were many things to be done. It would be another night without sleep. First, a call to SHAPE at Mons to tell them about the Pino affair. Then he would telephone Thomas Marks in Heidelberg. Finding the professor could hardly present a problem, even for Marks. The schedule of trains arriving at Heidelberg that evening from Frankfurt could be easily obtained, and one or two men placed at the *bahnhof* to intercept Oliver. For insurance, Marks could be sent to Oliver's room at the BOQ to wait for him.

Delvaux smiled a small, tired smile. Once again, the harried professor might have a surprise encounter with strangers in his room. This time, however, he would have no cause for complaint. Until Gideon Oliver was separated from the vital, deadly information he carried, his life was worth nothing. And the closer Operation Philidor's deadline came, the more danger he would be in.

Book 6: Heidelberg

19

AT TEN-THIRTY THAT NIGHT Gideon lay naked on his side, languorous and content. He was moving his hand down Janet's bare back in long, slow strokes, starting with firm pressure on her hair, then down the length of her torso, and ending with a gentle caress of her firm, smooth buttocks. Janet was sighing deep in her throat.

"I didn't know human beings could purr," he said dreamily.

"Was that me?" she said.

"Yup."

"I guess they can, then," she said, and made the sound again. "Ah, Gideon, I'm so glad you're here, it's scary. I don't like liking anyone this much."

Gideon had told her the entire story, from the first solicitation by NSD to Monkes's death and the theft of the radio. Afterwards, although they had made love earlier, they did so again, with a fierce, almost desperate tenderness on Janet's part.

At one point during their lovemaking, she had sobbed—a single, gasping sob, like a man's—and said with anguish, "They could have killed you," her voice muffled by his chest.

"What?" he had said.

"Nothing," she replied, but he had heard her, and his heart had constricted with pleasure and worry.

"Gideon," she said, "how did you get here so early? I thought your train wasn't due until eleven."

"I sat next to an army captain from USAREUR on the plane. His wife met him at the airport and they gave me a lift right to the door. That reminds me," he said, beginning to pull his arm from underneath her, "I'd better go down and register. I came straight to your room without stopping at the desk."

"You don't really want to get out of bed, do you? I'm not going to let you sleep in your room tonight anyway, so why don't you register in the morning?"

"But—"

"This way, you get the continued uninterrupted pleasure of my wondrously beautiful body."

"Well. . . ."

"Plus the immediate gratification of any perverse wishes you'd care to make known."

"Well. . . ."

"Plus you don't have to pay them six dollars for the night."

"Now *that's* a point," he said, snuggling down against her.

"I thought you'd think so," she said. Then, just as they were falling asleep again, she added, "I'll only charge you three."

"Do you charge extra for perverse wish gratification?"

"First two are on the house."

"Deal," he said, and fell happily asleep.

Forty feet down the hall in Room 15, Tom Marks was staring gloomily at his reflection in the mirror. He could already see the bags under his eyes, and wasn't the left one getting a little bloodshot? He looked at his watch: nearly 2:00 A.M., and he had to get up at 6:00. He was a man who needed his sleep. If he didn't get enough, it made his stomach queasy all day and he couldn't eat right. Even if he left right now and slept on the cot at the office, he'd only get three hours' sleep. How was he supposed to function on that? His work was very demanding, very detailed.

Damn. Where was Oliver? The Madrid plane had been on time and Oliver had been on it; they knew that. But the 11:00 train had arrived in Heidelberg without him, and the next one wouldn't be in until 9:20 A.M. He hadn't stayed over at the Rhein-Main Air Base Hotel, and so far the Polizei hadn't turned him up at any of the hotels in Frankfurt.

There was something fishy about that smart-mouthed professor, even if Delvaux didn't think so. One way or another, everything he touched got screwed up, including tonight. Delvaux had made it sound simple: "When he arrives, you will obtain the book from him and take it at once without opening it to Major Lauffer for deposit in the maximum-security vault." Simple, except what if he didn't arrive?

This was ridiculous. He was not a field operative used to all-night stakeouts. He was an official; he needed his sleep, and who knew when, if ever, Oliver would come? And when he finally came, he would naturally be without the book, and with some fantastic story of how he'd been set upon by Spanish pirates who had stolen all his jockey shorts at saber point.

And they'd check it out, and it would be true.

There was really no point in continuing to wait. He might have some idea of what to do, had Delvaux taken him into his confidence and told him what was so special about the book, but *le directeur*, in his wisdom, had chosen not to. It was the source for some code, probably. Well, enough was enough.

He left the room, slamming the door behind him. At the noise, the slow, steady snoring from the room across the hall fractured into a series of little hiccups and stopped. Good. Why should that sonofabitch sleep when *he* had to stay up all night? He hurried down the stairs, just in case the interrupted sleeper came out to see about the noise.

He got a sheet of paper from the sleepy attendant at the reception desk and wrote, "Oliver—Call me *at once* no matter what time. Do not let book, *Skull of Sinanthropus Pekinensis*, out of your sight. Extremely urgent. Tom Marks." He put the sheet in an envelope, sealed it, wrote "Oliver—urgent" neatly in its center, and gave it to the attendant.

"See that he gets this the minute he arrives."

"Check," the attendant said.

"Even before he registers."

"Right."

Marks formed his lips into a thin, tight line. "This is of the first order of magnitude," he said.

"I hear you, I hear you," the attendant said.

Marks glared at him a moment longer, then turned on his heel and went home for a few hours of hard-earned sleep.

Gideon was awakened by a gentle nuzzling high up between his shoulder blades. He lay on his side with Janet pressed close behind him, her hand resting on his hip, her soft belly against the base of his back, her knees fitting comfortably into the hollows behind his own.

So had he awakened peacefully with Nora on a thousand mornings. Nora. . . . A black shadow of grief and despair darkened his mind suddenly. His stomach twisted, and a violent shudder ran across his back from one shoulder to the other.

"Oh oh, it's awake, folks. Better stand back," Janet said, snuggling in even closer and moving her lips softly over his shoulders.

The black shadow passed on.

Gideon closed his eyes again and sighed. "Ah, Janet, how good you feel."

"Boy, do I ever," she said. She moved her hand to his chest— the touch excited him—and she pressed him still more tightly to her. "Mmm, I'm glad you have a hairy chest."

"Not always. I just wear it with girls who like truck drivers." He was sorry as soon as he said it and twisted to face her. He placed his fingertips on her mouth. "I'm sorry," he said. "That was stupid. I'm glad you like me, Janet. I don't think you have any idea how glad."

He took his hand from her lips and softly stroked her cheek. She lay still, watching him with glowing eyes. Her hair was tousled and her cheeks a little flushed. Something made Gideon's breath catch in his throat. He kissed her softly on the lips, a long, serene, relaxed kiss, with both their heads resting easily on her pillow.

This was getting serious. If he didn't watch out, he was going to find himself right up to his ears in a Meaningful Relationship, and with an odd female of whom he barely approved, if at all. Somehow, the prospect failed to repel him.

Her hand had stayed at his chest and now began to lightly caress his nipple. He leaned toward her and kissed her again, harder this time, and stroked her long, solid thighs.

She caught his hand and lifted it to her lips. "Don't get me excited. We don't have time for that stuff."

"It's six o'clock in the morning," he said plaintively. "And it's Saturday."

"We're going on the faculty Rhine cruise. They do it every year, with whoever's in town. I guess I forgot to mention it."

"Janet, I hate stuff like that—"

"I know, but I have to go. I'm on the administrative staff, remember, and Dr. Rufus likes all of us to be there. I just figured that you'd want to come along, so I booked a place. You don't have to if you don't want to."

"Well, I haven't seen the Rhine yet, but the idea of a group cruise—"

"It isn't, really. They've just reserved thirty places on one of the regular Rhine steamers from Rüdesheim."

"How do we get to Rüdesheim?"

"Most of the others are going up on an army bus, but we're driving up with John and Marti in their car."

"Who are they?"

"John Lau."

"John's married?"

"Sure. You'll like Marti. She's really off the wall."

"Do you know, I had no idea he was married?" It made Gideon feel vaguely guilty that he had never even asked. Had his relationship with John been as one-sided as that? "Okay," he said, "sounds good. I'm game "

"Great. We have to meet them at the Admin Building in half an hour. Let's go." She kissed him with a loud smack: the perfunctory sort of kiss shared by people who have kissed many times before and know that many more will follow. Then she reached down and gave his genitals an amiable little jiggle—as if she were scratching a friendly dog behind the ears—and jumped from the bed.

Gideon liked the possessiveness and indulgence implied by the gesture. Meaningful Relationships aside, he had wondered whether he would ever again share with any woman the comfortableness he was beginning to feel with this one.

With mixed feelings, all of them pleasant, he watched her walk toward the bathroom.

"Gideon, don't look at me when I'm not wearing any clothes," she said. "I look fat from behind."

"You don't look fat," he said with sincerity. "You look beautiful."

"No, I don't. My hips are fat." She ducked into the bathroom and got into the shower.

Gideon got up and came to the bathroom door. "But that's not any old fat. That's good, luscious, female adipose tissue, the kind of fat you can get a handful of, the kind of fat—"

"Gideon . . .!"

"No, I'm serious," he shouted above the sound of the water. "Anatomically speaking, all the things that look so great on women are fat, if you come right down to it—"

"Could we please talk about something else?" she shouted from behind the curtain.

"Okay, but I intend to look at your rear end a lot—every chance I get. And I want you to know how beautiful you are down there. There isn't a man in the world who wouldn't think so. You're so solid, so—"

"Thank you very much. Do you think we'll have nice weather today?"

"The thing is, women try to look slim-hipped like men, and they can't. Not if they have any female hormones. The very thing that makes a woman so lovely is exactly what you have: a big, beautiful trochanteric subcutaneous adipose tissue distribution."

Janet put her head out between the shower curtains. "Do all anthropologists talk like you? It's like listening to Elizabethan love poetry."

Through the parted curtains Gideon could see the water glistening on Janet's breasts and on one long, supple thigh.

"Hey," he said. "If we're short on time, why don't I jump in? Be faster if we shower together."

"Okay," said Janet, "but no fooling around."

Gideon practically leaped into the shower and pulled Janet's slippery body to him. "Would I fool around with a fat lady?"

"Ooh, you rat!" Janet cried, and pummeled his sides.

Laughing, they wrestled for a few moments, but then Gideon pinned her to the tile wall and kissed her wet mouth. They slid slowly down the wall, mouths pressed urgently together, not noticing the spray that drenched their hair.

They were late leaving her room, of course, and were out the BOQ's front door before Gideon remembered that he still hadn't registered.

"Well, make it as fast as you can," Janet said. "We're supposed to be meeting them right now."

Gideon hurriedly showed his TDY orders to the clerk, signed in, took the sealed brown envelope that was handed to him, and shoved it into his pocket. Then he ran back out the door, hand in hand with Janet.

Most of the staff members were congregated in the parking lot at USOC headquarters, awaiting the bus that would take them to Rüdesheim. Dr. Rufus, all rosy cheeks and high spirits, came over to them at once.

"Ah, I see you've convinced him to come along," he said to Janet. "Wonderful. It should be a glorious day; Bacharach, St. Goarshausen, the Lorelei, Rheinfels. . . ."

Janet's attention was engaged by someone else, and Dr. Rufus took Gideon's elbow, moving him to a more private place.

"My boy," he said, puffing out his cheeks, "I can't tell you how relieved I am to have you back in one piece." He mopped his brow with a handkerchief and grasped Gideon's elbow more tightly. "Warmer than I'd hoped, but there'll be breezes on the river." He smiled fondly at Gideon.

"I imagine you know what happened there, sir?" Gideon said.

"Well, I heard something about some people being killed. . . ."

"Dr. Rufus, Hilaire Delvaux told me—well, implied to me—that you've been working more closely with NSD than you told me."

Dr. Rufus's voice dropped. "Well, it's not the sort of thing one goes around talking about, my boy. Sort of, er, defeats the point of espionage, don't you think?"

"*Are* you an agent?"

The handkerchief came out again and blotted the moisture from Dr. Rufus's throat. "Gideon, you're putting me in a delicate position. . . ."

"I don't mean to do that, sir. But my radio was stolen last night. I think NSD had something to do with it, and—"

"Why on earth would you think that?"

"Because it happened to be taken during the time that NSD told me to stay away from my room. I doubt that it was a coincidence."

Dr. Rufus frowned at the ground, silent.

"Dr. Rufus, you *do* know about the theft, don't you?"

"Gideon," Dr. Rufus said, "I'm not very good at dissembling. I . . . well, I *was* informed of it, but . . . well, I can't tell you any more than that . . . except that I can *assure* you . . . unqualifiedly assure you . . . that NSD had absolutely nothing to do with it. When I heard about it last night, they . . . that is, we . . . were as puzzled as you. I really can't say any more. . . . I hope you understand my position. . . . Ah, Bruce," he cried with relief, "come and say hello to our world traveler."

"Well, well," said Bruce Danzig with a prunelike smile. "The peripatetic professor, put in from his peregrinations."

Dr. Rufus roared with laughter. "Wonderful, Bruce! How do you do that sort of thing?"

"I prepare ahead of time," Danzig said.

Gideon didn't doubt it. "Alliterative archivists always alienate," he said, rather pleased with himself.

"Touché," Danzig said with some surprise. Then, after a pause during which Dr. Rufus continued to chuckle, "Are those the books you borrowed last week? I have to go back inside for a moment; I can take them in for you."

"Actually, I brought them along hoping I could browse through them on the cruise. But I'm really only interested in one of them; you can have the other."

Danzig looked at the title of the book Gideon handed him. "Campbell, *Human Evolution,*" he read aloud. "So you're keeping the Weidenreich?"

"Just for a couple of days. I'm impressed; do you usually know your lent-out books by heart?"

"No," said Danzig evenly, "I just happened to remember because there's a rush request on that one, and I said it would be available Monday."

"I'll bring it in on Monday."

"Aren't you going to Izmir Monday?"

"All right, I'll drop it off tomorrow. It's not overdue, is it? What's the hurry?"

"Now, now," said Dr. Rufus uncomfortably, "let's not quibble. This is a big day."

"I thought I was the only one teaching anthro," Gideon said, studying Danzig. "Why would anyone else be interested in *The Skull of Sinanthropus Pekinensis?*"

"No, no, no, no," Dr. Rufus said. "Absolutely not. No arguing permitted today." He took them both by the arm. "The bus is here, and I'm getting on it with our alliterative archivist. You, sir," he said to Gideon, giving him a friendly shove in Janet's direction, "have the good fortune of being the object of that lovely lady's impatience."

He thumped Gideon on the back with robust good humor. "*Really* delighted you're back safe," he said, and marched off, pulling an annoyed-looking Bruce Danzig with him.

Book 7: The Rheingau

20

AT JANET'S SUGGESTION, THE four of them drove north via the Bergstrasse. Gideon was delighted with the road. Never more than a mile or two from the hectic *autobahn* and its dreary landscape, the Bergstrasse took them through a lovely world of ancient villages with names like Heppenheim and Zwingenberg and Bickenbach: little towns with crooked, half-timbered houses, and cobblestoned streets. Between the villages were neat little orchards that, according to Janet, were famous for blooming ten days before those anywhere else in Germany.

For a while they enjoyed the peace of the countryside, chatting casually and only occasionally. Gideon, who was expecting a sultry Chinese beauty, found Marti Lau a surprise. A gangling, coltish twenty-five-year-old with big hands and feet, whose maiden name had been Goldenberg, she was given to ejaculations like "yuckers" and "wowie-zowie." She had a frank, pretty face that dimpled engagingly when she smiled, which was every time they spoke to her, or looked at her, or looked as if they might look at her.

Other than smiles and wowie-zowies, her communications consisted of non sequiturs, mostly in the form of odd, abstract, unanswerable questions directed at Gideon. She had already asked him, in a broad Kansas accent, what human beings were going to look like in ten thousand years, and why there was more than one language in the world. At first he had tried serious replies, which seemed to delight her. After a while he simply smiled and shrugged. She appeared equally pleased.

Near Darmstadt they left the Bergstrasse and turned across the flat, industrial Rhine Plain below Frankfurt. The conversation turned to Gideon's adventures. John hadn't known about the attempted theft of the radio the night before and listened with absorption as he drove.

"Forget about NSD being responsible," he said. "That makes no sense at all. It's got to be the Russians. But why the radio?" he added under his breath. "Why the radio?"

"I have an idea," Janet said. "Why don't we try a little creative brainstorming on that question? Free association—whatever comes into your mind."

"Okay," John said, after a few moments of silence, "maybe he was stealing it to sell because his wife needed an operation."

"No," Gideon said. "This was really a cheap—"

Janet interrupted. "Hold it, hold it. That's not the way it works. No critical thinking, please. Just keep the ideas coming. Give your unconscious a chance."

"All right," said Gideon. He was happy and relaxed, and car games were fine with him. "Maybe he wanted to hear the soccer scores and his own radio was broken."

"Good," Janet said. "Or maybe he could hear it playing through the wall, and he hates music, and he was taking it to throw away."

"Or maybe," Gideon said, getting into the swing of it, "it sounded like it wasn't playing right, and he was taking it out to get a new battery for it."

"Hey, wow, got it!" Marti said. "How about if what's-his-name was in your room doing something that had nothing to do with the radio, but that he saw you coming—he could have, through the window, couldn't he?—and he just grabbed the radio and made off with it to keep you from figuring out what he was *really* doing."

It made a strange kind of sense to Gideon. He looked at Marti with respect. But what was he really doing?"

John cut in excitedly. "Using something else in your room as the dead drop . . . your suitcase, your shaving gear, your books, anything."

Gideon nodded. "It's possible," he said slowly. "They could

have deposited stuff in my room for me to carry off the base. Even with the alert, my pass was getting me through the gate pretty easily."

"So, if he took something, a radio, you'd assume he was just a thief," John said. "Hey, that's probably what happened to the socks, too. It'd never occur to you someone had been putting something *in* your room."

"I don't understand," Janet said. "You mean that's the way they smuggle things off the base? *You* carry it off for them?"

Gideon shook his head. "Do we really believe any of this, or are we just fooling around?"

"Funny, isn't it?" John said with a small, tight laugh. "It would mean you were the guy we were looking so hard for at Torrejón."

It was the Rüdesheim Gideon had read about in the travel books, but with a vengeance. What he'd read was "a lively Rhine village, with streets of wineshops and *bierstuben*, friendly and gregarious at all times of year." What he found was a riotous town jammed with tourists, bursting with tourists. Mostly German, mostly male, and mostly in large groups, they barreled along the streets in yellow- or green- or red-hatted brigades, tipsily following tour leaders with matching umbrellas held high.

"My God," he shouted over the clamor, "is it always like this?"

Janet assured him it was. "The Germans work hard," she shouted back, "and when they play, they work hard at playing hard."

And obviously, thought Gideon, this is where they come to do it.

"You ain't seen nothing yet!" John cried, pulling them along the street. "Come on, we only have twenty minutes before the boat goes."

They had to snake along single-file to get through the crowds of beefy, blond men, many of whom tramped along singing, with arms about each others' shoulders.

"Where to?" asked Janet. "The Drosselgasse?"

"You bet," John shouted.

Marti cheered: "Hot puppies!"

The Drosselgasse was Rüdesheim's most famous street. An alley, really, with no room for vehicles, it was packed along both sides from one end to the other with restaurants, *weinstuben*, and *bierstuben*. And all of them, or so it sounded, were full of people playing accordions and singing with all their might. The alley itself was so crammed with people that it seemed impossible to get through.

"I can't believe it," said Gideon. "It's only nine-thirty in the morning. What's this place going to be like at nine-thirty tonight?"

"The same," said John. "Let's go."

"You're nuts," Gideon said. "I'm not going in there."

"You can get the best bratwurst in Germany halfway down that street," John said, and pulled them into the throng.

The best bratwurst in Germany, it turned out, were served at a nondescript stand with the incongruous name of "Clem's." There, a scowling, elephantine man ferociously speared the sausages from the grill, tucked them deftly into split hard rolls, and for less than two marks each, thunked them down in front of a steady, appreciative line of patrons. Gideon, skeptical at first, changed his mind after the first crackling bite and ordered a second to fortify him for the struggle back down the alley.

He needed it. The crowd all seemed to be surging up the Drosselgasse in one direction, while the four of them were going in the other. Gideon suggested they turn around and go with the mass to the next corner, then turn up a side alley and come down another street, but Janet rejected the idea as unsporting.

Clutching his bratwurst in one hand and his copy of Weidenreich in the other, Gideon twisted and dodged his way out of several near-collisions with the uproarious German crowds. At the very end of the Drosselgasse, however, just when he thought he had safely made it, a thickset, blond man tore unsteadily around the corner and smashed heavily into him. The bratwurst flew one way, *The Skull of Sinanthropus Pekinensis* the other; Gideon himself was thrown backwards almost into the arms of a bald fat man who, seemingly thinking Gideon was going to fall, grasped him in a firm embrace and apologized effusively.

"*Verzeihen, Sie, bitte. . . .*"

The first man, to Gideon's surprise, was equally solicitous. He bent quickly, almost frantically, to retrieve the fallen book, but was held back by the crush of pedestrians. Meanwhile, Gideon—who disliked physical closeness with other men—twisted himself free and picked the book up himself, practically snatching it from the blond man's well-meaning fingers.

Gideon straightened up, composing a smile. Although annoyed—the bratwurst *had* been delicious, and he wasn't going back for another—he was prepared to exchange apologies with the two Germans, who had meant him no harm and had been so desperately quick to help. He was astonished to see that they were gone, already engulfed by the fast-moving crowds. He stood there in confusion for a moment, the smile dying on his face, dividing the oncoming foot traffic as a tree trunk might divide the waters of a flooding river.

John grabbed his arm and plucked him out of the crowded alley. "You want to get killed? Never get between a wine drinker and a *weinstube,* not in Rüdesheim."

"Don't look so sad," Janet said, laughing. "It was only a bratwurst. There'll be more on the boat."

"Ah, but not like Clem's," John said.

Arm in arm, like the German tourists, the four of them ran three blocks to the pier, arriving only a minute before the ship's departure.

To his initial dismay, the ship was packed with people: not only the USOC group and many German families, but two of the high-spirited, well-lubricated tour groups, one with yellow hats and one with orange hats. Nevertheless, Gideon enjoyed the trip. The finespun mist that hung in the Rhine valley, the fall colors, the vineyards running nearly vertically up from the river, and above all the castles—the ghostly, haunted, stunningly beautiful castles—all held him so enthralled that he barely noticed the racket on the boat.

After the first half hour, John and Marti went in search of wine and USOC company, but Janet stayed with him in the relatively uncrowded stern, watching the castles glide by. One after another they came, literally at every turn. There was hardly a time when two or three castles could not be seen perched high in the gorge.

When they approached the Lorelei, the great rock that juts into the Rhine like the prow of a stupendous ship, the loudspeakers squawked twice, announced "*Die Lorelei*," and emitted a series of hollow, tinny noises that were barely recognizable as Silcher's music to Heine's famous poem. At first it distressed Gideon. He had loved the song since his high school German class—it was almost all he remembered—and he found the scratchy rendering tasteless and commercial. The passengers paid no attention; they continued to shout, laugh, and pour huge glasses of wine and beer.

Then, as they neared the great rock, the clamor died down. One by one, the Germans softly took up the song, so that, as they passed the towering cliff face, the mournful, surpassingly sweet melody enveloped the ship like a sad, silvery cloud. Gideon was too overcome by the beauty of it to sing. Others were weeping as they sang, and he felt the tears come to his own eyes. Janet, her eyes shining too, leaned closer from her chair and tilted her head onto his shoulder.

"Oh, you neat, crazy man," she said, her voice furry. "It *is* glorious, isn't it?"

He squeezed her hand and leaned his cheek against the top of her head.

After a while in the hush that followed the song, she spoke again, her head still on his shoulder. "Do you know, everyone talks about how corny that is. Me, too. But in my heart I've always felt it was beautiful. I was afraid you wouldn't like it, but I should have known."

He must have dozed then in the peaceful filtered sunlight, because when he felt something brush heavily against his arm he sprang up, startled and ready to fight. What he saw were several yellow-hatted tourists lurching down the deck away from him.

"Easy, easy," Janet said, a gentle concern in her voice. "They just bumped you accidentally. They're a little pie-eyed, that's all."

192

"That's twice today," he said angrily. "Why don't they watch where they're going?"

"Be fair, now. It's not as if they were the same people."

"They look the same to me. That guy on the right, he sure looks like the one that practically ran me over on the Drosselgasse."

"How can you tell? You barely saw him."

"Well," he said, knowing how childish he sounded, "he's blond and big, and full of beer, and—"

"So are ninety percent of the passengers." She laughed, suddenly. "My, baby gets grumpy when he wakes up all of a sudden, doesn't he?"

He smiled sheepishly and sat down. "I guess I do. I'm not sure why you put up with me." He turned over *The Skull of Sinanthropus Pekinensis*. The back cover was partially torn off. "They nearly knocked it overboard, and my arm with it. Bruce will have a fit."

"Well, for all the reading you've done in it, you could have left it with him this morning."

"I know. I really did mean to read it, though."

"Go ahead; it won't bother me. I should go mingle for a while, anyway. I'll bring you back some wine later on."

After she had left, he realized that the boat was on its return trip; he had slept longer than he thought. When she returned with the wine half an hour later, the book lay on his lap, still open to page three. With a sigh, he closed it and willingly gave himself up to the Rhine, the wine, and Janet.

Gideon poured another glass of the superb 1971 Johannisberger Auslese from the little gray ceramic pitcher in front of him. Then he sat back, absently fingering the raised crest on the pitcher while he gazed at the famous vineyards that ran from the edge of the terrace down almost to the Rhine far below. He was utterly content. Russian spies and military secrets and threats of war and umbrella-guns were parts of another world.

At the table with him, John, Marti, and Janet looked equally relaxed with their own glasses and pitchers. In the middle of the table, two plates held some creamy white smears and a few dark specks, all that was left of a huge order of *weisskäse* and black bread.

They were on the Rheinterras at Schloss Johannisberg, a few miles south of Rüdesheim, refreshing themselves before continuing back to Heidelberg. The university had reserved five tables at the famous castle, home of the Metternichs since the early 1800s and prime source of one of the world's great wines. As he did every year, according to Janet, Dr. Rufus was paying for it out of his own pocket. There had been several toasts to the chancellor, and he had returned them copiously. He was, in fact, well into his fourth pitcher of wine, and more red-faced, amiable, and bearlike than ever, moving from table to table, back-slapping, guffawing, and mopping his beaming face.

"It's a good thing he's going to be riding home in the bus," John said, smiling, as they watched him roar delightedly over something a pretty history instructor had whispered in his ear.

"Yes," Gideon said. "It's nice to see him have a good time, though."

Marti spoke suddenly, directly to Gideon: "Hey, who invented wine?"

"Well, let's see," he said. "I'm not really sure. The Romans and Greeks had it—"

"Same kind of wine as this?" she said, holding up her glass.

"I wouldn't be surprised. I think Riesling goes back to the Romans, or to Charlemagne, at least. I know he planted vines right on these hillsides about 800 A.D."

John laughed, "Doc, now how the hell would you know that? You've never even been here before."

"Well, Charlemagne *did* plant vineyards in the Rheingau hills—everybody knows that—and the Rheingau isn't very big, and these are the only hills that are—"

He stopped suddenly as he was waving an arm over the scene. Two bulky men were walking onto the Rheinterras, looking casually about them. Gideon stared hard at them. Then he looked away. Janet had been wrong; he was sure of it now. The man who had bumped into him in Rüdesheim and the yellow-hatted tourist who had nearly knocked him from his deck chair had been the same. And here he was again, once more with the fat bald man who had pinned his arms on the Drosselgasse.

"What's the matter, Doc? What is it?" John spoke urgently, his eyes sweeping the terrace.

Gideon didn't reply. Out of the corner of his eye, he had seen them notice him and gesture inconspicuously at the wine glass near his hand. But why the wine glass? He looked down at the table; wine glass, pitcher, book. . . . The book!

He suddenly remembered the envelope he'd been carrying in the inside pocket of his jacket all day. Fingers trembling with excitement, he pulled it out and tore it open.

"Gideon," Janet said, "what *is* it? What's wrong?"

"Wait," he said breathlessly, "just let me. . . " He read the note urgently: *Do not let book*, Skull of Sinanthropus Pekinensis *out of your sight. . . .* Good God!

"Doc, for Christ's sake—"

"John, John!" he said, his thoughts tumbling wildly. "It's the book! The book!"

He grabbed it clumsily, almost dropping it, and riffled the pages. At once, near the back he found the half sheet of memo paper with writing in pencil on it. He read it aloud in a stunned whisper: " 'Deployment of tactical air forces. 1. Northern sector: Fighter-bombers, missile-equipped, 220 aircraft. . . .' God!" It finally clicked in his mind. He spun out of his chair to face the two men, and shouted to the others at the table. "Janet, watch out! John—"

He was too late. They were both running for him scattering people and knocking over the light metal tables. Glasses and pitchers shattered on the ground. Dr. Rufus, directly in the men's path, stood up and reached out a hand to stop them. Without breaking stride, the blond one knocked him to the stone floor with a brutal forearm blow to the face.

"He has a gun! Watch out!" Dr. Rufus shouted from the ground through blood-smeared lips, his voice shocked and weak.

John had risen from the chair and was reaching into his jacket when they got there. The bald one rammed his gun against

195

Marti's throat, making her cry out. John dropped back into the chair at once, his face gray. The blond one, flat-faced and powerful, shoved Gideon into his chair and snatched the book, with the paper inside, from the table. Then, from behind, he caught Janet's throat roughly in the crook of the same arm and forced her to rise, gasping. He jammed the gun hard into the small of her back; she winced and made a soft frightened sound.

Gideon's mind was raging with anger and panic. If they hurt her. . . . He tried to speak but choked on the words. Let her alone, he thought, take the damn paper, but let her alone, let her live. . . .

Marti was also pulled to her feet, and both women were dragged to the railing with guns pressed into their backs. The terrace was suffused with a weird, panting silence. Gideon's heart pounded terrifically. *Let her live, let her live. . .*

The blond climbed awkwardly over the railing, keeping his hold on Janet's throat. Breathing hoarsely, he began to pull her over the railing with him. Gideon gathered himself to leap, but John pushed him back down. The man looked quickly over his shoulder at the drop of three or four feet to the vineyard below. Janet, her face stony with terror, struggled suddenly, throwing him off balance. The gun gleamed evilly as he waved one arm to regain his equilibrium. The other arm shifted to get a more secure grip on Janet's throat.

And Gideon launched himself. It seemed to him that he flew the entire ten feet without once touching the ground. Certainly he was in the air when he struck, so that the full weight of his body was behind the rigid arm and outstretched hand that caught the man full in the face. His long, powerful fingers twisted, squeezed, and shoved at the same time. The man's arm flew from Janet's neck as he was flung backwards off the terrace to land jarringly on his feet in the dirt below.

Gideon swept Janet from the railing and onto the terrace floor with a backward swipe of his arm, and then fell on top of her and rolled on his side to shield her from the gunman. But the gunman wasn't shooting. He stood stunned for a second, then picked up the book, which had fallen to the ground, and began to run clumsily down the hill through the rows of grapevines.

The bald man, in the meantime, had managed to pull Marti over the railing, while keeping his gun pointed at John's head. When he dropped with her to the vineyard below, one of her heels caught in the soft, plowed earth, tearing off her shoe and twisting her sideways toward the ground. The man had her by one arm, trying to pull her to her feet, when he looked up to see John vaulting over the railing in a great, arching leap. He stumbled back out of the way, firing one jerky shot at the big airborne body coming down on him, but missed wildly. John landed awkwardly on one foot and one hand, and staggered off balance toward Marti, who lay face-down and still. The bald man fired and missed again, then began to run down the hill after the blond man. John fell as he reached Marti, but managed to take her in his arms. She hugged him fiercely. He buried his face in her shoulder for a moment, then stood up quickly.

Gideon began to get to his feet, and to help Janet up. As he did so, he saw three figures moving diagonally across the vineyard a few hundred feet below, running in a path that would cut off the two men floundering down the slope.

John pulled his pistol from a shoulder holster and shouted at the escaping men. "Stop! Halt! Police!"

They kept running. He fired once in the air, then took quick aim and shot at them.

"Oh, dear God," Janet said. Gideon pulled her to him and hid her face against his chest.

John fired again. Both men dropped into crouches behind a row of vines and returned several shots in a rapid spatter of gunfire.

The Rheinterras, which had been so strangely hushed, erupted with noise and action. Bullets ricocheted and clattered, tables overturned, people screamed and ducked. Gideon dropped to the floor again, with Janet still in his arms. On the ground just below the terrace, he could see John, seemingly unhurt, bent over low and trying to peer through the rows of grapevines. One of his hands was on Marti's shoulder, keeping her near the ground.

Gideon heard a far-off shout, unmistakably a command. He looked in the direction of the sound. Farther down the hill, behind a low stone fence near the road, were the three men he had seen cutting across the vineyard. They were pointing squat, ugly handguns at the crouching men. The three were in identical postures. Each was on one knee, calmly sighting along the gun held in his extended right hand while the left hand propped up the right wrist.

They were a different breed, those three. Gideon could see that from two hundred feet away. Not like the tense crouching men with the book; not like John, excitable and gallant; certainly not like Gideon himself, who could move from violent, courageous fury to hesitant timidity and back again, all within a few seconds. These three were professionals, emotionless, just doing their savage job, and terribly sure of themselves. Gideon knew the two crouching men would die. A cold droplet of sweat ran down the middle of his back.

The crouching men turned toward the shouted command, craning their necks to see through the vines. John held his fire and watched. The terrace was silent and breathless once again. The sound of a heavy truck shifting gears was somehow carried up from the Rheingoldstrasse along the Rhine, faint and strangely mundane. People on the terrace began to sit up or get tentatively to their knees. Janet pulled her face away from Gideon's body and started to rise. He put his hand on her arm to check her, and they both watched, leaning on their elbows.

The crouching men finally saw the ones at the stone fence and fired, once each, before the men began firing back. The sounds were flat and unimpressive on the open hillside, like the tiny explosions of penny firecrackers. But Gideon could see how the powerful repercussions jerked the hands of the men at the stone fence as if they were puppets with strings around their wrists. Only their hands moved. They didn't duck or flinch or shift their positions. They remained, each on one knee, straight-backed and impassive, firing slowing and steadily.

The blond, beefy man with the book was hit first. He stood up suddenly, almost angrily, his back slightly arched, and flung the book over his shoulder. Then he seemed to leap backwards off his feet, landing flatly on his back. He twitched and began to rise, getting as far as his knees and waving his gun drunkenly, but facing the wrong direction. He put a hand on a vine support to steady himself, then twitched wildly one more time and fell forward into the row of vines. There he lay still, his upper body supported and shaded by the trellis, his knees and feet on the ground. Gideon saw the gun slide gently from his fingers and knew he was dead.

The bald man, who had seemed momentarily benumbed by the sight of his partner dangling from the vines, now shook himself, snatched up the book, and began to sidle rapidly between two planted rows, scrambling along in the dirt on his hands and knees, his fat thighs pumping. The vines gave him little protection, Gideon saw; when he came to the end of the row, he'd be completely in the open. Gideon wished he would surrender. His naked skull looked very vulnerable and pink; it would stand up to bullets about as well as a soft-boiled egg.

The three men at the stone fence did not encourage him to give up. They had given him his chance; the choice was his. Dispassionately, they swung their weapons slowly to the right, following him. At the end of the row of vines, the bald man gathered himself. His intention was obvious. He would fire a few quick shots to cover himself, then dash across the ten feet of open space to the start of the next row. But what. then? *Give up*, Gideon urged silently. *Throw the gun down.* The man propped himself up like a racer, ready to make his run.

"Give up! Surrender!" Gideon was startled by his own hoarse shout, and strangely embarrassed, as if he had made some ill-bred noise. On the terrace, faces turned reproachfully toward him. Bruce Danzig, huddling under a table a few feet away, threw him a disgusted glance. He half-expected to be hushed by the others.

Angrily he shouted again: "Surrender, damn you! They'll kill you!"

The bald man paid no attention. He scrambled across the open space, firing a nervous shot as he ran. The men at the fence swiveled in calm unison, and their guns jerked at the same time, ending with little flourishes, as if they were a formal firing squad.

Nevertheless, the bald man made it across the open ground to the cover of the vines. He ran a few feet into the rows, then sat down with his back against a support post. Gideon saw him take a deep breath and let his chin sink to his chest as if he were quietly weeping.

Thank God, he thought, he's had enough. He's going to give up. He relaxed his tense shoulders and heaved a sigh of relief. At the same time, he was uncomfortably aware of a small dark part of him that was disappointed, that would have liked to see the thing carried out to its bloody end.

As he shook his head to clear the thought away, he saw the men at the fence rise and walk confidently forward, their guns held loosely. Puzzled, Gideon looked at the fat bald man. He had not moved, was not moving, was not looking at them. He still sat slumped against the post, his head drooping dispiritedly. The book lay open on his lap as if he were reading it.

And in the middle of his chest, just below his chin, a red flower of blood bloomed rapidly over his sky-blue shirt.

21

EVEN LESS COHERENT THAN usual, Dr. Rufus was the picture of consternation. And yet there was something about the agitated features, the contorted expression, that didn't quite fit, something that bothered Gideon, worried him. But he couldn't put his finger on what it was. He leaned forward and watched intently as the chancellor dabbed at his neck with a sodden handkerchief and babbled on.

He had already been babbling for some time. As soon as the shooting had stopped, one of the NSD agents had run up to the terrace—he was surprisingly young, seen up close—and brusquely herded the USOC group into the interior of the wine restaurant, there seating them at several long tables. In a strong Scottish accent, he had flung terse, excited questions at them: Had anyone recognized the two men? Were they already on the terrace when the group arrived? Who saw them first? What were they doing? Did they talk to anyone?

The responses had been listless and uninformative, and the agent, still flushed and edgy from the killings, quickly became hostile. Dr. Rufus, as protector of his brood, had sprung up and begun to prattle. But what *was* it about him . . .?

". . . and when I saw that he had a gun," he was saying, "or rather that *they* had guns . . . why, I . . . I was so startled I couldn't believe my eyes . . . in a place like this. . . . I still can't believe it, just can't believe it. . . ."

"I want to know exactly how he got his hands on the book," the agent said, looking at the floor.

"The book, yes, the book!" Dr. Rufus said. "Why ever would he steal a book? Why, he just ran right up to the table and . . . and. . . ."

It came to Gideon at last, with a shock that made him blink. He stared at Dr. Rufus for another few seconds, then leaped suddenly to his feet. The chancellor stopped in mid-exclamation; his eyes riveted on Gideon's face. The others looked up to see what had cut off the reassuring, familiar flow of words.

Gideon pointed a shaky finger at Dr. Rufus and spoke, his voice choked.

"It's you, isn't it? You're the one."

Every sound in the room stopped. There was a strained hush, an electric stupefaction. It seemed to Gideon they were all caught in a flash photograph; the only movement was the trembling of his finger, the only noise the pounding in his ears.

"The spy, the mole, whatever they call you," he said. "The USOC spy. The traitor."

Outraged noises burst from half the throats in the room. Eric Bozzini jumped up angrily, Janet turned an appalled face toward Gideon. John looked as if someone had hit him on the head with a mallet.

Gideon's confidence wavered. He shouldn't have been so impulsive; he should have waited, checked out his ideas, talked to John. His finger was still leveled dramatically at Dr. Rufus's nose. A little shamefacedly, he dropped his hand to his side.

Dr. Rufus finally found his voice. "Gideon . . . my dear boy, I know you don't really mean. . . . I hardly know what to say. . . ." His palms were lifted, his eyebrows raised in astonishment.

Gideon looked at him a little longer. "No, it's you all right," he said.

Another hostile roar came from the faculty. Bruce Danzig bobbed up from his chair and rapped his fist delicately on the table. "Damn you, Gideon!" he shouted precisely.

The agent strode to the center of the room. "That's enough now," he said. "Everyone sit down." The authority of sudden death still cloaked him. Everybody sat.

The agent looked at Gideon with dull eyes. "Now," he said. "Just you."

Gideon spoke directly to the agent, working hard to keep his voice steady. "It's Dr. Rufus who's working for the KGB, who had that information put in my book, who arranged those two—"

It was too much for Danzig. He was on his feet again, his little breast heaving like a bird's. "You idiot, you don't know what you're talking about—"

Gideon cut him off. With his heart in his mouth, he took a gamble. "Bruce, you said there was a rush request on the Weidenreich book. Who was asking for it?"

"Well. . . ." Danzig darted a sudden look at Dr. Rufus.

Gideon pressed him. "It was Dr. Rufus, wasn't it?"

Danzig spoke carefully. "Well, it was the chancellor's *office*. But that happens all the time. His secretary—"

Gideon pushed on. "And before I left for Torrejón, Dr. Rufus sent me to the library. He said you were holding some books for me. Where'd you get them? Who suggested the titles?"

Danzig stammered wordlessly, but his confused glance at Dr. Rufus was answer enough. He sat down slowly, blinking.

"That's an awful lot of interest in my books," Gideon said, talking more to himself than Danzig. "And I remember something else. I wasn't planning on taking any books with me to Sigonella either. But he pressed me—remember, Bruce?—he told me what a fine library you had, how you'd be hurt if I didn't take any. And he made sure he knew just which books I did take. . . ."

He had been dreading looking at Dr. Rufus. Now he turned to him. ". . . didn't you?" he asked quietly.

A look at the chancellor drained the belligerence from Gideon

202

as if someone had pulled out a plug. Dr. Rufus was staring at him, trembling all over and blowing his lips in and out like a hooked fish lying on a pier. He looked about as much like a spy as Santa Claus did. Gideon's heart went out to him. He had liked Dr. Rufus, really liked him. He still did.

"I think we three should have a private little talk," the agent said without expression. He made a curt hand motion to Dr. Rufus, a wordless "Get up, you." Better than words, it summarized the sudden, awful role transformation that had come to the chancellor of United States Overseas College. It saddened Gideon to see him obey the rude gesture.

They walked toward a small private room. The agent pointedly waited for Dr. Rufus to precede him, even giving the shambling, red-faced figure a casual, gratuitous nudge.

Gideon followed, his feelings turbulent and paradoxical. He, who had just publicly denounced and humiliated Dr. Rufus, burned with rage at the agent's supererogatory disrespect. And he, who had been so vilely betrayed; why should he feel like the betrayer?

"So it was the books," Janet said, looking out the car window at the dark, nearly deserted *autobahn*.

"Yes," said Gideon, "both times. They'd pick out some wide-eyed kid and tell him he was serving his country by stealing something from the computer room or the control room and sticking it in one of my books. A patriotic act. Apparently Dr. Rufus was a pretty convincing *Times* reporter."

"Yeah, sure," said John, "with some money thrown in in case the kid wasn't a true-blue patriot."

Janet frowned. "But do you mean that Dr. Rufus flew down to Sigonella and Torrejón himself, and then flew right back?"

"Sure," John said, "no problem there."

Marti shook her head. "Now wait a minute, you guys. Gideon, what made them think you wouldn't find it when you read the book?"

"That's why they had to know the exact books I had with me. They put the information in them on Thursday night both times, after I'd had my final class, and they picked a book I wouldn't need for my next course, assuming that I wouldn't be reading it."

A car zoomed out of the night, passed them, and disappeared in seconds, going at least a hundred miles an hour. "God, these German drivers," John said.

"I still don't get it," Marti said.

"I had the Weidenreich with me for the course in Torrejón. My next class, in Izmir, deals with Upper Paleolithic population distributions, so naturally I wouldn't be expected to be reading a book on *Homo erectus javanensis*."

"Naturally," John said. "Any fool could see that. I'm surprised at you, Marti."

"Rat piddle," she said. "How could they be sure you wouldn't want to read it anyway?"

"Obviously, they couldn't," Janet said. "In fact, that's just what happened this time. You kept the book, and they came after it."

"Boy, did they," Gideon said with a sigh. He was very tired. The agent had made him wait, alone, until Delvaux had arrived by helicopter about 9:00 P.M. Three hours of questions and putting the pieces together had followed. Then, at midnight, Gideon had been offered a ride back to Heidelberg in the helicopter with Delvaux. He had declined, unable to face the prospect of having Dr. Rufus as a handcuffed fellow passenger, and had started the drive back with the others at a little before one in the morning. For a while they had talked excitedly, but then their fatigue had caught up with them as they headed south from Frankfurt, and they sat quietly for many minutes at a time.

Once Gideon was awakened from a doze to hear John ask quietly, "Did Delvaux tell you how the NSD guys got here so fast? Were they following you?"

Janet's hand, lying in his own, jumped; Gideon knew she had been asleep too. "No," he said, "they didn't know where to find me. They were following Bruce. Delvaux thought maybe he was their man."

"Because of the books. Yeah," John said.

Gideon gently pulled Janet's head to his shoulder and sat, comfortable and warm, watching the dark flat landscape go by.

A little later it was Janet who stirred and sat up. "Wait a

minute," she said. "Dr. Rufus *warned* you, remember? And he tried to stop them, and took a pretty good crack in the face. Was that an act?"

"He said he didn't know there'd be guns, and he was afraid we'd be hurt. I believe him, you know; but I think Delvaux thinks it was just an act."

Marti spoke quietly: "What'd he do it for, money?"

Gideon nodded, then realized she couldn't see him in the dark. "Yes," he said, "so he says."

At about 2:30 A.M., famished, they stopped at an automated roadside AAFES canteen for sandwiches and milk. Their first bites revived them, and they began talking again.

"Mmm," Janet said, chewing her egg salad sandwich with such evident pleasure that Gideon, who was already eating a roast beef sandwich, searched his pockets for change to buy one. "Mmm, question," she said. "If Dr. Rufus went all the way to Sigonella and Torrejón anyway, why didn't he have these kids bring the information directly to him, or go on base himself and have it delivered to him there? Why involve a middle man?"

John answered for Gideon. "Too much risk. The kids were amateurs. They'd be nervous, and an alert guard could tell something was wrong." He bit off a huge corner of his pastrami sandwich and chewed happily for a while until he could speak again. "And as for Rufus taking it off the base himself"—Gideon noted the dropping of the honorific title; one more indignity Dr. Rufus would have to get used to—"why take the risk when ol' Gid could take it for him? There was always a chance the stuff would be found by a guard, after all."

"Does anyone have a quarter?" Gideon asked. Janet gave him one, and he went to the machine for an egg salad sandwich. He pulled unsuccessfully on the plastic wrapper, then tore at it with his teeth. A memory came suddenly to his mind, and he sat thoughtfully with the plastic wrapping in his mouth.

"Want some mustard to go with that?" Janet said. "Brings out the flavor."

He removed the wrapping. "I was just thinking about how Dr. Rufus snowed me. When I went in to see him and he calmly . .

205

and damn cleverly . . . sat there while *I* talked *him* into letting me take the Torrejón assignment. And all the time I was playing right smack into his hands."

They ate and drank quietly for a while. John finished his sandwich and milk, and brought coffee for them all. He sat down with a great sigh and looked straight at Gideon.

"Okay, Doc, lay it on me. I guess I can stand it now."

Gideon looked blankly at him.

"Marti," said John, "you ask him. I can't bring myself to do it."

"Yowzah, Massa John," Marti said. "We're all dying to know how you did it."

"Did what?" Gideon said.

"How you knew it was Dr. Rufus, you turkey!" Janet said.

Gideon laughed. "Oh no, you don't. Every time I try to tell John about the marvels of modern scientific inference, he argues with me."

"No," John said, "I've learned my lesson, Doc. I promise I won't say a thing."

Gideon had looked forward to this scene. He took his time, adding a little powdered cream to his coffee, tasting it, and then carefully stirring in a little more.

"I'll give him ten more seconds. Then I hit him," Janet said.

"I'll tell you, but you're not going to believe me," Gideon said, looking at John.

"I knew it, I knew it," said John, "I'm already sorry I asked."

"Do you remember," Gideon said, "how Dr. Rufus was sitting there telling the agent about what happened, and how amazed he'd been, and so on?"

All three of them eagerly nodded at the same time.

"How surprised he looked? Raised eyebrows, wrinkled brow, big eyes, mouth open and puffing away?"

They all nodded at once again, encouraging him to go on. It was like being in front of a good class.

"Well, that's the classic expression of surprise, all right, except for three things: his upper eyelids were completely raised—"

"He was surprised," John said. "When you're surprised, your eyes open up wide."

"No, and that's my point. Most people think that surprise

results in a pop-eyed stare. It doesn't. It raises your upper eyelids only partway, like this."

"That looks like a pop-eyed stare to me." John said.

Gideon turned to Marti. "Didn't I hear him say he wasn't going to argue?"

"Shut up, Lau," she said. Then to Gideon, "You said there were three things."

"Yes. Number two: the lateral ends of his eyebrows were raised, as you'd expect, but the medial corners weren't."

"I don't follow. Demonstrate, please, Professor," Janet said.

"I can't. Most people can't voluntarily raise the medial corners of their eyebrows. That's my point."

"Dammit, Doc," John said excitedly, his hands chopping away at the air. That's the second time you've said that. *What's* your point?"

"Will someone kindly control this person?" Gideon said.

"Goddammit, Doc—"

Gideon laughed and patted John's arm. "My point is that Dr. Rufus's surprise was fabricated. He was faking it." He sipped his cooling coffe. "He *knew* those men were going to come after me, and he *knew* about the book. *Ergo*, he was the spy."

John shook his head doubtfully. "I don't know. . . ."

"What's point three?" asked Janet.

"That his facial expressions were asymmetrical; much more pronounced on the left side."

"I see," Janet. "So you assumed that the neurological pathways were subcortical in origin. Very clever, if I do say so myself. How—"

"Argh," Marti said. "I'm going bonkers. Will somebody let us poor mortals in on this?"

Gideon laughed. "There are two separate paths from the brain to the facial muscles, one for deliberate expressions and the other for involuntary ones. And they result in different faces. Involuntary expressions are usually very symmetrical. Deliberate ones are almost always more pronounced on the left side."

"Doc," John said, "no disrespect intended, but is this a little theory of your own, or is there any scientific basis for it?"

"That's an excellent question . . . finally. There's plenty of

207

evidence. Duchenne did some preliminary work on the facial muscles in the 1860s, and Izard was analyzing facial expressions in the 1920s in the U.S. But the main work's being done by Ekman at UC—the University of California—and by Friesen. Ekman's even talked to the CIA—"

"All right, all right, you win." John was quiet a few moments. Then he said, "Okay, I admit it. I'm impressed."

Gideon stood up and stretched. "And now that one and all have been astounded by feats of scientific legerdemain, why don't we hit the road and get home?"

In the dark car, John turned on the ignition, then shut it off and turned to Gideon, his arm on the back of his seat.

"Here comes the rebuttal," Gideon said to no one. "I thought it was too easy."

"No rebuttal, Doc. I'm just not clear about everything yet. It doesn't make sense that the Russians were trying to kill you. They were getting their information through you, right? So why would they want you dead, huh?"

"Yeah, huh?" said Marti.

Gideon smiled, although he knew no one could see it. "The need-to-know principle," he said softly. "The great standard of the espionage world. It just turns out that the Russians are as dumb as we are."

When he was silent for a few moments, Janet said, "If that was an explanation, I'm afraid I missed something."

"You know how NSD got mixed up?" Gideon said. "How Intelligence was protecting me because I was working for them, but Bureau Four was after me because they thought I was a spy?"

There were murmurs of assent.

"Well, the same thing—the exact same goddamn thing—happened to the Russians. Their espionage people knew I was their source, but espionage and counterespionage don't talk to each other—just like us—and as far as counterespionage was concerned, I was a danger, an NSD operative."

"Which you were," John said.

"Which I was." He sighed. "Which I sure was. I was hunting

like mad for the KGB source . . . and it was me. And I was searching everywhere for the dead drop . . . and I had it. 'One for the books,' Delvaux said."

"Huh," John said.

"Jumpin' Jehoshaphat," said Marti.

Book 8: Heidelberg

22

IMMERSED IN THE *International Herald Tribune* the next morning, Gideon started when a pair of hands were laid gently on his shoulders. "Janet!" he said. "Hi, sit down. You look great in yellow."

She took his empty cup to the coffeepot at the back of the faculty lounge and filled it, along with one for herself. She didn't often wear summery frocks, but it was unseasonably warm. Her bare arms were brown and firm and very smooth.

He smiled at her when she returned and sat down.

"That's not a smile; that's a leer," she said. "I know leers, and that's one."

"Hey, lady, can I lick your arm? Did anyone ever tell you you have extremely sexy arms?"

"I can't handle any more compliments," she said. "I still haven't gotten used to the one about the subtrochanteric what-ever-it-was."

"Trochanteric subcutaneous adipose tissue distribution. Mmm, that's nice, too."

"What's with you? You didn't seem very interested last night. You were asleep before the lights were out."

"I was tired. I'm wide awake now." He reached out and stroked her arm.

She covered his hand with her own and squeezed it. With a quick glance around to make sure they were alone, she leaned forward and kissed him gently.

When they pulled back, a lump rose suddenly to his throat. "Ah, Janet, I'm afraid you've gotten to me, and I didn't want to be gotten to. It's going to be a long four days in Izmir without you."

Her eyes shining, she smiled at him. "Listen, I need to tell you about the staff meeting."

"It was a short one, wasn't it? You were only in there half an hour."

"Yes, but big things happened. In the first place, Eric Bozzini is going to be acting chancellor until they get a replacement."

"Eric?" You're kidding! That's ridiculous."

"He'll do fine," Janet said. "There's more. First, I'm going to be acting logistics director. Acting acting director, I guess it is."

She seemed so pleased with the appointment that he congratulated her. "Is it a good position for you?"

She laughed with a tinkling, pealing laugh he had not heard before. He hoped he would hear it many times again. "Who cares about the position?" she said. "The point is, with the Russian thing off and the alert over, we go back to our normal schedule. Isn't that great?"

"I guess so," he said, "but am I missing something?"

"You bet you are. It means that the logistics director has to get out of her office and start making field visits. And guess which base hasn't been visited in two years?"

He sipped his coffee, giving himself time to determine whether he was feeling happy or anxious. He decided easily on happy. "It wouldn't be Izmir?" he said.

"It sure would," she said, and then looked at him for a long time. "Is that all right?"

Her hands were clenched on the table. He covered them with his own, and she turned her palms up to clasp his fingers.

"Yes, that's all right," he said, with a fine, painful tightness in his throat. "I guess I'm getting kind of used to you." He paused. "Did I ever tell you what beautiful *orbicularis oculi* you have?"

Mystery . . . Intrigue
. . . Suspense

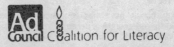